This Small Corner of Time

Works of historical fiction and fantasy by
Sarah Woodbury

The After Cilmeri Series

Daughter of Time
Footsteps in Time
Winds of Time
Prince of Time
Crossroads in Time
Children of Time
Exiles in Time
Castaways in Time
Ashes of Time
Warden of Time
Guardians of Time
Masters of Time
Outpost in Time
Shades of Time
Champions of Time

The Lion of Wales

Cold My Heart
The Oaken Door
Of Men and Dragons
A Long Cloud
Frost Against the Hilt

Gareth and Gwen Medieval Mysteries

The Bard's Daughter
The Good Knight
The Uninvited Guest
The Fourth Horseman
The Fallen Princess
The Unlikely Spy
The Lost Brother
The Renegade Merchant
The Unexpected Ally
The Worthy Soldier
The Favored Son
The Viking Prince

The Last Pendragon Saga

The Last Pendragon
The Pendragon's Blade
Song of the Pendragon
The Pendragon's Quest
The Pendragon's Champions
Rise of the Pendragon
The Pendragon's Challenge
Legend of the Pendragon

This Small Corner of Time

The *After Cilmeri* Series Companion

by

Sarah Woodbury

with
Dan Haug

The Morgan-Stanwood Publishing Group
Pendleton, Oregon

This Small Corner of Time

To my mom

you are loved

Table of Contents

Acknowledgements   vii
Chapter One: Introduction   1
    How it All Started   3
    The Writing Process   5
    Making Mistakes   7
    The After Cilmeri Series   9
Chapter Two: The Historical World of the After Cilmeri Series   11
    The Conquests of Wales   13
    Religion in Medieval Wales   17
    The Life and Death of Llywelyn ap Gruffydd   21
    Historic Timeline: 1196-1284   27
Chapter Three: The Welsh Language   29
    Pronunciation Guide   30
    Specific Names and Places   31
Chapter Four: The People of After Cilmeri   33
Chapter Five: The Landscape   47
    North Wales   49
    South Wales   59
    Scotland and Northern England   65
    Southeast England   69
    Ireland   71
    Additional Places   75
Chapter Six: Fifteen Journeys   77
    Making Sense of the Timelines and Maps   79
    Prequel: Daughter of Time   81
    Book 1: Footsteps in Time   85
    Book 1.5: Winds of Time   91
    Book 2: Prince of Time   93
    Book 3: Crossroads in Time   97
    Book 4: Children of Time   101
    Book 5: Exiles in Time   105
    Book 6: Castaways in Time   109
    Book 7: Ashes of Time   113
    Book 8: Warden of Time   117
    Book 9: Guardians of Time   121
    Book 10: Masters of Time   125
    Book 11: Outpost in Time   129
    Book 12: Shades of Time   133
    Book 13: Champions of Time   137
Chapter Seven: Conclusion   141
    Works Cited and Further Reading   142

List of Characters

Aaron ben Simon ... 45
Alexander Callum ... 37
Anna ... 35
Bevyn ... 44
Bronwen Llywelyn ... 37
Cassie McKay Callum ... 37
Chad Treadman ... 45
Christopher Shepherd ... 38
Dafydd ap Gruffydd ... 39
David ... 35
Edmund Mortimer ... 41
Gilbert de Clare ... 40
Goronwy ap Heilin ... 44
Gwenllian ferch Llywelyn ... 38
Heledd ... 44
Humphrey de Bohun ... 39
Huw ap Aeddan ... 44
Hywel ... 44
Ieuan ap Cynan ... 37
James Stewart ... 43
John Balliol ... 42
King Edward ... 39
Lili ferch Cynan ... 36
Llywelyn ap Gruffydd ... 34
Mark Jones ... 38
Mathonwy ap Rhys ... 36
Meg ... 34
MI-5 ... 45
Nicholas de Carew ... 41
Red Comyn ... 43
Robbie Bruce ... 43
Roger Mortimer ... 42
Rupert Jones ... 45
Samuel ben Aaron ... 45
William de Bohun ... 40
William de Valence ... 42

List of Places

Abbey Cwm Hir ... 59
Aber ... 49
Anglesey ... 49
Avalon ... 75
Beaumaris Castle ... 49
Bective Abbey ... 71
Beeston Castle ... 50
Boyne River ... 71
Brecon Castle ... 59
Buellt Castle ... 60
Bwlch y Ddeufaen ... 50
Caerhun ... 50
Caernarfon Castle ... 50
Caerphilly Castle ... 60
Carew Castle ... 60
Carlisle Castle ... 65
Castell y Bere ... 50
Château Niort ... 75
Chepstow Castle ... 60
Cilmeri ... 61
Criccieth Castle ... 51
Deheubarth ... 61
Denbigh Castle ... 52
Dinas Bran ... 52
Dolbadarn Castle ... 53
Dolwyddelan Castle ... 53
Dover Castle ... 69
Drogheda ... 71
Dublin ... 72
Earth Two ... 75
Gwynedd ... 53
Hadrian's Wall ... 65
Healing Waters Spa ... 61
Hythe ... 69
Land of Madoc ... 75
Llangollen ... 54
Lyons (Holt) Castle ... 54
Menai Strait ... 54
Montgomery Castle ... 55
Mugdock Castle ... 66
Offa's Dyke ... 62

Painscastle   62
Powys   62
Radnor, Pennsylvania   75
Rhuddlan Castle   55
Roche (Castle Roche)   72
Roscommon Castle   72
Saint Gwenffrewi's Well   56
Skipton Castle   66
Snowdon (Yr Wyddfa)   56
Tara (Hill of Tara)   72
Tesco (Bangor and Caernarfon)   57
The March   61
The Pale   72
The Royal Llys   56
Trim Castle   72
Umatilla Indian Reservation   75
Valle Crucis Abbey   57
Westminster Palace   69
Windsor Castle   69
Ysbyty Gwynedd   57

David's Campaign in the Marches   88
Travel to Lancaster   89
Meg's Return to the Middle Ages   91
Sailing to Scotland   93
David and Ieuan in Scotland   94
Return to Wales   95
Journey through Pennsylvania   95
Dinas Bran to Buellt and Anna's escape   98
Battle of the Severn   99
Chasing William de Bohun   99
Travel to the Bohun Wedding   103
From Healing Waters to Chepstow   103
Callum to Scotland   105
Callum and Cassie in Scotland   106
Loch Ard to Duncraggan   107
David's Shipwreck   109
The Battle of Windsor   111
Arrival in Oregon   113
Travel from Oregon to Cardiff   114
Battle of Aberglaslyn   115
Conflict in Southeast England   119
Caernarfon and Bangor   122
Peter and Bridget's Investigation   123
Escape from Chateau Niort   125
Road Trip through France   126
Portsmouth to London   127
All Travels in Ireland   129
Christopher   130
Robbie to Trim   130
William and Huw to Drogheda   130
Meg and Llywelyn to Skyrne   130
James   130
Escape from Trim   130
James and Robbie to Roche   130
David and Callum to Dublin   130
Ambush near Dinas Bran   133
Pursuit of Anna's Abductors   134
Anna in Avalon   135
David's Adventures in Avalon   137
Marching on Skipton Castle   138
Battle of Skipton Castle   139

List of Maps

Aberglaslyn Pass   7
Annan and the cliffs   8
The British Isles   46
North Wales   48
South Wales   58
The March   61
Scotland and Northern England   64
Southeast England   68
Ireland   70
Criccieth to Castell y Bere   81
The Abduction of Meg   82
Castell y Bere to Brecon   82
Llywelyn's Confrontation with Clare   83
Attempt on Llywelyn's Life   83
Cilmeri to Castell y Bere   85
Llywelyn's Campaign against King Edward   86
David's Wayfinding   86
Anna flees Castell y Bere   87
David's Abduction   88

List of Photos

Holyhead, on Anglesey — I
The River Wye from Chepstow Castle — II
The mists rolling in over Tre'r Ceiri — IV
Overlooking the Clwyd River valley — V
A chamber in Valle Crucis Abbey — VI
The Menai Strait southwest of The Swellies — ii
The Menai Strait from Beaumaris — iv
A chamber in Bective Abbey — vi
Arched chamber in Valle Crucis Abbey — viii
Gwynedd from Llys Rhosyr on Anglesey — x
The cloister in Bective Abbey — 2
Writing in September of 2011 — 5
Tower remains at Montgomery Castle — 6
Aberglaslyn Pass, looking north — 8
View from Dolforwyn Castle — 10
Peat cut from a bog — 12
Lligwy Burial Chamber — 13
Reconstruction of circular huts at St Fagan's — 13
A pre-Roman hut circle on Anglesey — 14
Temple of Mithras near Hadrian's Wall — 14
Roman ampitheatre in Caerleon — 15
Medieval lodge at Penarth Fawr — 15
The castle and town of Conwy — 16
Deganwy from Conwy Castle — 16
St. Michael's Church near Castell y Bere — 17
Welsh Bible — 18
Tintern Abbey — 18
St. Mary's Church on the Menai Strait — 19
Llywelyn's castle at Criccieth — 20
Llywelyn's sarcophagus lid? — 21
Castell Dolbadarn — 24
The damaged plaque at Cilmeri in 2012 — 24
Sarcophagus of Joan, wife of Llywelyn Fawr — 25
Plaque over Joan's sarcophagus — 25
View from Dun Lligwy on Anglesey — 26
Castle Square in Caernarfon — 28
The Welsh / English border in Knighton — 30
The dry moat of Rhuddlan Castle — 32
Llywelyn's keep at Criccieth: front gate — 34
Llywelyn's monument at Cilmeri — 34
The minivan Anna "drove" to Wales — 35
Looking down the valley from Castell y Bere — 36

Wallowa Mountains, where Cassie hunts — 37
Christopher's car — 38
Site of William's arrival in Avalon — 40
The ruins of the Mortimer castle at Wigmore — 42
Carrickfergus: Stewart's Castle in Ireland — 43
The keep at Dolwyddelan — 44
Samuel's visit to Scotland — 45
Mount Snowdon overlooking Menai Strait — 47
Aber from Beaumaris Castle — 49
Beeston Castle — 50
Bwlch y Ddeufaen — 50
Caernarfon Castle — 51
Castell y Bere — 51
Criccieth Castle — 52
Dinas Bran — 52
Dolbadarn Castle — 52
Llyn Padarn, in Gwynedd — 53
Dolwyddelan Castle — 53
Llangollen from Dinas Bran — 54
Menai Strait — 54
Montgomery Castle — 55
Rhuddlan Castle — 55
Conwy City Walls sign — 56
What remains of Llys Conwy — 56
Mount Snowdon, summit in the clouds — 56
Saint Gwenffrewi's Well — 56
Valle Crucis Abbey — 57
Bangor Tesco — 57
Llywelyn's memorial at Abbey Cwm Hir — 59
The infamous balcony at Chepstow Castle — 60
Carew Castle — 60
Cilmeri street sign — 61
The well at Cilmeri — 61
Offa's Dyke — 62
Offa's Dyke plaque — 62
The old gate at Chepstow Castle — 63
Carlisle Castle — 65
Hadrian's Wall — 65
Skipton Castle — 66
Mugdock Castle — 66
Stirling Castle — 66
Rievaulx Abbey — 67

List of Figures

Westminster Palace — 69
Bective Abbey — 71
St. Laurence's Gate, Drogheda — 71
Castle Roche — 72
Roscommon Castle — 72
Trim Castle reflected in the River Boyne — 73
Wallowa Mountains at dusk — 74
Wiston Castle — 77
Panoramic view from Deganwy — 79
The standing stone at Bwlch — 83
Reginald's Tower, Waterford, Ireland — 87
Welsh coast from the Irish Sea — 89
Near Marty's landing site — 91
Carlisle Castle — 94
Hadrian's Wall — 94
Twyn y Garth — 95
Looking west from Dinas Bran — 97
The Severn Estuary — 99
Chepstow Castle — 101
Ambush site, south of Kilsyth — 105
Looking west and south from Stirling Castle — 106
Loch Ard — 107
The current bridge at Duncraggan — 107
Windsor Castle — 110
Bridge over the Thames in Windsor — 111
Near Pendleton, Oregon — 113
Ieuan's route to Aberglaslyn — 115
Dover Castle — 117
Canterbury: from Castle to Cathedral — 118
Caernarfon Castle latrine — 121
Whittington Castle — 121
Menai Bridge from Anglesey — 123
Temple Church in London — 127
The Round Tower of Kells — 131
Dinas Bran from the south — 133
The Hill of Tara — 135
Beaumaris Castle — 137
Black Mountain from Skipton — 139
Chepstow Castle and the River Wye — 140
Looking down from Beeston Castle — 143

Recipe for Welsh Mead — 11
Letter from Llywelyn to Peckham — 22
Found at the Llywelyn Memorial in Cilmeri — 31
Welsh Royal Family Tree — 35
CIA memo after Christopher's escape — 38
Strongbow Family Tree — 39
Stained glass from Carew Castle — 41
Chad's diagram of parallel universes — 45
Timeline: The After Cilmeri Series — 76
Roscommon Castle and former lake — 79
Timeline: Daughter of Time — 80
Timeline: Footsteps in Time — 84
Timeline: Winds of Time — 90
Timeline: Prince of Time — 92
Timeline: Crossroads in Time — 96
Timeline: Children of Time — 100
MI-5 Memo: Callum's disappearance — 102
Timeline: Exiles in Time — 104
Timeline: Castaways in Time — 108
Timeline: Ashes of Time — 112
Timeline: Warden of Time — 116
Timeline: Guardians of Time — 120
Timeline: Masters of Time — 124
Timeline: Outpost in Time — 128
Timeline: Shades of Time — 132
Welsh Cakes Recipe — 134
Timeline: Champions of Time — 136

Acknowledgements

I have so many people to thank for helping me along this journey ...

My study of Wales began as a homeschool project with my daughter. The legend in my family had always been that, while Woodbury is clearly a Saxon name, somewhere in our history we were Welsh. In 1998, my daughter and I made our first foray into family genealogy to determine the truth for ourselves, with no idea that this process of discovery would eventually become a twenty-year odyssey, not to mention a career.

The family tree was only the first step, for both me and my daughter, as it turns out. While she grew up and eventually majored in medieval history in college, even writing her senior thesis on Gerald of Wales and the March, I spent the subsequent eight years reading everything I could get my hands on about Wales. Initially, it was out of a fascination with the people and culture, and then out of a real grief at the tragic history I discovered. The more I read, the more involved (some would say obsessed) I became. I had finished my Ph.D. in anthropology in 1995, focusing on issues of ethnicity and nationalism, and I easily pivoted that focus to the history of Wales.

It took until 2006 for me to put pen to paper (or rather, fingers to keyboard) and write what eventually became *Footsteps in Time*. Perhaps unsurprisingly, the story arose out of a desire to write something my children would enjoy reading, and though I would never presume to think that I am one of their favorite authors, all four continue to read my books even after dozens of stories. What's more, they *edit* them willingly. That's love, I tell you.

So thank you first to my daughter, Brynne, for her love and support in a million different ways. It was her creativity that sparked my own and even the title of this book is down to her.

Thank you to my son Carew, whose fourteen-year-old self was the inspiration for the character of David. Twelve years on, he continues to be a kind, honest, upright, justice-seeking, brilliant man.

Thank you to my son Gareth, who became a teenager the year I started publishing my books. Not only has he been a supportive office mate, but his insight into the human condition and what makes people tick has been a constant source of inspiration for the characters in my books.

Thank you to my son Taran, whose arrival changed my world so profoundly and set me on a path that ultimately led here. He has spent his life being neglected by his novel-writing mother and still loves Wales almost as much as I do. He is also an excellent and highly tolerant traveling companion.

Thank you to my husband, Dan, who told me to give it five years and see if I still loved writing. Twelve years on, I still do. Without him, this journey wouldn't have been possible. He is also the co-author of this book, which is his project as much as mine.

Thank you to my parents, Melissa, Ron, Jolie, and Peter, who couldn't be more supportive if they tried.

Thank you to my sisters, Deborah and Linda, for editing my books and providing expertise when I need it. Thank you also for *reading* them, and thank you for putting up with knowing more about Wales than you ever wished to.

Thank you to Anna for being my writing partner, shoulder to cry on, and lifeline. Thank you for being there.

Thank you to my posse of editors and proofreaders: Claudia, Olivia, Mark, Yvonne, Cassandra, Venkata, Jolea, and Lily.

Thank you to all the writers who gave me the courage to write, to keep writing, and to publish my own books. Because of you, I have had community, support, and friendship along this path.

Thank you to my Facebook book club, a group of wonderful people, for their love, ideas, and endless enthusiasm.

And thank you to every one of my readers for making my job the best in the world.

I am lucky to have you, and I am grateful.

Sarah Woodbury

Whatever else may come to pass,
I do not think that on the Day of Direst Judgement
any race other than the Welsh,
or any other language,
will give answer to the Supreme Judge of all
for this small corner of the earth.

—Gerald of Wales
quoting an unnamed Welshman
Description of Wales, AD 1194

Chapter One: Introduction

This quote in the *Description of Wales* from an un-named Welshman struck enough of a chord in Gerald's heart, despite his love/hate relationship with his own heritage, for him to make it the final line of his book. Furthermore, that unnamed Welshman had a clear enough concept of his own identity and that of his countrymen, despite the way Wales at the time was divided into many kingdoms, to make the comment in the first place. More amazing still, the sentiment continues to resonate for many Welsh people and lovers of Wales eight hundred and twenty-four years later.

This comment, in fact, is placed at the end of the book as a warning to Gerald's Norman masters that conquering the Welsh landscape was one thing, but conquering people's hearts and minds was another matter entirely.

Wales *was* conquered, however, and the story of that conquest presents a problem for the medieval fiction writer. I love history and reading about history, but *real* history often ends badly for the heroes—and pretty much always ends badly in medieval Wales with a main character who dies an unpleasant and premature death. That can make it difficult to craft a tale that is an enjoyable read.

And few endings have had a greater impact on the progress—or lack thereof—of a country than the death on December 11, 1282 of Llywelyn ap Gruffydd, the last Welsh Prince of Wales, at a little place west of Builth Wells called Cilmeri.

From the moment of Llywelyn's death, King Edward I of England endeavored to temper—and even eliminate—that Welsh sense of self, indicated in Gerald's book, to the point of expunging any mention of Aber Garth Celyn, the Welsh royal court, from public documents. Though he never succeeded in extinguishing Welsh nationalism, as many a Welsh person could tell you, he was ruthless in his efforts. Unlike the twenty-firsters in the *After Cilmeri* series, King Edward was trying to meld a united kingdom out of disparate peoples by making England and English culture pre-eminent. He took the crown, the piece of the true cross, and even the title, *Prince of Wales*, which he bestowed on his own son.

The *After Cilmeri* series follows a different path. It takes the ambush and assassination of Llywelyn ap Gruffydd, throws in some time travel, and asks *what if?* What if Llywelyn survived Cilmeri? What might happen afterwards to the two teenagers who saved him?

Of all the key points in Welsh history, that one day, that single hour, when Llywelyn was lured into an ambush and assassinated, stands out to me as a turning point.

Most moments in history aren't as pivotal. Sometimes it's hard to say when the tide definitely turned.

But even at the time, it was said that had Llywelyn lived only a few more weeks, all of Wales would have flocked to his banner. Not only would King Edward have run out of money for his war, but with the defeat at the Menai Strait only a month earlier, Edward's barons might have withdrawn their support. Llywelyn could have solidified his hold on the whole country, and Edward might have given up his quest to conquer Wales. After all, it was December 11th, with true winter coming on, and the failure of the assassination plot might have been the final nail in the coffin of a war that had not been going well for England.

Orson Welles once said, "If you want a happy ending, that depends, of course, on where you stop your story."

My problem is that I didn't want the story to stop where it did—with the death of the hero. The life and death of Llywelyn ap Gruffydd was a story that desperately needed someone to rewrite it. At least I thought so.

And so I did.

This story has obviously evolved over the subsequent twelve years of writing fifteen books, but I have always endeavored to stay true to that original vision. *Daughter of Time* has been called a 'love letter to Wales'. The comment was meant as a criticism, but after nearly twenty years of spending more than half my time in medieval Wales, I have no choice but to embrace the notion unapologetically.

I do love Wales. I love England and Scotland too. I have loved writing these books, and it is my sense that many readers have loved reading them. Thus, I thought it was time to dive deeply into the world that I created. The following pages include a discussion of Welsh history, timelines, descriptions of characters and castles, family trees, maps, photographs, and a peek into the process of writing the books themselves. Welcome to *The After Cilmeri Series Companion*.

How it All Started

Sometimes, as with the death of Llywelyn, it's easy to pinpoint that moment where everything changes. When you look across the room and say to yourself, I'm going to marry him. Or stare down at those two pink lines on the pregnancy test, when you're only twenty-two and been married for a month and a half and are living on $800 a month because you're both still in school and *my God how is this going to work?* Because, as my writing partner, Anna, says, "Nothing goes better with no money and no idea where we're going to be living in 9 months than a new baby, right?"

And sometimes, it's possible to see that moment of change only in retrospect. Until I was eleven, my parents tell me they thought I was going to grow up to be a hippie. I wandered through the swampy woods of our 2 ½ acres, making up poems and singing them to myself. By the time I'd turned twelve, however, whether because of family pressures or the realities of school, I

put all that creativity and whimsicalness into a box on a high shelf in my mind. And once I reached my late teens, I routinely told people that I didn't "have a creative bone in my body." It makes me sad to think of all those years where I thought the creative side of me didn't exist.

When I was in my twenties and a full-time mother of two, my husband and I took our family to a picnic with his graduate school department. I was pleased at how friendly and accepting everyone seemed. And then one of the other graduate students turned to me out of the blue and said, "Do you really think you can jump back into a job after staying home with your kids for five or ten years?"

I remember staring at him, not knowing what to say. It wasn't that I hadn't thought about it, but that it didn't matter—it couldn't matter—because I had *this* job to

do, and the consequences of staying home with my kids were something I'd just have to face when the time came.

Fast forward ten years and it was clear that this friend had been right in his incredulity. I was earning $15 an hour as a part-time contract anthropologist, trying to supplement our income while at the same time holding the fort at home. I remember the day it became clear it wasn't working. I was simultaneously folding laundry, cooking dinner, and slogging through a report I didn't want to write, trying to get it all in before the baby (number four, by now) woke up. I put my head down, right there on the dryer, and cried.

It was time to seek another path. Time to follow my heart and do what I'd wanted to do for a long time but hadn't had the courage or the belief in myself to make happen.

I had spent the previous four years slowly working my way back to creativity. In 2002, we moved to a small town in Oregon. Because we lived on the dry side of the state, I started learning everything I could about low-water plants and designing what sixteen years later is still a beautiful garden.

I then moved on to quilting, something I could do with my children, and though I never got particularly good at sewing anything but a straight line, I learned to love the colors and the feel of the fabric and to use my instincts to create something that again I believed to be beautiful.

Then, at the age of thirty-seven, on April 1, 2006, I started my first novel, just to see if I could. I wrote it in six weeks, and it was bad in a way that all first books are bad. It was about elves and magic stones and will never see the light of day. My family knows not to publish it after my death. But it taught me many things, among them: *I can do this!*

In the five years that followed, I discovered that I loved writing, despite experiencing a humbling amount of rejection along my newfound path. Over seventy agents and then dozens of editors (once I found an agent) read my books and passed them over. Again and again.

Meanwhile, I wrote. I started another series. When I cried on my husband's shoulder at how many rejections I received, he told me, "Give it five years."

At the time, I thought he meant *give it five years and see if you're making any money*. What he actually meant, of course, was *give it five years and see if you still love it*. Regardless, I wrote more books, for a total of eight. And still ... received nothing but rejection from the powers-that-be.

Then, in the autumn of 2010, my agent gave the book he was trying to sell, *The Last Pendragon*, back to me and told me that if I had something else to give him, he'd try to sell that, but we had nowhere else to go with the book. Although I did send him one of my other books, internally I was at a crossroads and faced a stark choice: let *The Last Pendragon* molder in the bottom of my laptop for eternity with my first novel—or publish it myself.

I chose the latter. In September of 2010, I uploaded my book to Barnes & Noble Nook for free.

The response was immediate, and I gave away ten thousand books in three months. Then, at the end of December, a reader emailed me and said two things: 1) she loved my books, and 2) please don't give them away anymore. They were too good for that.

I still give away thousands of books every year, but I took her advice on the rest and started publishing my books myself.

And then, on March 31, 2011, one day short of five years from the day I first put fingers to keyboard, I received my first payment from Amazon for the sale of my books. My husband had been right.

While I think of myself as staid, even somewhat conservative, my extended family apparently has decided that those years where I showed little creativity were just a phase. The other day, my husband told me of several conversations he either overheard or had with them, in which it became clear they thought I was so alternative and creative—so far off the map—that I didn't even remember there *was* a map.

I haven't really forgotten. It's just that the maps I'm interested in are the ones in this book.

The Writing Process

Possibly the most common question I'm asked is to explain my writing process, followed immediately by where my ideas come from. Because I don't want to offend the questioner, I don't usually answer with the truth, which is that I find talking about my writing process boring, and that ideas are a dime a dozen.

The hard thing isn't coming up with an idea; it's coming up with an idea that can carry me through 350 pages and fifteen books.

But I thought I'd answer the questions here anyway, since when I'm not being obnoxious, I really don't think there's such a thing as a stupid question. Maybe not even a boring one.

In American culture, writers are often placed on a pedestal. Spurred on by some authors of hallowed literary fiction, who are or were depressed and unhappy people, writers are often viewed as solitary souls, pounding away on a typewriter for years at a time, crafting every word and sentence until they are satisfied that they have achieved some level of perfection. A famous story from Oscar Wilde was that his hard day of work consisted of spending all morning putting in a comma and all afternoon taking it out again.

Unfortunately, the story is often taken seriously, rather than for the joke it was (if he even said it).

Writing in September of 2011

I don't write that way. I don't think that way either. And while good stories always to one extent or another lay bare my own personality and experiences, I don't write to exorcise my own demons. I write to entertain myself and my readers, as my favorite quote from Donna Tartt states:

> The first duty of the novelist is to entertain. It is a moral duty. People who read your books are sick, sad, traveling, in the hospital waiting room while someone is dying. Books are written by the alone for the alone.

I've always been a drafter, which means I write drafts. Some writers I know feel the book is all but finished by the time they reach the last line because they have gone over the entire text many times before they finally come to the end. By contrast, every book I've written has gone through literally dozens of drafts as I work through the book from beginning to end and then go back to the beginning to start working through it all over again. In general, I don't even know what the story is truly about until after the second draft.

When I'm actively writing a novel, I write 1000 words a day, every day. That might sound like a lot at first, but it's only four pages double-spaced. Some days it takes me a few hours to do, and some days, when I'm on a roll, only an hour and a half.

Because writing, when it's going well, is like magic. Usually, when I put my fingers to the keyboard in the morning, I have only the vaguest idea—and sometimes no idea at all—what comes next in a story. And then I start typing. Maybe it's just the first sentence, maybe it takes a whole page before the magic kicks in, but when it works, what comes out of my fingers are ideas, characters, and scenes about which I had no notion five minutes before.

From the outside, it might sound like a crazy way to work, but after forty novels, I have learned to trust the process.

Making Mistakes

When it comes to the information in my books, I'm very much a perfectionist. I obsess over little details, and some days when I'm in the middle of writing and come across something I don't know, I can spend two hours researching a factoid that takes up half a sentence. At the same time, while I endeavor to make the details in my books as accurate as possible, the desire to get the story out into the world eventually becomes paramount. As in most endeavors, there is a point of diminishing returns.

That said, there are clearly times when I simply make a mistake. An easy out would be to say that my setting is an alternate universe where things are different, but that doesn't make them correct. Sometimes I catch errors, either at the last moment before publication or immediately thereafter. Sometimes it is a reader who kindly points out the mistake to me, and I hastily make the correction. Sometimes I don't learn of them until long after release. Thankfully, those appear to be few and far between.

In the last year, however, I have had to come to terms with two significant geographical mistakes in the *After Cilmeri* series, neither of which is correctable within the context of the books. I am well aware that I am geographically challenged. When I write *north*, half the time I really mean *south*. The same is true for *east* and *west*. During the editing process, I globally search my books for cardinal directions to make sure that I *really* mean what I wrote.

In *Ashes of Time*, Llywelyn rides through the pass at Aberglaslyn on the old Roman road on the eastern side of the river. Having seen the place for myself, while not necessarily impossible, in our world the Roman road actually ran on the western side of the river.

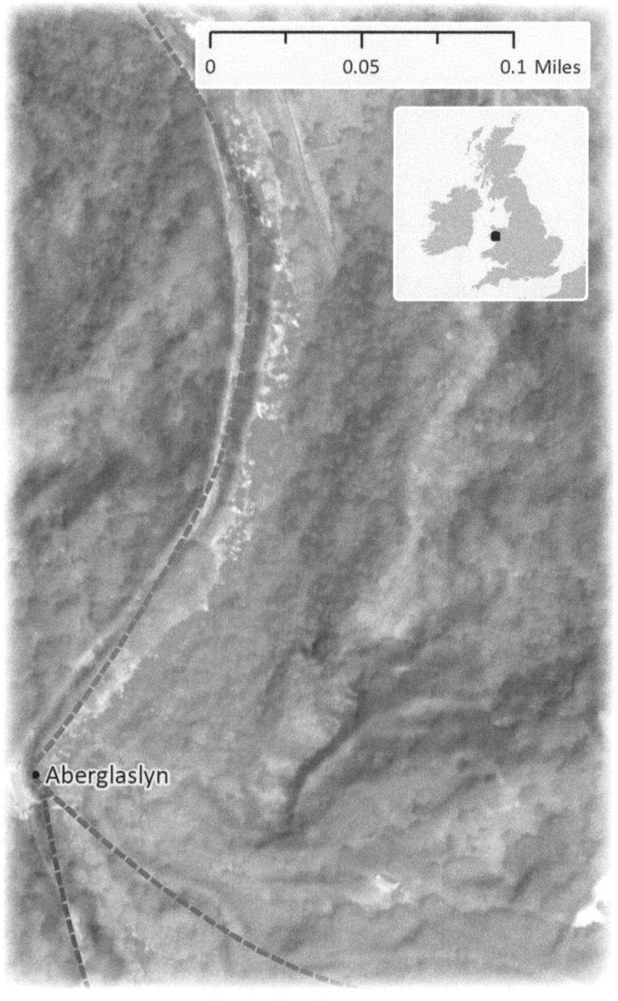

Aberglaslyn Pass

Aberglaslyn Pass, looking north

The second geographical mistake is that Annan, the village where David and Ieuan dock in the beginning of *Prince of Time*, is in the wrong place. Or rather, the actual village of Annan is where I meant for them to dock, but the geography that I wrote into the book—particularly a cliff off which David could jump with Ieuan in his arms—is some sixteen miles to the west of where the village actually lies.

That I could make these kinds of mistakes arises out of a confluence of lack of information and neglect. In both instances, I hadn't visited the place before publication to confirm for myself what it looked like. At the time of the writing of *Prince of Time* in 2007, the satellite imagery that I use now was not available. When I published the book in 2011, the data was available, but being geographically challenged, I simply forgot to double-check my information.

In both cases, the details I weave around the geography make the locations impossible to change or modify for future versions of the books. I have to say as well that there will *always* be mistakes. Undoubtedly there are some nobody has yet caught, and the book I'm writing right now will have them too. Hopefully, the more I write, the fewer mistakes I make, but mistakes are part of life, arguably even a necessary one, though I'm not trying to turn them into a virtue! In this regard, I can only promise that I will do my best not to make them, and hope for your understanding and forgiveness.

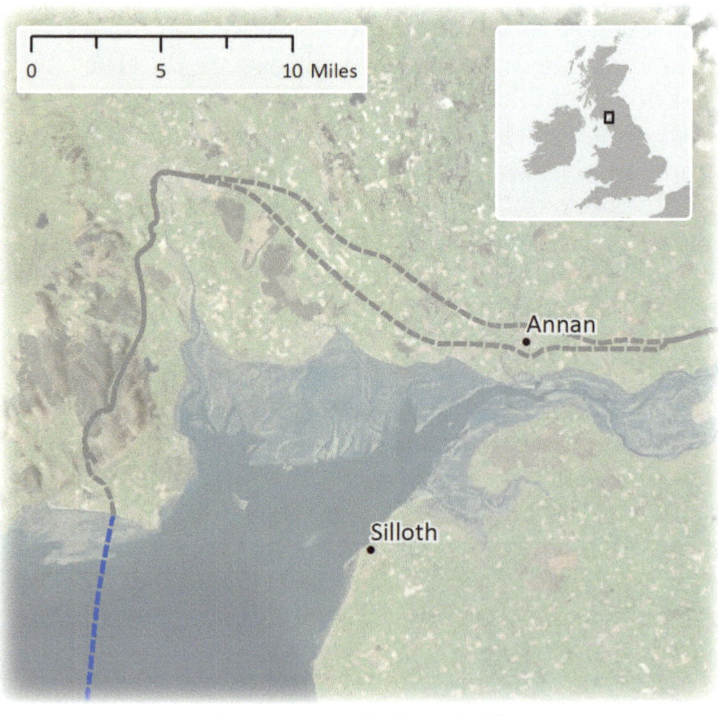

Annan and the cliffs

The After Cilmeri Series

The *After Cilmeri* series begins with Meg, a young, troubled American widow, who, at a moment of catastrophic danger, falls through time and into the life of Llywelyn ap Gruffydd, the last Prince of Wales. A strong and charismatic leader, he saves her, and she in turn saves him, thanks to her knowledge of future events. Although powerful forces seek to divide them, by working together, Meg and Llywelyn navigate the dangerous and shifting alliances that constantly undermine his rule and threaten the very existence of Wales.

But before they can create a future which avoids the predetermined death of Llywelyn, Meg is ripped from his world and returned to her own—in time to give birth to their son, David.

David and his older sister, Anna, as teenagers, return to the medieval world to save Llywelyn yet again. This time, Norman lords have lured Llywelyn into the fateful ambush at Cilmeri. Without warning, David and Anna are thrown into a world they do not understand, among a people whose language and customs are totally unfamiliar. Before long, David is recognized as Llywelyn's true son, and he and Anna begin to make a life for themselves in this new world, which ultimately proves to be an alternate universe, one they come to call Earth Two. And ultimately they realize that Meg, Anna, and David (as well as David's son, Arthur) time travel when their lives are in danger.

Over the course of fifteen novels, many new characters, both medieval and modern, are introduced. These include Math (Lord Mathonwy), Llywelyn's nephew, who marries Anna (*Footsteps in Time*); Ieuan, David's captain, who travels with him to the modern world (referred to as Avalon) (*Prince of Time*); and Lili, Ieuan's sister, who becomes David's wife (*Crossroads in Time*).

From Avalon comes Bronwen, an anthropology graduate student, who marries Ieuan (*Prince of Time*); Callum, an MI-5 agent suffering from PTSD, who attempts to prevent Meg and Llywelyn from returning to Earth Two (*Children of Time*); Cassie, a Native American woman, who was plucked from the mountains of Oregon in the wake of Meg's plane crash (*Winds of Time*) and must survive on her own in medieval Scotland (*Exiles in Time*); a busload of twenty-firsters, who make the mistake of traveling on the same bus as Meg and Anna and end up in Earth Two (*Ashes of Time*); Meg's family, including Christopher, David's cousin (*Masters of Time*), and three twenty-firsters, George, Andre, and Sophie, who work for Chad Treadman (*Shades of Time*).

The fact of having Meg, Anna, David, and their family and friends in Earth Two by definition transforms it. Not everyone appreciates the burgeoning equality, universal education, and democracy, however, and throughout the books, the twenty-firsters face threats both from outside their inner circle and from within it. Those adventures make up the journeys of the *After Cilmeri* series.

Chapter Two: The Historical World of the After Cilmeri Series

The books in the *After Cilmeri* series each take place during the few days of adventure in the midst of daily living. That is, of course, the point. When a character is traveling back and forth from a modern world to a medieval one, the bits in between, where life happens, are far less exciting.

From a modern perspective, life in the Middle Ages appears not to have had a lot to recommend it. For example, the lives of the majority of women consisted of unceasing labor, hand-to-mouth existence, and a total lack of political representation. This was also true for the majority of men, provided they were landless. Everyone experienced the restrictions of the all-encompassing Catholic Church, societal acceptance of physical abuse, and the very real possibility of dying of disease, in war, or in childbirth at a young age, such that the median lifespan during this time was in the middle forties.

But people did *live* then. They loved their children, they cared for one another, and it does seem from what has been passed down to us that they found beauty and pleasure in their lives.

Digging deeper into history, there is far more going on in the past than simply that life was Hobbesian: "solitary, poor, nasty, brutish, and short". This quote, by the way, has been taken out of context for most of its life. Hobbes wasn't describing life in the Middle Ages; he was explaining what life would be like without a strong monarch, without which it would be a war of "man against man" (1909).

Recipe: Welsh Mead

4 pint glass bottle
3.5 pints warm water
1 inflatable pig's bladder*
3 Cups honey**
1/2 Cup fermented currents***
1 tsp. each cinnamon/nutmeg****

Pour warm water into glass bottle. Add honey, currents, and spices. Stir well to dissolve the honey and then cap and shake to aerate. Prick three tiny holes in the pig's bladder, uncap the bottle, and afix the bladder to the opening. Leave in a warm place.

Leave for three weeks. Over time the bladder will inflate, and the liquid should clear and turn dark gold. Serve at the next feast!

*Or a balloon
**Must be unpasteurized/unprocessed
***Or Young's all-purpose dried active yeast for wine and beer-making
****Or Jamaican Allspice

Recipe for Welsh Mead

Peat cut from a bog

three main social groups: the *uchelwyr* (the upper class), the *bonheddwyr* (the freemen), and the *taeogion* (the unfree peasants).

The *taeogion* lived mostly in the fertile lowlands of south Wales and Anglesey, supplying the needs of the nobility who oversaw them. The lowlands were linked to the mountains economically in that herding, rather than farming, formed the foundation of the Welsh agricultural economy, and herding was controlled by the *bonheddwyr*, the freemen. Like herders the world over, entire communities moved from their settlement in the lowlands to their upland pastures each spring and then back again in the autumn.

The freemen lived in kinship groups that controlled specific areas of land. They performed military service for princes and kings but did not do menial tasks like the *taeogion*. The upland farms enabled the Welsh to keep their economic and political independence when Marcher lords occupied the fertile lowlands and instituted Norman feudalism, at which point the *taeogion* essentially ceased to exist, becoming, for the most part, *villeins* within the Norman system.

Although fewer in number, Welsh towns did develop over time, more often in Marcher lordships because these areas were richer and allowed for settled agriculture. But the Welsh kings and princes also encouraged the development of towns, often near their castles in the mountains. Trade increased in conjunction with these towns, and Wales exported goods such as cattle, hides, wool, and cheese. Imports included necessities like salt, wheat, and iron. Ultimately, reliance on these imports would be a weakness when King Edward began his assault on Gwynedd.

To tie back to Hobbes' quote, the reign of King Edward could be viewed as the pinnacle of what a strong monarch and central government in the Middle Ages should look like. His rule was free of war within England itself, but he led many wars against other nations, and, in Wales in particular, the end result was a far less free and materially wealthy society than it had been before the Edwardian conquest, making life, ironically, *more* nasty, brutish, and short.

In fact, if one looks at the consequences of the Industrial Revolution in the 18th and 19th centuries, the lives of average people, in terms of nutrition, longevity, cleanliness, etc. were (on the whole) far, far worse than their lives would have been as peasants in the Middle Ages.

Life for the average English medieval peasant centered around villages and farms, and much of the daily routine occurred outdoors. Houses, barns, and animal pens clustered near the center of the village, which was surrounded by plowed fields and pastures. Common effort was the key to an individual's survival, and most people worked, married, had children, and died within a few miles of where they were born, rarely venturing beyond the boundaries of their native village.

Every village had a lord, even if he didn't make the area his permanent residence, and after the Norman conquest of England in 1066 AD, castles dominated the landscape. Medieval peasants were either classified as free men or as "villeins," those who owed heavy labor service to a lord, were bound to the land, and subject to feudal dues.

By contrast, Wales had few villages, and land ownership was more egalitarian. Welsh society consisted of

The Conquests of Wales

Lligwy Burial Chamber

We have no knowledge of what the Celtic tribes called themselves, only what the Romans called them: the Ordovices, the Deceangli, the Gangani, the Demetae, and the Silures. Although today, the Welsh, Irish, and Scots epitomize what we think of as Celts, when the Celts settled in Wales, Ireland, and Scotland, these countries were on the fringes of a vast culture, the center of which was located in what is now Germany, Austria, and Switzerland.

The Celts left remains of their society all over Britain. They often lived in hilltop enclosures or hillforts, defended by banks and ditches. Their houses were round, made of stone or wattle and daub, with wooden roofs thatched with straw or reeds and clay or earth floors. They farmed and herded, worked metal, and wove fabric on looms.

It goes without saying that Wales was conquered. The whole of Britain was settled by a succession of invading groups over the course of ten thousand years. We know very little about these initial settlers, and what we do know often comes from the monuments they left behind, such as, most famously, Stonehenge. In chronological order, the conquering civilizations were the Celts, the Romans, the Saxons (and related groups), and finally, the Normans.

The Celts

The first group about whom we know anything substantial are the Celts, who appeared in Britain and Ireland by 400 BC, superimposing their culture upon whatever native peoples were already there and likely intermarrying with the local inhabitants rather than exterminating them.

Reconstruction of circular huts at St Fagan's

A pre-Roman hut circle on Anglesey

The Romans

By the time the Romans invaded Britain in 43 AD, the people the Romans encountered were homogenous enough that they were all *Britons*. The Romans employed a shock and awe type of warfare, and in the initial wave of invasion, eleven tribes of southeast Britain surrendered to the invaders.

From there, the Romans moved west and north, establishing their capital at Camulodunum (Colchester). It wasn't until late in 47 AD that the new governor of Britain, Ostorius Scapula, began a campaign against the tribes of modern day Wales. He had limited success at first, but the Romans continued to strike deep into Welsh territory through the next decade of conquest.

The druids, in particular, were of concern to the Romans, because they were the leaders of all the tribes, and they encouraged an ongoing resistance. Remember, there were no lines on a map separating England, Scotland, and Wales at this time. It was all just *Britain*. The Romans began an overt campaign to wipe out all the druids and marched onto the island of Anglesey, the seat of the druidic religion. Eventually, the entire island fell to the Roman legions, the sacred groves of trees were razed to the ground, and a garrison was stationed on the island to ensure the native peoples' continued subjugation.

As a harbinger of things to come, despite this great victory on Anglesey, throughout the entire Roman period, the conquerors continued to have difficulty controlling the people of western Britain, particularly in what is now Gwynedd. The remains of the Celtic hillforts, many of which were never conquered, are still evident today, and except for a few instances in the south, such as at Caerwent, Carmarthen, and Caerleon, the Roman occupation of Wales was an entirely militaristic endeavor.

By 390 AD, things were falling apart in the center of the Roman world, and all Roman troops were withdrawn, first from Wales, and by 410 AD, from the whole of Britain.

The Fall of Rome

Rome dominated Europe (and parts of Africa and Asia) for nearly 800 years, but by the 400s AD, it had gone into serious decline, resulting ultimately in its sacking by Alaric the Visigoth in 410.

The consequences for Britain were profound. The Romans had controlled the island for nearly four hundred years, during which time the legions had provided all the security and force of law needed or allowed. With their departure, the Britons were left to fend for themselves—with no soldiers, no army, and no overarching government by which to organize or defend their country. The Romans had created this situation deliberately in order to prevent uprisings within the local populace, but their departure left the country wide open to invaders.

Below is a passage by Gildas, a 6th century British cleric, and another by Zosimus, a Byzantine historian from Constantinople, writing between 491-518 AD:

Gildas: From Britain, envoys set out with their complaints, their clothes (it is said) torn, their heads covered in dust, to beg help from the Romans.... The Romans ... informed our country that they could not go on being bothered with

Temple of Mithras near Hadrian's Wall

Roman ampitheatre in Caerleon

such troublesome expeditions; that Roman standards, that great and splendid army, could not be worn out by land and sea for the sake of wandering thieves who had no taste for war. Rather, the Britons should stand alone, get used to arms, fight bravely, and defend with all their powers their land, property, wives, children, and, more importantly, their life and liberty. Their enemies were no stronger than they, unless Britain chose to relax in laziness and torpor; they should not hold out to them for the chaining hands that held no arms, but hands equipped with shields, swords and lances, ready for the kill. This was the Romans' advice.

Zosimus: When Alaric neither gained peace on the terms he proposed nor received any hostages, he again attacked Rome … and finally captured it…. Honorius sent letters to the cities of Britain, urging them to fend for themselves.

The following years in Britain were marked by retreat from the civilization the Romans had created and flight from the cities the Romans had established—because a new conqueror had come.

The Saxons

It is a matter of record that the Saxons invaded Britain in the last years of the Roman occupation and then in full force after the Roman legions marched away, seemingly without a backward glance, leaving the Britons—after 400 years of occupation—to fend for themselves. These invaders were not, in fact, all 'Saxon', but a combination of Jutes, Angles, Saxons, Franks, and Frisians, each hailing from a different region of the northwestern coast of Europe. The Battle of Mt. Badon (whether or not fought by Arthur) is said to have occurred around 500 AD, and legend has it that the British victory there held back the Saxon tide for a generation.

After that, however, it was unstoppable.

Scholars are not united in the exact timeline of the spread of Saxons throughout the island or the extent of the violence. Regardless, over time, eastern and southern Britain became dominated by Saxon culture,

Medieval lodge at Penarth Fawr

The castle and town of Conwy

language, and law, and the Britons themselves were pushed steadily westward and northward until they were confined to Wales. Ironically, the identity itself, *Welsh*, derives from the Old English, Wealh, which means *foreigner*. Certainly, the transition to Saxon England had been entirely accomplished by the eighth century when Offa's Dyke was built and the border between the two countries definitively established. The native Britons had become foreigners in their own land.

The Normans

Although the Saxons took over six hundred years to completely conquer England, it took only six years for their kingdom to fall to the next invaders, the Normans, descendants of the Vikings.

William the Bastard (William the Conqueror; William the Norman) won his first battle for the conquest of England at Hastings in October 1066. He defeated the army of the Saxon king, Harold Godwinson, who'd force-marched his men from Stamford Bridge after defeating an invasion by King Harald Hardrada of Norway. The Saxon forces almost held, but in the end, their discipline did not, and Harold Godwinson himself died on the battlefield.

Wales, however, held out for quite a bit longer. For over two hundred years, the Welsh fought what amounted to a guerilla war against these Anglo-Norman aggressors. Unlike their long-ago ancestors, they were prepared for this new fight by six hundred years of war with the Saxons.

The Chronicle of the Princes, from the *Red Book of Hergest*, states in its entry from 1095:

> And then, the second time, William, King of England, assembled innumerable hosts, with immense means and power, against the Britons. And then the Britons avoided their impulse, not confiding in themselves, but placing their hope in God, the Creator of all things, by fasting and praying and giving alms, and undergoing severe bodily penance. For the French dared not penetrate the rocks and the woods, but hovered about the level plains. At length they returned home empty, without having gained anything; and the Britons, happy and unintimidated, defended their country.

Thus begins the saga of the 'French' conquest of Wales, culminating in 1282 with the death of Llywelyn ap Gruffydd, which marked the end of Welsh independence from the English crown.

Deganwy from Conwy Castle

Religion in Medieval Wales

Before the coming of the Romans to Britain, the Celts were pagans, and their religious leaders were druids. Even though the Romans themselves were pagan, they exterminated the druids in order to gain control of the island. Ultimately, the Romans converted to Christianity—and some percentage of Britons did too—but when the Romans left, the Britons were once again cut off from the rest of the world. Consequently, they developed their own traditions and laws as Christians, which didn't always conform to official doctrine from Rome.

Though more organized by the mid-600s, Christianity in Wales was a religion based around cells of monks and hermitages, with few, if any, churches as we understand them today. Over time, a system of priests and monasteries grew up, but these were dominated by the Cistercians, whose mother church was in France, not England, and whose proponents actively sought out remote places where they could be independent and self-sufficient.

The conflict between the Welsh and the Norman/Roman Church became, in large part, a cultural one. Among the Welsh, for example, illegitimate sons could inherit equally with legitimate ones, an anathema to the Norman Church, and women had a much higher status. Divorce was easier, lords levied fines instead of executing criminals as punishment for crimes, and the punitive forest laws of Anglo-Norman feudalism were absent.

Welsh priests were also known to conduct services in Welsh instead of Latin, and the Welsh venerated their own saints as much as the official Roman ones.

St. Michael's Church near Castell y Bere

Welsh Bible

One of the reasons, late in the 1282 war, that the Archbishop of Canterbury, John Peckham, involved himself was because he deeply desired to bring the Welsh Church into conformity with Rome. Of course, his attempts at unification were hindered by the fact that King Edward had asked the Pope to excommunicate Llywelyn when he wouldn't submit. Even then, the Cistercians, in defiance of Rome, refused to put out the candles in their churches.

David, in the *After Cilmeri* series, is very aware of Avalon's history and how the death of his father was averted when Anna drove their aunt's minivan into his attackers at Cilmeri. It is furthermore very important to David to ensure that what happened at Cilmeri can not happen in Earth Two in any fashion. One way he attempts to ensure that it doesn't is by changing medieval society.

Probably his foremost concern, and one that as King of England he has the most direct control over, is freedom of religion. He begins in *Footsteps in Time* by asking his father to welcome Jewish refugees into Wales. While pursuit of religious freedom puts him at odds with the Catholic Church, which at the time is the only Christian Church available in Europe, David believes so strongly in this right that, if necessary, he is willing to implement the Reformation several hundred years early to ensure it.

History of the Jewish People in Britain

Jewish peoples had lived in England during the Roman and Anglo-Saxon periods, but not as an organized community. When William the Conqueror arrived in England in 1066, he encouraged Jewish merchants and artisans from northern France to move to England, which they did, seeking prosperity and a haven from anti-Semitism. Serving as special representatives of the king, these Jews worked as moneylenders and coin dealers. Over the course of a generation, Jews established communities in London, York, Bristol, and Canterbury, though they generally lived in segregated areas.

From the charter by King John (1201), for which he received 4000 marks:

> John, by the grace of God, &c. Know that we have granted to all the Jews of England and Normandy to have freely and honourably residence in our land, and to hold all that from us, which they held from King Henry, our father's grandfather, and all that now they reasonably hold in land and fees and mortgages and goods, and that they have all their liberties and customs just as they had them in the time of the aforesaid King Henry, our father's grandfather, better and more quietly and more honourably. [Jacobs, 1893]

This goodwill, if it ever really existed, began to disintegrate almost immediately. Throughout the thirteenth century, Edward, as had his father before him, began to

make life more and more difficult for the Jewish population through a series of pogroms. First, he reduced the ability of Jewish people to secure a livelihood. They had been allowed to become physicians, merchants, bankers, and traders, but not to own land. Through apprenticeship and education, which was of supreme importance to the Jewish community, many had accumulated a great deal of wealth, in disproportion to their routinely uneducated gentile counterparts. Of course, this engendered animosity among the gentiles, who saw only the wealth and not the effort required to attain it.

This did not stop the gentiles from borrowing money, however, and the king allowed Jewish merchants in England to charge interest on loans (called usury). In turn, the king would exact huge taxes from them. As the taxes became more burdensome, it forced them to both raise the interest rates which they charged their debtors, and, when taxed to excess, to call in those loans.

As had happened throughout history, the Jewish people were scapegoated in an attempt to create unity among gentiles and relieve the nobility of their debt, leading to massacres such as the one Gilbert de Clare led in Canterbury during the Second Barons' War. Simon de Montfort had already expelled the Jewish community from Leicester in 1231 and again in 1253. During Montfort's ascendancy, he encouraged attacks on Jews throughout England. The confiscated wealth then filled Montfort's treasury.

In 1278, Edward ordered the arrest 600 Jewish men for coin clipping and hanged 270 of them. Edward then claimed their wealth for himself, to the tune of over 16,000 pounds (Jacobs 1903). That equaled 10% of the annual income of the entire realm. The money Edward took was an amount almost identical to the huge cost of defeating Llywelyn in the 1277 war.

Once Edward had taken all their money, he began to pass more laws restricting the lives of the Jewish peo-

St. Mary's Church on the Menai Strait

ple. They were required to wear specific clothing and badges, could not own land, practice money lending, join any guild or business, or pass on their assets to their children. In 1290, Edward completed his pogrom by expelling the Jewish population from England (although a few paid bribes in order to be allowed to stay). England was the first country in Europe to do this, though France and Germany followed suit within twenty years.

These expulsions are one reason why Spain had so many Jewish people to persecute 200 years later during the Spanish Inquisition, and also why, by 1935, millions of Jews lived in Poland, which had welcomed them after the Black Death.

In the *After Cilmeri* series, Meg becomes friends with Aaron, a Jewish physician. One consequence of their friendship is that Llywelyn agrees to allow Jews to come to Wales. As Llywelyn says to David in the beginning of *Champions of Time,*

> "When you insisted that I welcome the Jews into Wales, I agreed. But it was more to show you that I respected your ability to make decisions than because I understood your reasons. I understand them now." He looked around the table. "We all do, now."

Llywelyn's castle at Criccieth

The Life and Death of Llywelyn ap Gruffydd

Llywelyn ap Gruffydd was born sometime between 1222 and 1228. Amazingly, historians are unsure of either the actual date of Llywelyn's birth or the true identity of his mother—although there are enough hints to conclude that she was, in fact, Senana, his father's wife. Llywelyn's brothers were Owain, the eldest, Rhodri, who never asserted any claim to power in Wales, and Dafydd, who was born in 1238, only two years before the death of the boys' grandfather, Llywelyn ap Iorwerth (Llywelyn Fawr), the great Prince of Wales.

Llywelyn Fawr had two sons himself, Gruffydd, eldest but illegitimate, and Dafydd, younger but born to Llywelyn Fawr's lawful wife, Joanna, herself the illegitimate daughter of King John of England. Upon Llywelyn Fawr's death, both Dafydd and Gruffydd vied for the right to rule Wales.

Although Welsh law decreed that inheritances should be divided equally among all sons regardless of legitimacy, the kings of Gwynedd had usually designated a single heir to rule after them. Llywelyn Fawr instructed that only his younger son would follow him as Prince of Wales. This decree was supported by King Henry III and the Church, which was continually campaigning for the enforcement of Norman inheritance law in Wales. This law was not the only conflict between Welsh tradition and the Church, but it was certainly one of the most contentious.

As had generations of brothers before him, Gruffydd objected to his disinheritance and set about undermining Dafydd's rule. Dafydd retaliated by imprisoning Gruffydd and his eldest son, Owain, in Criccieth Castle. In response, Senana journeyed to King Henry to beg for her husband's deliverance.

King Henry appeared initially to listen to her plea and offered the family asylum in England. When they arrived, however, King Henry threw Gruffydd and Owain into the Tower of London. Llywelyn, Gruffydd's second son, had by this time become a man (in Welsh law, age fourteen). Rather than follow his father and elder brother into captivity, he ran away to his uncle's court. That single action set him apart from his brothers and ensured that he was in Gwynedd, ready to take over, when his Uncle Dafydd died unexpectedly without an heir in 1246.

Llywelyn's sarcophagus lid?

(Translated from the original Latin)

To John Peckham, Archbishop of Canterbury from Llywelyn, Prince of Wales

November 1282, Garth Celyn

To the most reverend father in Christ... out of the love you bear to us and our nation, we render you grateful thanks, all the more since, as you have confided to us, you come against the king's will. You ask us to come to the king's peace. Your holiness should know that we are ready to do so, provided the lord king will truly observe that same peace as is due to us and ours.

The realm of England may well be the special object of the Roman curia's affection, but the aforesaid curia has yet to learn, and must learn, and the lord pope likewise, what evils have been wrought upon us by the English, how the peace formerly made has been violated in all the clauses of the treaty, how churches have been fired and devastated, and ecclesiastical persons, priests, monks and nuns slaughtered, women slain with children at their breast, hospitals and other houses of religion burned, Welsh people murdered in cemeteries, churches, yes at the very altar, with other sacrilegious offences horrible to hear.

...As to the assertion that we are acting against God, and ought to repent as true Christians, seeking God's grace, if the war continues it shall not be set at our door, provided we can be indemnified as is our due. But while we are disinherited and slaughtered, it behoves us to defend ourselves to the utmost. Where any genuine injuries and damages come into consideration upon either side, we are prepared to make amends for those committed by our men, provided the like amends are made for damages inflicted upon us.

We fight because we are forced to fight, for we, and all Wales, are oppressed, subjugated, despoiled, reduced to servitude by the royal officers and bailiffs, in defiance of the form of the peace and of all justice ...

You should not believe all the words of our enemies, holy Father, the very people who by their deeds oppress and ill-use us, and in their words defame us by attributing to us whatever they choose. They are ever present with you, and we absent, they the oppressors, we the oppressed. In accordance with divine faith, instead of quoting their words in all things, we should rather examine their deeds.

Llywelyn

Letter from Llywelyn to Peckham

Llywelyn's father, Gruffydd, had already died in 1244 thanks to a broken rope which he was using to scale down from his window in the Tower of London. After her husband's death, instead of returning to Wales, Senana made the fateful decision to stay in England, under the continued patronage of the King of England, and keep her younger sons with her. That act left the field open for Llywelyn and Owain to establish an uneasy truce and to split Gwynedd between them.

Llywelyn, however, had inherited his grandfather's vision of a united Wales along with the arrogance to put himself at its head. For the next twenty years, he tirelessly pursued hegemony over all Wales, coupled with resistance to English rule.

This dream put him into conflict with his brothers. Dafydd and Owain united against him in 1255 in the Battle of Bryn Derwin. Llywelyn defeated them and imprisoned Owain for over twenty years. But Llywelyn released Dafydd after one year and gave him estates, ultimately bowing to his younger brother's right to rule a portion of Gwynedd. At the time, Llywelyn perceived Owain as the greater threat and the mastermind behind the rebellion.

Dafydd ap Gruffydd

As the youngest of the four sons, born at least a decade after Llywelyn, Dafydd spent the majority of his life in England where his family lived when his father was imprisoned. Dafydd grew up in the Tower of London and was a close companion and friend to King Henry's son, Edward, the future King of England, who was only one year younger than Dafydd.

Thus, Dafydd was a prince of Wales but one who'd never really lived there. He believed in his right to rule, however, and appeared to alternately admire and resent his elder brother for what he had achieved.

Dafydd rebelled against Llywelyn three times: in 1255, when he allied with Owain; in 1263, when he defected to England unexpectedly; and finally, as the ultimate betrayal, in 1274, when he conspired with a prince of Powys to assassinate Llywelyn and take his throne. The timely intervention of a snowstorm averted that attempt. As in 1263, Dafydd fled to Edward.

From Brynne Haug (2012):

> Dafydd's choice to turn to Edward in 1263 and again in 1274 was self-serving in that he believed his chances better with the king than with Llywelyn. Llywelyn had little choice but to accept Dafydd back when he changed his mind: in 1267 Edward stipulated it in the Treaty of Montgomery, and it was again a condition in 1277.

Dafydd, in fact, bears a measure of responsibility for all three wars Llywelyn fought against England.

The End of an Independent Wales

By 1267, Llywelyn had conquered most of Wales, to the point that he was recognized by King Henry III of England as its prince. Unfortunately for Llywelyn, that was the high water mark of his power. In 1272, Henry died, and Edward was crowned king—and set his sights on the complete subjugation of Wales. In 1277, he put together an enormous army and ultimately forced Llywelyn to sue for peace.

In the subsequent treaty, Edward not only required Llywelyn to accept Dafydd's return to Wales, but he reduced Llywelyn's lands to those west of the River Conwy and gave Dafydd a portion of land to the east, centered on Denbigh Castle. Also as a result of the peace treaty, however, Llywelyn was finally able to marry Elinor de Montfort, whom Edward had abducted and held as part of his attempt to get Llywelyn to do what he wanted.

For the next five years, Llywelyn remained uncharacteristically quiet, seemingly content to rule his portion of Gwynedd in peace. Although Llywelyn had never fathered a child before, Elinor did become pregnant in 1281. Unfortunately, she did not survive the child's birth in June of 1282, and the child was a girl. It appears that these events prompted Llywelyn to throw in with Dafydd, who, chafing at the restrictions Edward—his ally—had placed on him, had instigated a coordinated attack on several English castles.

Over the course of the next six months, Llywelyn succeeded in regaining virtually all of the land he'd ceded to Edward in 1277, to the point that writers at the time claimed that, had he lived only a few more weeks, all of Wales would have flocked to his banner. Things were going so well, in fact, that Archbishop Peckham began corresponding with Llywelyn, looking for a way to mediate a peace. These efforts were further bolstered by a significant Welsh victory in November at the Menai Strait, where Welsh forces repulsed an English army that had attempted to cross the Strait on a bridge of boats.

The *Chronicle of the Princes* states:

> The king and his host came to Rhuddlan. And he sent a fleet of ships to Anglesey, and they gained possession of Arfon. And they made the bridge over the Menai; but the bridge broke and countless numbers of the English were drowned and others slain.

Emboldened by the victory, Llywelyn sought to expand on it by moving east into more reliably Marcher and English territory. More specifically, he set out with an army for the region of Buellt (Builth Wells), lured by a promise of allegiance by Roger and Edmund Mortimer.

Unfortunately, as J. Beverly Smith writes, "Intimations of treachery, of breach of faith, are so often conveyed darkly, and no chronicle, nor any other source, provides the unequivocal testimony which might enable us to unravel the threads in the various accounts of the tragic happening in the vicinity of Builth." These include the next comment in the Chronicle of the Princes, shortly after the victory at the Menai, "And then was affected the betrayal of Llywelyn in the belfry at Bangor by his own men."

What exactly happened in the belfry of Bangor is lost to time, but the implication is that it had something to do with his death. In any case, the Hagnaby Chronicler, an important source for the events of the day on which Llywelyn died, was quite definite that Edmund Mortimer "drew the prince there by beseeching him to come to the neighbourhood of Builth to take his homage and that of his men. Along with other lords, he hatched a plot to corner Llywelyn and kill him" (Smith 1998:551).

The entry from the *Chronicle of the Princes* tells a stark tale of December 11, 1282:

The damaged plaque at Cilmeri in 2012

And then Llywelyn ap Gruffydd left Dafydd, his brother, guarding Gwynedd; and he himself and his host went to gain possession of Powys and Buellt. And he gained possession as far as Llanganten. And thereupon he sent his men and his steward to receive the homage of the men of Brycheiniog, and the prince was left with but a few men with him. And then Edmund Mortimer and Gruffydd ap Gwenwynwyn, and with them the king's host, came upon them without warning; and then Llywelyn and his foremost men were slain on the day of Damasus the Pope, a fortnight to the day from Christmas day; and that was a Friday.
> —*Brut y Tywysogyon*, Peniarth manuscript 20 (*The Chronicle of the Princes*)

Llywelyn's head was carried to King Edward, who ordered that it be displayed on a pike in London—where it remained for over twenty years. The rest of his body was purportedly buried at Abbey Cwm Hir to the north of Cilmeri.

Dafydd carried on for a few more months, but the English finally captured him in 1283. Edward had him hanged, drawn, and quartered, and dragged through the streets of Shrewsbury, the first man of noble standing to be given such a death. And with Dafydd's death, the last hope of an independent Wales died too.

Dafydd's young sons were imprisoned for the rest of their days in Bristol Castle, and Gwenllian, Llywelyn's daughter and only child, was abducted from Garth Celyn (Aber Castle) and sent to a convent in England, where she remained a prisoner for the rest of her life, knowing nothing of her history or her people.

Castell Dolbadarn

Sarcophagus of Joan, wife of Llywelyn Fawr

The Aftermath of the Norman Conquest

King Edward had started building his Iron Ring of Castles after the 1277 war, beginning with several in far eastern Gwynedd, castles such as Flint, Rhuddlan, Buellt, and Hawarden. After 1282, he ordered work to begin on a host of others, among them Conwy, Caernarfon, Denbigh, Harlech, and ultimately Beaumaris. Each was built with the deliberate intent to project the power of the English crown and to intimidate and oppress the local populace.

Determined that no Welshman ever claim the title *Prince of Wales* again and having eliminated the male line of the royal house of Gwynedd, Edward arranged for his own son, Edward II, to be born at the unfinished Caernarfon Castle. From then on, the only Prince of Wales would be the son of the English king.

Over the following decades, the people of Gwynedd suffered under English overlordship, with debilitating taxation and policies which effectively made them "outsiders in their own country" (Davies 1988). This disempowerment was exacerbated by the construction of walled, English boroughs associated with the Norman castles. These towns became the centers of commerce and industry in north Wales, but Welsh people were not allowed to live in them, thus furthering the Welsh populace's impoverishment.

The people of Gwynedd, including members of the religious houses at Llanfaes and Conwy, were evicted forcibly, their homes and communities razed to the ground to make way for the English castles and towns.

English law was also brought to Wales, though not in its entirety until the sixteenth century. Some particular changes after 1284, however, included the disinheritance of illegitimate children and the application of English felony law. All of north Wales was administered by Englishmen, and while the lands west of the Conwy River came under Edward's direct control, other regions, such as those lands Dafydd had controlled east of the Conwy, fell to various of Edward's strongest supporters, such as Henry de Lacy at Denbigh.

Life became even harsher with the rebellion of Owain Glyndŵr at the start of the fifteenth century. In response to his rise to power, the English parliament passed the Penal Laws of 1402, which prohibited the Welsh from carrying arms, holding office, and dwelling in fortified towns. These laws applied not only to Welshmen but to Englishmen who married Welsh women.

It wasn't until the last year of the twentieth century, 1999, that Wales finally was granted its own parliament and the right to control elements of its governmental, commercial, and educational systems.

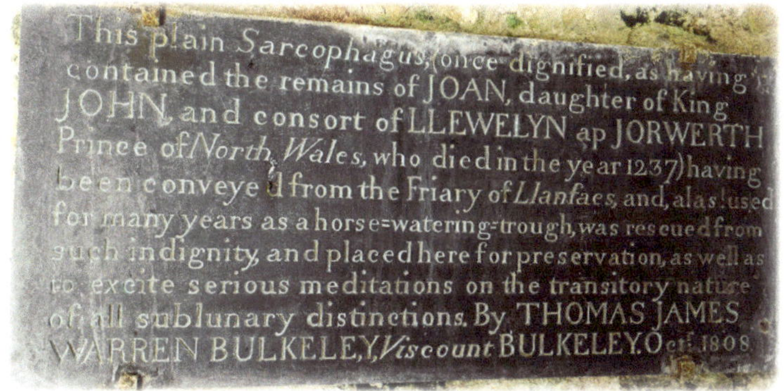

Plaque over Joan's sarcophagus

Historic Timeline: 1196-1284

1196-1240: Llywelyn ap Iorwerth (Llywelyn Fawr) rules as Prince of Gwynedd and later most of Wales.

1215: English barons force King John to sign Magna Carta.

Circa 1228: Llywelyn ap Gruffydd born to Gruffydd ap Llywelyn, eldest (illegitimate) son of Llywelyn ap Iorwerth.

1240: Llywelyn ap Iorwerth dies. Succeeded by his legitimate but younger son, Dafydd.

1244: Gruffydd ap Llywelyn dies when a makeshift rope breaks as he attempts to escape from the Tower of London.

1246: Dafydd ap Llywelyn dies unexpectedly without an heir. Llywelyn ap Gruffydd stands in his stead.

1255: Battle of Bryn Derwin. Llywelyn defeats his brothers, Owain and Dafydd, becoming sole ruler of Gwynedd. Imprisons both brothers.

1256: Llywelyn releases Dafydd from prison.

1258: Llywelyn accepts the allegiance of the princes of Deheubarth, styles himself *Prince of Wales*.

1263: Dafydd ap Gruffydd defects to the English.

1267: Treaty of Montgomery signed by Henry III, ratifying Llywelyn ap Gruffydd's claim to the title Prince of Wales. Dafydd restored to Llywelyn's favor as part of the treaty.

1271: Edward, Prince of England, goes on Crusade.

1272: King Henry III dies. Edward crowned king while still in the Holy Land, begins to make his way back to England, arriving in 1274.

1274: Dafydd plots with Owain ap Gruffydd ap Gwenwynwyn to assassinate Llywelyn. The plot is foiled by a snowstorm, and Dafydd and Owain flee to England. Sensing blood, King Edward demands that Llywelyn pay homage to him before he will recognize him as the Prince of Wales. Llywelyn refuses.

1276: King Edward declares Llywelyn a rebel.

1277: Edward gathers an enormous army and invades Wales. Llywelyn is forced to sue for peace, resulting in the Treaty of Aberconwy, which restricts Llywelyn to lands in Gwynedd west of the River Conwy and restores Llywelyn's brother Dafydd and Gruffydd ap Gwenwynwyn to their lands in Wales (with Dafydd's seat at Denbigh; Gruffydd in Powys).

1278: Llywelyn marries Elinor, daughter of Simon de Montfort.

1282 (Palm Sunday): Dafydd grows dissatisfied with subservience to Edward and rebels against him, joined by other Welsh lords who are discontented with Edward's rule.

1282 (June 19): Elinor, wife of Llywelyn, dies in childbirth. Their daughter, Gwenllian, lives. Llywelyn takes up the mantle of leader of the rebellion against England.

1282 (December 11): Ambush and death of Llywelyn at the hands of Edmund and Roger Mortimer.

1284 (April): Edward II born at Caernarfon Castle.

Chapter Three: The Welsh Language

Linguistics tells us that languages evolve. They are also arbitrary. This does not mean language isn't important, or that it isn't integral to culture. It does mean that there is nothing inherent in the word 'spoon' that denotes the rounded tool with which English speakers cook or eat.

Medieval Welsh, or Middle Welsh, was the language spoken in Wales in the 12th to 14th centuries and is the language of much of Welsh literature, including, as one example, *The Four Tales of the Mabinogi,* although the tales themselves are much older. As when a modern English-speaker attempts to read Chaucer in English (though it is usually read in translation), it is possible for a modern Welsh speaker to read middle Welsh.

The root of the changes between medieval and modern Welsh lies in what linguists call 'mutations', mostly in initial consonants. Old Welsh, on the other hand, is different yet again and not readily intelligible to Welsh readers. This period of the language dates from around 800 AD through the 12th century.

It is important to point out, in all this, that it is very hard to know if the pronunciation of words changed over time as much as the writing of those words changed. We cannot hear people reading these ancient documents out loud. They may have pronounced words similarly to modern Welsh, but simply spelled the words differently.

Primitive Welsh dates to 550 AD and derives from what linguists call British, or Brythonic, one of the Celtic insular languages, which also includes Breton and Cornish. This language borrowed heavily from Latin, not surprising since Rome ruled Britain for nearly four hundred years. An easy example of this influence is the Latin word *draco*, which becomes *draig* in Welsh and *dragon* in English. Many of these words with Latin roots have to do with religion, again not surprising given the use of Latin in the Christian Church and the fact that

many Britons, under the influence of Rome, converted to Christianity after 311 AD: the Latin *sacramentum* becomes *sacrafen; episcopus* (bishop) becomes *esgob; ecclesia*, the Latin word for *church*, becomes *eglwys; altare* becomes *allor*; and so on.

The language spoken by the earliest Britons can only be guessed at as some proto-Brythonic, pre-Celtic language. The people of Britain, prior to the coming of the Romans, were not literate, so there is no record of them or their history, beyond the material remains uncovered by archaeologists.

I want to emphasize that how *you*, as a reader, choose to pronounce the words in my books is completely up to you. Pronouncing Welsh names and places 'properly' is by no means a requirement, and I completely understand if saying Llywelyn the Welsh way is a barrier to enjoying the story.

Pronunciation Guide

If you've reached a point where you'd like to know better how to pronounce the words as the characters themselves would, below is a rough pronunciation guide to help you on your way:

a 'ah' as in 'rah' (Caradog)

ae 'eye' as in 'my' (Cadfael)

ai 'eye' as in 'my' (Owain)

aw 'ow' as in 'cow' (fawr)

au 'eye' as in 'my' (Dau)

c a hard 'c' sound (Cadfael)

ch a non-English sound as in Scottish 'ch' in 'loch' (Fychan)

dd a buzzy 'th' sound, as in 'the' (Ddu; Gwynedd)

e 'eh' as in 'met' (Ceri)

eu 'ay' as in 'day' (Ddeufaen)

f 'v' as in 'of' (Cadfael)

ff as in 'off' (Gruffydd)

g a hard 'g' sound, as in 'gas' (Goronwy)

i 'ee' as in 'see' (Ceri)

ia 'yah' as in 'yawn' (Iago)

ieu sounds like the cheer, 'yay' (Ieuan)

l as in 'lamp' (Llywelyn)

ll a breathy /sh/ sound that does not occur in English (Llywelyn)

o 'aw' as in 'dog' (Cadog)

oe 'oy' as in 'boy' (Coel)

rh a breathy mix between 'r' and 'rh' that does not occur in English (Rhys)

th a softer sound than for 'dd,' as in 'thick' (Arthur)

u a short 'ih' sound (Gruffydd), or a long 'ee' sound (Cymru—pronounced 'kumree')

w as a consonant, is an English 'w' (Llywelyn); as a vowel, an 'oo' sound like in 'book' (Bwlch); wy has been known to be 'oy' as in 'boy', but wyn is 'win'.

y the only letter in which Welsh is not phonetic. It can be an 'ih' sound, as in 'Gwyn,' is often an 'uh' sound (Cymru), and, at the end of the word, it is an 'ee' sound (thus, both Cymru—the modern word for Wales—and Cymry—the word for Wales in the medieval period—are pronounced 'kumree').

Specific Names and Places

Abergavenny — Ah-bare-gahv-ENN-ee
Aberystwyth — Ah-bare-IH-stwith
Angharad — An-GAR-ad
Bevyn — BEH-vin
Bronwen — BRON-wen
Buellt —BEE-eh/sh/t
Bwlch y Ddeufaen —Boolk -uh- THEY-vine
Cadair Idris —CAH-dire EE-drees
Cadwaladr — Cad-wall-A-der
Caerleon — Kire-LEH-on
Caernarfon — Kire -NAR-von
Caerphilly — Kire-FILL-ee
Cariad — car-EE-ad
Conwy — CON-wee
Cymru — CUM-ree
Cymry — CUM-ree
Dafydd — DAH-vith ('th' as in 'the')
Deheubarth — deh-HAY-barth
Dewi — DEH-wee
Dinas Bran — DEE-nahs Bran
Dolbadarn — Dol-BA-darn
Dolgellau — Doll-GE/sh/-eye
Gruffydd Fychan — GRIFF-ith VICK-an
Gwenllian — Gwen-/sh/EE-ahn
Gwladys — Goo-LAD-iss
Gwynedd — GWIN-eth ('th' as in 'the')
Hywel — HUH-well
Ieuan — YAY-an
Llywelyn — /sh/ew-EL-in
Marged — MAR-ged (hard 'g')
Mathonwy — Math-ON-wee
Owain — OH-wine
Rhiannon — Ree-AH-non
Sion — Shawn
Tywi — TUH-wee
Usk — Isk
Ynys Mon — UN-iss mon

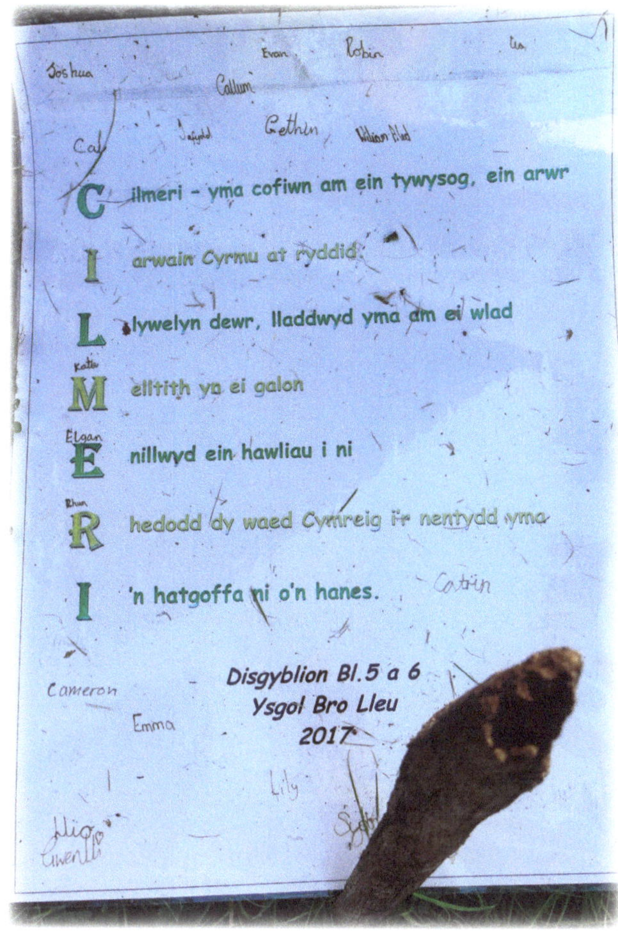

Found at the Llywelyn Memorial in Cilmeri

Chapter Four: The People of After Cilmeri

The *After Cilmeri* series includes both historical and fictional characters. The three who drive the story at the start are, of course, Meg, Anna, and David. They are fictional characters, but they interact in a vividly realized historical world. I always say that my books are as historically accurate as I can make them *except when they aren't*. That has to be particularly true in a story where the characters time travel from a world called Avalon to one called Earth Two. And while the starting point for a given historical figure must be what happened to him in 'real life', because the books take place in an alternate universe, his or her character can't help but diverge from our world's known past.

The most obvious example of this is, of course, the character of Llywelyn ap Gruffydd, whose life ended in our world on December 11, 1282, while he is saved by Anna and David in the opening of *Footsteps in Time*. Other historical  figures fare according to the needs of the story, with births and deaths and adventures following, in some cases, similar paths to what happened in 'our' world, and in other cases diverging extensively.

 — indicates historical figure

Llywelyn ap Gruffydd

The historical life and death of Llywelyn ap Gruffydd provides the framework for the *After Cilmeri* series, and his and Meg's love is the pivot around which the story revolves. Initially, Llywelyn falls in love with Meg almost despite himself, and while he is twenty years older than she is, as their relationship evolves, they grow to become equals. Their years apart (between the events of *Daughter* and *Footsteps*) are traumatic for them both, and *Footsteps in Time* begins where the known historical events involving Llywelyn leave off.

Once Anna and David—and then Meg—return to Earth Two, Llywelyn finds himself with renewed purpose and reason for living. He becomes King of Wales and the father of the King of England. His health drives the time travel in *Children of Time,* but he recovers, and Meg is determined to keep him healthy in Earth Two as long as possible. David asks his father to come to Ireland in *Outpost in Time* to help mediate the conflict with the barons, little knowing the rebellion that is imminent. Had he known, such is Llywelyn's character that he would have come anyway.

Meg

Meg was raised in a household with two parents of Welsh descent, though neither spoke much Welsh beyond the occasional word or phrase. When Meg was seventeen, her father died, which sent her into something of a tailspin. At only eighteen, she married her boyfriend, Trevor Lloyd. Though he abused her, and she left him

Llywelyn's keep at Criccieth: front gate

initially because of it, when their daughter, Anna, was two years old and Trevor was diagnosed with pancreatic cancer, Meg consented to return to him during his treatment.

Several months later, after an argument, Trevor hits Meg and storms out of the house. He has alcohol and medication in his system and is killed while driving.

Freed from her marriage, Meg returns to live with her mother and sister, Elisa.

Llywelyn's monument at Cilmeri

Then, only a week after the funeral, on the way to taking Anna to buy ice cream, Meg finds herself driving down the same road upon which Trevor died. As she approaches the stop sign, the car skids. But instead of crashing into the embankment as Trevor had done, Meg slides *through* it into the thirteenth century.

Meg lives in Earth Two for ten months. Secretly married to Llywelyn, she becomes pregnant with their child, but when she goes into labor, she is transported back to her mother's house in Pennsylvania. She gives birth to David and afterwards embarks on a journey towards self-discovery and self-empowerment. Returning to college and then graduate school in medieval history, she eventually achieves a Ph.D. in medieval studies, her focus throughout on the time of Llywelyn ap Gruffydd. She never (re)marries and tries to teach her children about Wales and the Welsh language but with limited success, since she is unable, of course, to tell them the truth.

Having become an accomplished scholar and much more sure of herself and her own identity, Meg returns to Earth Two and Llywelyn at the age of thirty-seven. Once there, she marries Llywelyn again and takes up the mantle of the Queen of Wales. Both David and Llywelyn rely heavily on her knowledge and guidance as they forge a new path for Wales and Britain as a whole.

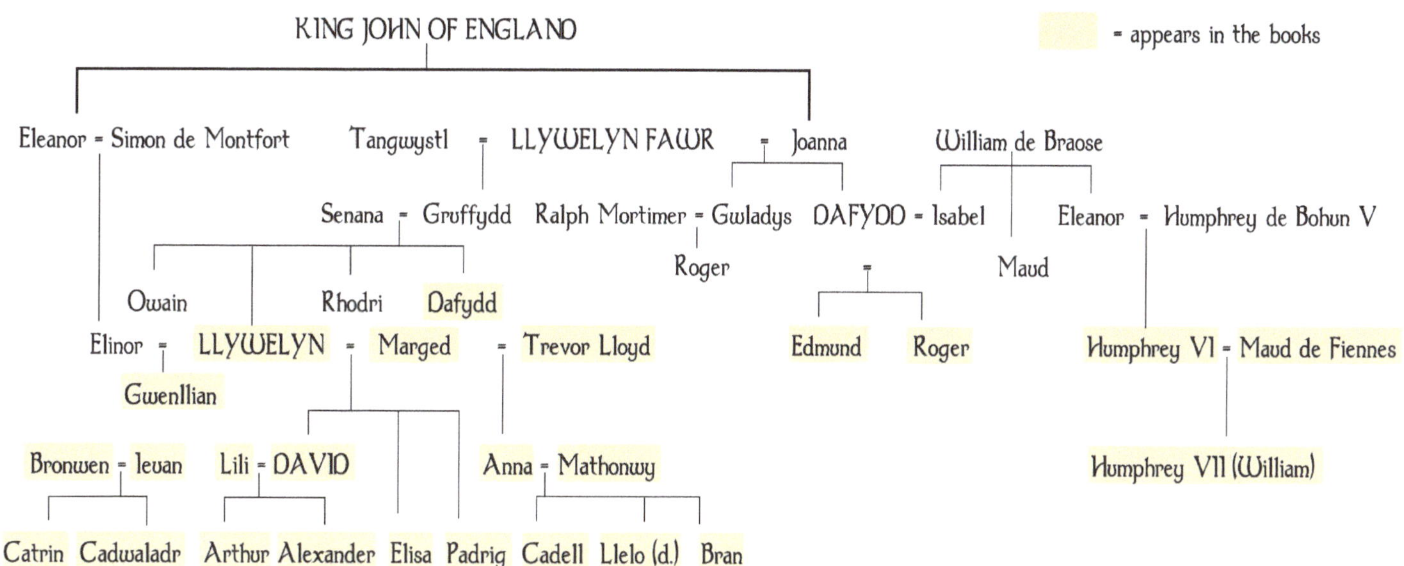

Welsh Royal Family Tree

Anna

Born to Trevor Lloyd and Meg in August 1993, Anna is Meg's eldest child. In January 1996, at only 2 ½, she is transported with her mother to Earth Two. While there, she proves to be resilient, but after their return to the modern world and her brother's birth, she refuses to speak Welsh or mention Llewelyn, whom she had grown to love as a father. Over time her memories of Wales fade.

However, on December 11, 2010, just after David's fourteenth birthday, Anna is driving with him to pick up their cousin Christopher when she bursts through a snowbank and ends up at Cilmeri in 1282. Their appearance—and quick dispatch of the English attackers—saves Llywelyn's life. While Llywelyn understands instantly who she and David are and what they have done, he doesn't reveal the truth to the siblings until a month later.

It is only then that some of Anna's suppressed memories, particularly of Llywelyn and Goronwy, Llywelyn's seneschal, return. As the series progresses, Anna comes more and more into her own. By the time she and her mother time travel to Avalon in *Ashes of Time* and then by herself in *Shades of Time,* Anna has spent twelve years negotiating the politics and society of Earth Two and finds herself a capable diplomat in her own right in dealing with Chad Treadman.

David

The story of the long-lost son who returns to claim the throne is one that has resonated down the ages. Sometimes, as in the King Arthur story, he is deliberately hidden and is able to return to his kingdom only after his father is dead, often at the hand of a treacherous uncle. Welsh history certainly has its share of such uncles, but David's story wouldn't be as fulfilling and complete without the finding of his true father.

David is born in the modern world because his mother returns there at the onset of labor. He grows up not knowing anything at all about his mother's past or his real father. At the age of fourteen, he is riding with his sister when she drives their aunt's minivan into medieval Wales and saves the life of Llywelyn ap Gruffydd. While they realize fairly quickly that they've time traveled, it isn't until Llywelyn confesses the truth to them that David learns of his true heritage.

The minivan Anna "drove" to Wales

They all stared at each other, or rather, the men stared at David. They seemed frozen to their horses, and Anna looked up at David, trying to see what they saw. He had turned fourteen in November, but his voice hadn't yet changed. Nor had he grown as tall as many of his friends. At 5' 6", he was still four inches taller than she, however. David had sandy blond hair, cut short, and an athletic build, thanks to his continuous efforts in soccer and karate. Anna's friends at school considered him cute in a geeky sort of way.   *—Footsteps in Time,* Chapter 1

Being a prince of Wales isn't something for which David was trained or in any way prepared, and yet, he embraces his responsibilities (for the most part), and continually seeks a way to unite and blend the modern and medieval within him. Although he can be uncomfortable with his growing power and the push from those around him to claim more and more of it, he understands why he must do so. He is driven by his sense of right and wrong, what his sister might call his stubborn sense of righteousness, as well as the heavy responsibility he feels to make the world a better place in a way that he knows only he can.

Mathonwy ap Rhys

Wary initially at being summoned to Castell y Bere to mentor a cousin he never knew he had, Math quickly recognizes that David is not only something special, but crucial to the survival of Wales. He takes his duties seriously, and, in the process, becomes one of David's staunchest supporters. He also falls in love with Anna, finding her combination of beauty, intelligence, and sincerity irresistible and unique for a woman of the court.

Math's surety and solidity provide a constant support for David, who starts out idolizing him and grows to view him as a best friend and counselor. Throughout the series, Math acts as a second-in-command—and sometimes regent when David or Llywelyn is absent—ruling from his seat of Dinas Bran in eastern Gwynedd with Anna by his side.

Lili ferch Cynan

Sister to Ieuan, with a troubled relationship with her father, Lili grew up following her older brother around. Ieuan taught her archery, and she continues the practice because it is something for herself alone—a place of peace and a chance to be herself in a way she often isn't allowed to be.

> Her first arrow went wide, and then her second. Then she shot over the target on purpose—out of frustration and guilt, and maybe even a bit of fear—losing the arrow in the trees beyond the range. Ieuan was riding into danger, and she was loosing arrows at a target, safe at Buellt. She didn't want to be safe. She wanted to yell and fight and blow up a curtain wall like they had at Painscastle. Her life was so sedate, so set, and not what she wanted. She would have screamed in frustration if the air wasn't so still that someone on the castle ramparts might have heard her and come running out to see what was the matter. *—Crossroads in Time,* Chapter 2

Lili ultimately works out her relationship with David in such a way that they are partners in life as well as King and Queen of England. Beloved in a way David cannot be, over time Lili grows into the role of queen in her own right. She is the mother of Arthur and Alexander, to whom she is fiercely devoted, despite societal pressures on a queen that might preclude her taking an active role in their lives.

Looking down the valley from Castell y Bere

Wallowa Mountains, where Cassie hunts

Bronwen Llywelyn

Bronwen is the first modern person David attempts to convince that the alternate universe of Earth Two not only exists but is a place to which he can travel back and forth. Her training in archeology makes her, like Meg, a perfect candidate for adaptation to a medieval world, and, with the encouragement of Ieuan, with whom she eventually falls in love and marries, she abandons her unsatisfactory life in Avalon. Vaulted into a position of authority through her friendship with David and marriage to Ieuan, she uses her intelligence and compassion to promote equality and justice in her new world. She is the only one of the original twenty-firsters who has never returned to Avalon.

Ieuan ap Cynan

Promoted to captain of David's guard in *Prince of Time*, Ieuan immediately becomes one of David's closest companions and genuine friends. Ieuan is the first medieval person to time travel with David, and he overcomes his initial bewilderment to not only accept the truth of David's station, but embrace it. He also has the good sense to adjust to the idea that men and women are equal in intelligence, and his marriage to Bronwen is a true meeting of the minds. Through association with the twenty-firsters, he becomes more progressive than any other man of his time.

Alexander Callum

Callum arrived in Earth Two by accident, trying to fulfill his duties as an MI-5 agent. Although initially more lost than many of the twenty-firsters, he eventually finds his feet in Earth Two as adviser to David, who considers him one of his closest companions and anoints him the Earl of Shrewsbury to give him the necessary stature to act as a diplomat. As Mark Jones notes:

It wasn't just David who'd had destiny thrust upon him. Callum had done his best in the modern world, but it hadn't been until he'd traveled to the medieval world that he'd come into his own. David had made him the Earl of Shrewsbury, and Mark was pretty sure that was his real identity, not the mild mannered MI5 agent he'd been in Avalon.—*Shades of Time*, Chapter 8

Cassie McKay Callum

Cassie is another twenty-firster who arrives in Avalon by accident and is given no choice but to stay, having been caught up in the plane crash that brings Meg to Hadrian's Wall. Cassie, however, is dumped in Scotland, west of Stirling Castle, and forced to carve out a life for herself in a way that none of the other twenty-firsters had to do. She survives on her skills as a linguist, an archer, and a diplomat, finding ways to overcome obstacles in a landscape that is entirely alien to her.

When Callum's party is ambushed on the road to Stirling, Cassie pulls him out of a ditch and takes him to her cabin. They soon discover how well they work together, and Cassie consents to leave her mountains in order to marry him. While she sees this decision at first as a betrayal of who she is, she ultimately comes to realize that not only does she love Callum, but the world she's fallen into is much larger than she'd imagined—and there is much good she can do on a larger stage.

Cassie travels with Callum and David to Avalon in *Castaways in Time* and remains behind after Callum is shot, eventually becoming an MI-5 agent herself (and a better driver than Callum). She, along with Callum and a busload of twenty-firsters, returns to Earth Two in *Ashes of Time*.

Christopher's car

Christopher Shepherd

Christopher decided when he was seven years old (*Prince of Time*) that his goal in life was to travel to Earth Two with his older cousin David and become a knight. Throughout his teenage years, much of his energy is directed towards that end, but when he rescues Gwenllian and Arthur, who have time traveled to Avalon, he takes it upon himself to see that they return home safely.

> "I've pretty much given Gwenllian and Arthur the grand tour of the twenty-first century, haven't I?"
>
> "How's that?" Mark said.
>
> "Chocolate chip pancakes and a visit to a car wash."
>
> —*Masters of Time*, Chapter 26

Although the circumstances leading up to the journey are accidental, as is the killing of Gilbert de Clare at Westminster Palace with his car, it is clear to him—more than to many of the other twenty-firsters—that nothing about their time travel happens by accident.

Once in Earth Two, Christopher strives with a will to acclimate to the medieval world. While he would not have sought out the events of *Outpost in Time* and *Champions of Time,* he rises to the occasion when presented with challenges and is well on his way to becoming the knight he'd always dreamed of being.

Gwenllian ferch Llywelyn

Of all the medieval people affected by the arrival of David and Anna into Earth Two, Gwenllian is perhaps the most changed. Because her father lived, she was not abducted as an infant and imprisoned in a convent for the rest of her life. And once Llywelyn survives, because Anna had the necessary fortitude and intelligence to escape with her from Castell y Bere, she lives to become a confident young woman.

In *Masters of Time*, Gwenllian takes it upon herself to time travel to Avalon with her little nephew Arthur, rather than allow him to be used or harmed by Gilbert de Clare. The growing equality of women in Earth Two has encouraged her to think beyond marriage and children as her only career path, and she has dreams of attending university in either world.

Mark Jones

A loyal lieutenant of Callum, sometimes despite himself, Mark prefers Avalon to Earth Two and makes no apologies for it. He travels the first time to Earth Two on the Cardiff bus in *Ashes of Time*, back to Avalon in *Guardians of Time,* where he stays behind, and then back to Earth Two in *Shades of Time*. He is unhappy about the lack of modern amenities and computers, and resents the fact that David has asked him to return. As he tells Callum in *Champions of Time*, "David can't always get what he wants." That said, he acknowledges the important role he plays in David's reign, appreciates that he can make a difference, and feels as if the other twenty-firsters are a genuine family for him.

TRANSCRIPT -- CLASSIFIED DOCUMENT--DO NOT CIRCULATE
Interview with Jon and Paul Fischer
TIME TRAVEL INITIATIVE
T.L. Nowak

TLN: When did you first encounter Christopher Shepherd?

Jon: Well, I mean, we've been friends since we were little.

Paul: They went to kindergarten together.

TLN: This latest incident, when you met with Christopher, who was with him?

Jon: You know who! We've told you this six hundred times!

Paul: Jon--

Jon: You know we have, Dad! He was with Gwenllian and Arthur. Gwenllian is David's half-sister and Arthur is his son, so I suppose that makes Arthur her nephew.

TLN: Did you doubt they were who they said they were?

Jon: No.

TLN: If you don't mind elaborating ...

Jon: They spoke Welsh. Who else speaks Welsh?

[note, the subject here folded his arms across his chest and refused to say anything further]

TLN: Paul, what was your impression of Gwenllian and Arthur?

Paul: They were kids. I mean, Christopher said they were his cousins

cont. page 2

1

CIA memo after Christopher's escape

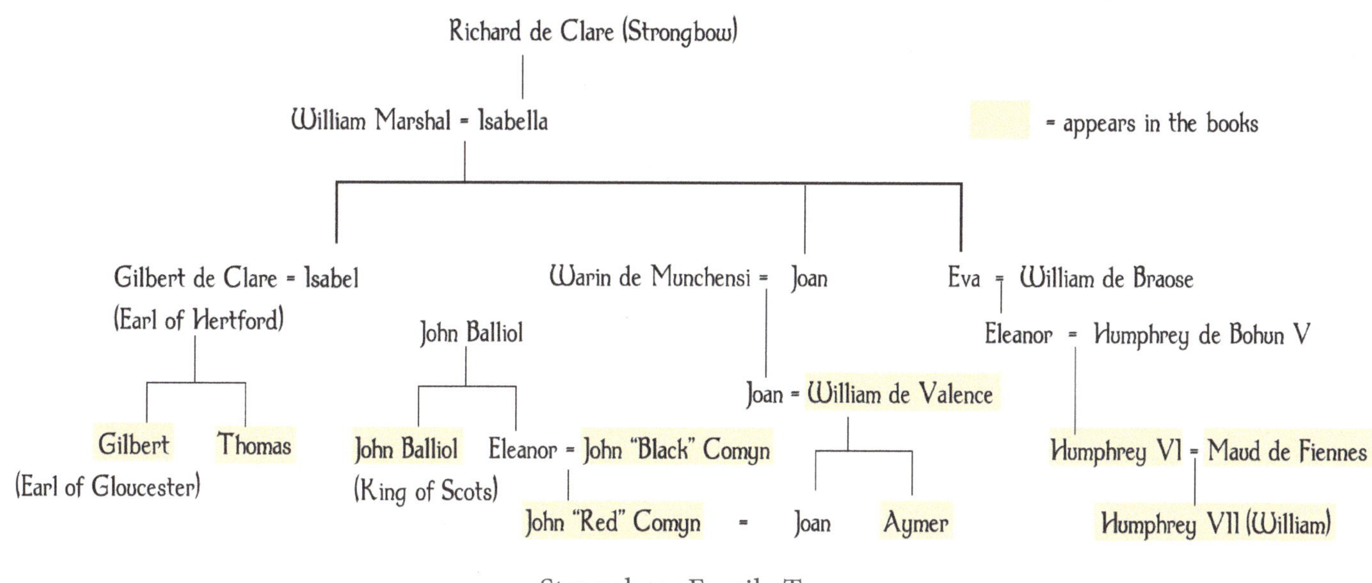

Strongbow Family Tree

King Edward

King Edward was a giant of his time, standing head and shoulders above the kings who came before and after him. To the English, he was a great king. To the Scots, Irish, and Welsh, not so much. For the Welsh, he stands opposite Llywelyn as the antagonist in the story. While on one hand, Edward was organized, a law-giver (codifying within English law existing statues into a more cohesive system of law), and judicious in his approach to managing his kingdom, on the other hand, he was fiercely determined to bring every person or people who challenged him to heel. He was the most successful medieval ruler at controlling the four regions that surrounded England: Scotland, Ireland, Wales, and Aquitaine. Without Edward, there would have been no death of Llywelyn at Cilmeri.

In *Footsteps in Time,* Edward is a powerful antagonist, but he dies not by the actions of David or Llywelyn, but at the hands of his Jewish food taster, out of revenge for his longstanding persecution of the Jewish people.

Dafydd ap Gruffydd

By 1282, when the events of *Footsteps in Time* take place, Dafydd has grown from the eight-year-old boy he was in 1246, to a forty-four-year-old man who has spent half his life supporting Llywelyn and half his life fighting him. In *Daughter of Time,* he attempts to woo Meg away from Llywelyn, and then, when she refuses him, he abducts her. Although he appears loyal again at the beginning of *Footsteps in Time,* he defects to the English yet again and dies with Edward at the encampment near Lancaster.

Humphrey de Bohun

Humphrey de Bohun, both as a historical figure and as a character in the *After Cilmeri* series, has a complicated history and personality. In 1265 as an idealistic teenager, he watched his father die supporting a cause he believed in: the Second Barons' War and Simon de Montfort. As a Marcher baron, he was predisposed to intrigue and distrust, both of which he learned at the feet of his grandfather, also named Humphrey, who was very protective of his own rights and honors, and who himself had a history of opposing the king.

Humphrey is introduced in *Daughter of Time* as a young man who exposes a plot to murder Llywelyn. Years later, in *Prince of Time,* he conspires against Llywelyn and plots to take the throne of England. However, over the subsequent books in the series, he comes to realize that not only do his interests and David's align, but he trusts David, cares about the future of his country, and wants to be part of David's world.

Humphrey … had changed in the last few years since David had become King of England, almost as if the sharp edges, which the dog-eat-dog world of the March required in order for him to survive, had been worn down and softened, revealing a more vulnerable man beneath—a man he'd spent his adult life trying to hide. David's mother had assured David it was there, because she'd seen it. A few years of David's honesty and justice had been required to convince Humphrey that it was safe to show it again.

—*Masters of Time,* Chapter 12

Site of William's arrival in Avalon

William de Bohun

Born in 1276, Humphrey de Bohun (nicknamed William in the *After Cilmeri* series), was a supporter of the king, but as a Marcher baron, he was determined to maintain his privileges and ensure that the king adhered to Magna Carta. He was a major player in the Scottish wars for independence, fighting for Edwards I and II, but also a companion to Robbie Bruce. When King Edward abducted Robbie's wife to assure Robbie's good behavior, Humphrey and his wife, Elizabeth of Rhuddlan, Edward's daughter, were her custodians.

In the *After Cilmeri* series, William feels the heavy burden of his family's legacy and constantly strives both to live up to it and to deserve it. He has spent his life trying to please his father and feeling as if he never quite measures up. He sees himself as a pawn in *Crossroads in Time,* but with the events of *Outpost in Time,* he begins to come into his own. In *Champions of Time,* David tells him that Avalon is a future world and exposes him to the person he became in Avalon's past. At that point, William achieves a sense of peace with himself and the man he hopes to become.

Gilbert de Clare

One of the greatest Marcher barons of the Middle Ages, Gilbert de Clare came into his inheritance as a young man after briefly being a ward of Humphrey de Bohun IV. He married first Alice de Valence, daughter of William de Valence, but after producing two daughters, their marriage was annulled, at which point Gilbert married Joan of Acre, daughter of King Edward himself. Gilbert was six years older than Humphrey de Bohun VI, and while the two men started out as allies in the Second Barons' War, Gilbert switched allegiances, and they were rarely anything but adversaries from then on.

Gilbert's relationship with Llywelyn ap Gruffydd was equally complicated in that, during the Second Barons' War, Gilbert, Llywelyn, and Simon de Montfort drafted a plan to split England and Wales among the three of them. But once Gilbert switched sides, he fought equally hard for Edward, who himself had initially supported Simon de Montfort before the actual fighting started. In 1268, Llywelyn burned Gilbert's nascent castle at Caerphilly, and in 1282, Gilbert himself led the English forces against Llywelyn in south Wales.

In the *After Cilmeri* series, Gilbert appears for many years to be a staunch ally of David, supporting his claim to the throne of England and acting as a stalwart adviser. In *Masters of Time,* however, he allies with the brother of King Philip of France, arranges for the assassination of both Philip and David, and ultimately dies on the front end of Christopher's car as Christopher time travels into Westminster Palace.

Nicholas de Carew

In the 13th century, Sir Nicholas de Carew was a high ranking officer and distinguished soldier. He fought on behalf of the king in Ireland and in Europe, but does not appear to have played much of a role in the Welsh wars up until 1282. He was responsible for much of the medieval construction of Carew Castle between 1280 and 1310.

In the *After Cilmeri* series, very early on, Nicholas sees the way the wind is blowing and chooses to side with David and Llywelyn instead of King Edward. He is well rewarded for his loyalty with lands in both England and Wales, and, over time, his cynicism gives way to admiration and appreciation for David's goals. As a close confidant of David, he acts as regent for him when he is absent.

> Carew laughed. "My motives are clear. I'm interested in power."
>
> "Edward can give you more of it than we can," David said.
>
> "But Edward is interested in only power too. That means we don't work well together. You, on the other hand, care so little about power it's hard to believe you are a prince. I understand you not at all, but I do trust you. That makes the difference."
>
> David raised his head to look at his father, who lifted his eyebrows and gave him a small smile.
>
> "Fine," David said. "You can come."
>
> "Good," Carew said. "You won't regret it."
> —*Footsteps in Time*, Chapter 20

Edmund Mortimer

As the second son of his father, Roger, Edmund Mortimer never thought he was going to be the heir to the Mortimer estates and went to Oxford to become a cleric. When his older brother died, he left school to take up the mantle of the Mortimer dynasty. He and his brother, Roger, were the primary conspirators in the plan to lure Llywelyn ap Gruffydd to Cilmeri. In Avalon's history, they succeeded.

From a letter to King Edward from Archbishop Peckham:

> Sire, know that those who were at the death of Llywelyn found in the most secret part of his body some small things which we have seen. Among other things was a treasonable letter disguised by false names. And that you may be

Stained glass from Carew Castle

The ruins of the Mortimer castle at Wigmore

warned, we sent a copy of the letter to the Bishop of Bath, and the letter itself Edmund Mortimer has, with Llywelyn's privy seal, and these things you may have at your pleasure …

[Martin 1884]

In Earth Two, Llywelyn is saved, King Edward dies, and Edmund finds himself in a less favorable situation in relation to the other Marcher barons and the regents of England. After his brother Roger imprisons him in his own castle, Anna allies with Edmund and escapes into Wales. As a result, Edmund sees which way the wind is blowing and, with his cousin Humphrey de Bohun, allies permanently with David.

Roger Mortimer

The third Mortimer son, Roger, is as ambitious and conniving in Avalon's history as I have written in Earth Two. In Avalon, he conspired with his brother Edmund to assassinate Llywelyn and himself carried Llywelyn's head to King Edward. In Earth Two, after Roger's initial attempt to gain standing by working with barons such as Roger Bigod and William de Valence, he manages to evade punishment, in part by acquiescing to the plan to put David on the throne of England. To all appearances, he retires quietly to his estates, but, in reality, he has not changed and resents being out of favor with the new king. In *Shades of Time*, he is revealed as the leader of the English conspiracy to assassinate David.

John Balliol

In both Avalon and Earth Two, John Balliol was the compromise choice for King of Scots. In Avalon, King Edward chose him in hopes that he would be an ineffective king and humiliated him routinely. In turn, Balliol was despised by his own barons because they felt he was too accommodating to King Edward. Once Balliol was deposed, King Edward invaded Scotland.

In Earth Two, after the events of *Exiles in Time*, Balliol wins the election, in part because the delegates are divided between the claims of the Bruces and the Comyns. Despite his victory, Balliol resents David's power as King of England and convinces himself that David is only biding his time until he invades. Rather than wait for that to happen, he conspires with barons in England and Ireland to assassinate David and take the English throne. He is defeated in *Champions of Time,* and David's choice of punishment is to humiliate him rather than kill him.

William de Valence

William de Valence was the fourth son of Isabella of Angouleme, by her second husband, Hugh X de Lusignan, making him and King Henry III of England half-brothers. Over time, his influence over the English royal court grew, as did the honors heaped upon him by Henry, which caused resentment among the barons without ties to France and led ultimately to the rebellion of Simon de Montfort and the Second Barons' War. From his base in Pembroke, he was heavily involved in the 1282 conquest of Wales and oversaw the final surrender of Castell y Bere to royal forces in 1283.

In *Crossroads in Time*, Valence resents the loss of his lands in Wales and conspires with other barons to regain power. His conspiracy shifts to outright rebellion in *Children of Time* and ultimately leads to his death.

James Stewart

As the fifth High Steward of Scotland, James Stewart became one of the Guardians of Scotland during the disputed succession to the throne in 1290. Though he submitted to King Edward in 1297, he was a supporter of William Wallace and then Robert Bruce, in whose service he died in 1309.

In the *After Cilmeri* series, James becomes a staunch friend and ally of Alexander Callum, King David, and Robert 'Robbie' Bruce. As chaperone to Robbie, Christopher, and their friends, he survives the massacre at Trim Castle in Ireland in *Outpost in Time,* and his forces play an invaluable role in the siege of Skipton Castle in *Champions of Time*.

Robbie Bruce

In Avalon's history, Robert the Bruce is one of the greatest of Scotland's kings in the medieval period, though it was his father who first put in a claim to the throne after the death of King Alexander and his granddaughter, Margaret. However, in *Exiles in Time,* during the disputed succession to the throne of Scotland, the elder Robert Bruce dies. At the time, Robbie is too young to claim the throne, and his grandfather is too old. Thus, the Scots vote for John Balliol.

The historic rivalry with the Comyns continues, however, and in *Outpost in Time,* Robbie plays an important role in turning back Red Comyn's attempt to assassinate David and become High King of Ireland. During the Battle of Tara, Robbie attacks Red Comyn and tries to kill him, but David stops him.

Red Comyn

The Comyns were one of the most dominant families in Scotland even before John Balliol, a relation by marriage, became king. The Bruces were their main rival, for the throne and in life. Initially, the Bruces and the Comyns ended up on opposite sides of the war with King Edward, with Robert Bruce supporting Edward from the royal castle at Carlisle and the Comyns attacking it. Later, both clans deserted King Edward, though they maintained their hatred of each other.

In Avalon's history, Robbie Bruce murders Red Comyn in a church. When King Edward hears of it, he sends Aymer de Valence, Red's brother-in-law, to avenge himself upon the Bruces. Despite this effort, Robbie is crowned King of Scots in 1306 and then wages a guerilla war against King Edward—and then Edward II—until his victory at Bannockburn in 1314.

In the *After Cilmeri* series, Robbie Bruce idolizes David and becomes his companion and supporter. Robbie participates in the dispute over the succession in *Exiles in Time*, and then is instrumental in David's victory over the combined forces of the rebelling Scot, Irish, and English barons in *Outpost in Time* and *Champions of Time*.

Carrickfergus: Stewart's Castle in Ireland

Goronwy ap Heilin

A longtime companion of Llywelyn ap Gruffydd, in Avalon's history, Goronwy was faithful to the Welsh cause throughout the reign of Llywelyn and, after his death, the subsequent claim to the principality by Dafydd ap Gruffydd. Goronwy held on to the Welsh cause to the bitter end, as he was among those who led guerilla raids against the English forces, even after the fall of Castell y Bere in the spring of 1283.

In the *After Cilmeri* series, Goronwy is with Llywelyn when he rescues Meg from her car in *Daughter of Time*. He adores Anna and acts as her surrogate uncle.

> When Prince Llywelyn put David down, he looked at Anna. "Do you remember anything of your time in Wales?"
>
> "My first memories aren't until David was a baby, except—" She paused, thinking hard, "—did I know Goronwy then?"
>
> Llywelyn smiled. "You did. And you called me Papa. You liked me to put you on my shoulders. You would grasp my hair with your fists to hold on."
>
> Anna gazed at him through several heartbeats. "I don't think you want to carry me anywhere, but I will call you Papa again, if you'd like."
>
> "Yes." He smiled. "I'd like that."
>
> *—Footsteps in Time*, Chapter 5

As the series progresses, though his health isn't always what it once was, he continues to be a staunch ally and friend of both Llywelyn and David and acts as custodian of Llywelyn's holdings in Gwynedd.

Hywel

As a stable boy in *Footsteps in Time*, Hywel follows Anna out of Castell y Bere and leads her north to Dolwyddelan Castle. He proves himself to be dependable, intelligent, and courageous—and absolutely loyal. Recognizing these qualities and wanting to reward them, David takes him on as his valet. Ultimately, Anna and Math promote him to steward of Dinas Bran.

The keep at Dolwyddelan

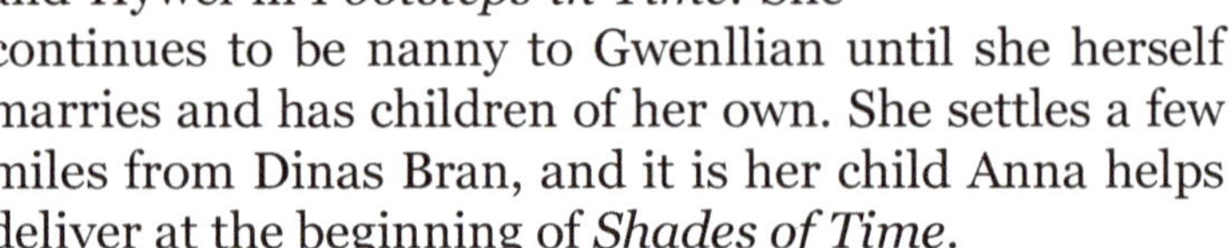

Heledd

As Gwenllian's wet nurse, Heledd agrees to flee Castell y Bere with Anna and Hywel in *Footsteps in Time*. She continues to be nanny to Gwenllian until she herself marries and has children of her own. She settles a few miles from Dinas Bran, and it is her child Anna helps deliver at the beginning of *Shades of Time*.

Huw ap Aeddan

In *Footsteps in Time*, Huw's family rescues David from the men who abducted him and comes with him to Dinas Bran. Huw joins the Order of the Pendragon, and is among those who aid Lili in *Masters of Time*. His role matures further when he becomes a close friend and companion to Christopher and is knighted with him after the Battle of Tara in *Outpost in Time*.

Bevyn

A young man in *Daughter of Time*, Bevyn is designated as Meg and Anna's protector during the ambush at Coedwig Gap. After David and Anna save Llywelyn's life in *Footsteps in Time*, he becomes David's mentor and trainer. He is one of the founders of the Order of the Pendragon, and his loyalty to David leads him to conspire in the death of David's cousin, a pretender to the throne of Wales. Although this results in a period of estrangement between him and David, eventually David recognizes that what Bevyn did was out of love for him, and they reconcile, returning Bevyn to David's inner circle as one of his most loyal lieutenants.

> He was well into middle age, and he knew enough of men by now to understand that someone like Dafydd came along once in a hundred years, if not longer. King Llywelyn was a remarkable leader, as had been his grandfather, Llywelyn Fawr. But Dafydd was the result of a special kind of alchemy, where the universe—and God—had conspired to produce someone so suited to his time and place that it was impossible to imagine the world without him. While he'd been born in Avalon, in that country called America, he belonged to Britain. To place him anywhere else would be to completely misunderstand who he was.
>
> *—Champions of Time,* Chapter 10

Aaron ben Simon

Meg meets Aaron in *Winds of Time* on the ship from Scotland to Wales. He helps her with her seasickness, and the pair aid each other when their boat capsizes in a storm. He becomes Llywelyn's court physician, and, through his influence, David asks Llywelyn to allow Jewish refugees to come to Wales. Ultimately, Aaron becomes one of the founders of the teaching hospital, Ysbyty Gwynedd, in Llangollen.

Samuel ben Aaron

The son of Aaron, as a young man Samuel rejected his faith and learned to pass as a Gentile in order to become a soldier. Under David's reign, the restrictions against Jews serving in the army are lifted, and David sends Samuel with Callum to Scotland in *Exiles in Time*. Through that adventure, Samuel and Callum become friends and companions, and Callum designates him Sheriff of Shrewsbury. Samuel participates in the rescue of the hostages at Beeston Castle in *Champions of Time*.

Rupert Jones

> Here Rupert was, the premier newsman in England, for God's sake, in the world even, muffled by a jumped-up dictator. Rupert mouthed the words to himself: *the world's premier newsman.* He would have put it on his office door at Westminster Castle if he could have done so without David mocking him mercilessly for it, or more likely, giving him the raised eyebrow look he had that meant he didn't have to say anything.
>
> –*Masters of Time*, chapter 32

An investigative reporter, Rupert tenaciously chases down every lead associated with the twenty-firsters, to the point of sneaking onto the Cardiff bus on a hunch that he will discover the truth about who and what they are. He is, therefore, on the second level of the double-decker bus when Cassie drives it into a pillar on the Menai Bridge and travels back to Earth Two in *Guardians of Time*.

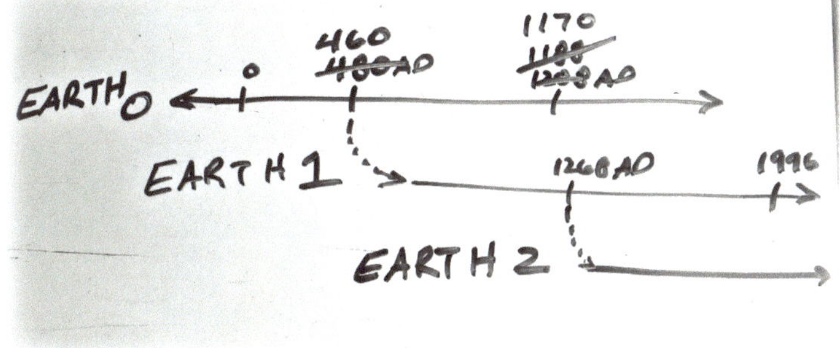

Chad's diagram of parallel universes

Samuel's visit to Scotland

Although at first he is daunted, not to mention terrified, to find himself in Earth Two, he quickly realizes that he has a front row seat on the greatest story he's ever encountered and commits wholeheartedly to developing an independent media in his new world.

MI-5

Though not a single person, the Security Service, known also as MI-5 or simply Five, plays a significant role in the *After Cilmeri* series. MI-5 (motto: *Keeping Our Country Safe*) is the branch of the British government charged with internal security. In the twenty-first century, its primary role has been to evaluate and eliminate terrorist threats and espionage on British soil. Throughout the *After Cilmeri* series, agents from MI-5 have alternately pursued and helped the time travelers, and many of the twenty-firsters who have chosen to stay in Earth Two are former MI-5 agents.

Chad Treadman

CEO of Treadman Global, Chad Treadman recruits Ted Shepherd, Christopher's father and Meg's brother-in-law, to work for him as his CIO. Through Ted, he learns about the defunct Time Travel Initiative and offers, first to Anna and then to David, to put his considerable resources to work for them—as an alternative to working with MI-5. On one hand, he is as good as his word and does everything he promises. On the other, David and Anna both can't help thinking he has an ulterior motive they don't yet understand.

In *Shades of Time*, Anna travels back to Earth Two on Chad's airplane and thus brings three more twenty-firsters—Sophie, Andre, and George—to Earth Two. Though David has concerns that their ultimate loyalty remains with Treadman, the three appear to be sincere in their desire to help Earth Two and share, at least in part, David's hopes for the future.

The British Isles

Chapter Five: The Landscape

Wales is known for its snow-covered mountains, deep lakes, hundreds of miles of coastline ... and a long, brutal history of rebellion and conquest. That conquest is reflected in the landscape and is why many of the places listed below are castles. It is important to point out that the castles built by the native Welsh kings and princes, such as Llywelyn ap Gruffydd and his grandfather, Llywelyn Fawr, were built more as administrative centers than to dominate the populace. The traditional Welsh 'castle' was actually a *llys*, a palace, rather than the massive stone bastions of the Edwardian era.

The stone bastions *are* impressive, however, and many are still standing with some semblance of what they looked like when they were built. The descriptions in this book also reflect the particulars of the *After Cilmeri* series, a fictional world, and I have indicated where the fictional world diverges from the 'real' one. Sadly, all of the photographs are from our world, since I am unable to time travel with Meg, Anna, and David.

Anglesey
Beaumaris
Menai Strait
Aber
Ysbyty Gwynedd
Caerhun
Rhuddlan
Saint Gwenffrewi's Well
Caernarfon
Dolbadarn
Denbigh
Snowdon
Dolwyddelan
Beeston
Gwynedd
Lyons Castle
Valle Crucis
Dinas Bran
Criccieth
Llangollen
Powys
Castell y Bere
The March
Montgomery
England
Offa's Dyke

North Wales

North Wales

Aber

Aber, or Garth Celyn, was one of the primary seats of the Kings of Gwynedd dating back to the twelfth century. It was less a castle than a *llys*, meaning palace (see *Royal Llys*). With the fall of the Royal House of Wales and the subsequent conquering of Wales by Edward I, the location of Aber was lost to history. It is only in the last twenty years that a large manor house overlooking the Menai Strait has been identified as the site of the palace. A single medieval tower still stands, known locally as 'Llywelyn's Tower'. It is all that remains of the once extensive site.

Culturally speaking, one of the most important records of Garth Celyn is found in the letters written in the last months of Llywelyn's life to King Edward I and John Peckham, the Archbishop of Canterbury.

Aber Castle plays an important role in the *After Cilmeri* series, since it remains Llywelyn's seat on the Welsh north coast, and it is one of the few castles that is featured in Avalon as well (*Guardians of Time*).

Anglesey

The name for Ynys Mon was deliberately changed to Anglesey by the Anglo-Norman conquerors, but that fact belies the extent to which Anglesey remains resolutely Welsh, with 7 out of 10 residents speaking Welsh to this day. Because of its function as the bread basket of Gwynedd, the populace suffered greatly over the millennia from foreign invaders, culminating with

Aber from Beaumaris Castle

the wars of 1277 and 1282, when it was conquered as a stepping stone to Snowdonia, the stronghold of Llywelyn ap Gruffydd.

After the 1282 war, the Normans deliberately razed to the ground much that was Welsh, including the royal palace at Aberffraw, the prosperous town of Llanfaes, Llanfaes Abbey, and the gravesites of Princesses Joanna and Elinor. Beaumaris Castle and its English borough were constructed near the former town of Llanfaes to subdue the hostile populace.

Beaumaris Castle

Beaumaris was begun in 1294, in response to a new rebellion in Wales. The castle, along with its associated English borough, was established near the ruins of the village of Llanfaes, which the English deliberately destroyed because it was the most populated and wealthy town in north Wales, and Llanfaes Abbey had been patronized by the kings and princes of Gwynedd. The

Beeston Castle

town's population was moved in its entirety to a new location in western Anglesey, and, for many years, the sarcophagus of Joanna, Llywelyn Fawr's wife, was used by English soldiers as a horse trough.

Beaumaris plays no role in Earth Two because it was built well after 1282, but David and William de Bohun appear here in Avalon in *Champions of Time*.

Beeston Castle

The hill upon which Beeston Castle is built dominates the surrounding landscape, and there is evidence of habitation in this location dating back to the Iron Age. The current castle was begun in the 1220s by Ranulf of Chester, and, during the medieval period, the castle acted as a jumping off point for conquests in Wales, especially since it was part of the Earldom of Chester, which was under royal control.

In *Shades of Time* and *Champions of Time*, Beeston Castle is the seat of Robert FitzWalter, who has conspired with Roger Mortimer and John Balliol, King of Scots, to overthrow David's rule.

Bwlch y Ddeufaen

From ancient times, the people of Wales crossed the River Conwy at Caerhun and headed into the hills,

Bwlch y Ddeufaen

reaching Bwlch y Ddeufaen, marked by standing stones on either side of the road (Bwlch y Ddeufaen means *pass of the two stones*). The road then descends out of the hills, arriving at Aber, at which point, travelers could either cross the Menai Strait at low tide or follow the road west towards Bangor and Caernarfon.

The topography of North Wales is such that, before modern blasting techniques, no significant road could run along the coastline due to the cliffs that come right down to the Irish Sea. Even the Romans found the topography impossible and chose to improve the ancient British road rather than attempt to build an entirely new one closer to the coast. A thousand years later, the Normans faced the same difficulties—and it was that difficult topography that allowed the princes of Gwynedd to maintain their seat at Aber almost uncontested. Protected by the mountains, their llys was accessible only by the pass of Bwlch y Ddeufaen or from the sea.

Caerhun

Caerhun was an important ford on the River Conwy, used since ancient times to connect Anglesey to Chester along an ancient road that traveled through Bwlch y Ddeufaen. The Romans recognized the ford's significance and built their fort of Canovium to guard it.

Caernarfon Castle

Beginning in 1277, King Edward began the construction of a series of castles to control the populace, particularly Gwynedd, which had always been a hotbed of Welsh resistance and resentment of English authority. Caernarfon Castle was begun in 1283 and became one of his most impressive monuments. As with Beaumaris, in the process of building the castle, the previously established Welsh community was destroyed. Instead, Edward imported English settlers to form an 'English borough'. Caernarfon then became King Edward's primary seat in Wales, and it was here that his son, Edward II was born—intentionally—so Edward could say that his son was the Prince of Wales, a title that from thenceforth was bestowed only on the eldest son of the English monarch.

To the delight of my Welsh nationalist friends, Caernarfon Castle is blown up in *Guardians of Time*.

Castell y Bere

My daughter, when she first saw Castell y Bere, informed me that it was in the middle of *freaking nowhere*! That is true for us now, but when it was built, the castle enabled the princes of Gwynedd to control the upper Dysynni valley and all the territory from Cadair Idris to Dolgellau as well as the Dyfi and Mawddach estuaries. The castle was luxurious for the time,

Caernarfon Castle

King Edward maintained the castle (to the tune of 265 pounds) from 1286 to 1290, but, as Adrian Pettifer (2000) states, "the castle proved too remote to be supplied in times of siege." It was burned during Madog ap Llywelyn's uprising in 1294 and never restored.

Castell y Bere is the first castle to which Llywelyn brings David and Anna in *Footsteps in Time*. Later in that book, the English burn it to the ground.

Criccieth Castle

Criccieth Castle was built by Llywelyn ap Iorwerth (Llywelyn Fawr) before 1239. Gruffydd ap Llywelyn was kept prisoner here, first by his father and then by his half-brother, before being transferred to the Tower of London. Llywelyn ap Gruffydd augmented the castle during his reign, as did Edward I after the Norman conquest of Wales.

Meg appears at Criccieth Castle after time traveling from Avalon in *Daughter of Time*. Her car ends up in a swamp, where it is found by Goronwy and Llywelyn.

"By all that is holy!" Goronwy saw the vehicle for the first time. "What is it?"

with stained glass windows, inlaid tile, and stone carvings (Davis 1978).

Llywelyn Fawr began Castell y Bere in 1221, after he decided his son Gruffydd had mismanaged the region and removed it from his control. His grandson, Llywelyn ap Gruffydd, added to the work, eventually creating a sprawling complex of buildings, surrounded by a system of walls and ditches that made the castle virtually impossible to assault. It was, in fact, the last castle to fall to English forces, though in 1283 it surrendered to King Edward's army without a fight.

Castell y Bere

Criccieth Castle

> "I don't know. A chariot of some kind, carrying two from the looks."
> —*Daughter of Time*, Chapter 2

Denbigh Castle

The present Denbigh Castle was built after 1282 by Henry de Lacy, a loyal lieutenant of King Edward, and became one of the Iron Ring of Castles that Edward built to surround Gwynedd and control the Welsh populace after the conquest of Wales. The castle was constructed on the site of a *llys* (or palace) for the rulers of Gwynedd, dating back at least several hundred years. Building the new Norman castle on this site was a deliberate attempt to project the power of the King of England, and, in that vein, Denbigh was built in a typically massive style. It's construction also included an English borough.

A rebellion, led by Madog ap Llywelyn, captured the partly-built castle in 1294, but the castle reverted to English hands after the rebellion and was repaired.

Dinas Bran

> He came up from a full somersault into a runner's crouch in the grass, and as he caught his breath, the blades in the tuft directly in front

Dinas Bran

of his nose came into focus. A drop of rain plopped onto it, and David shot a glance at the sky. It was raining instead of snowing, and low hanging clouds surrounded him.

> He knew instantly where he was: the castle of Dinas Bran sat silhouetted against the sky ...
> —*Guardians of Time*, Chapter 24

The first settlement at Dinas Bran was an iron age hill fort, from which the castle gets its name. *Dinas Bran* is variously translated as *Crow Castle, Crow City, Hill of the Crow*, or *Bran's Stronghold*.

Dinas Bran first appears in historical documents as early as 1073. While the current castle itself, such as it is, dates to 1260 to 1277, the encompassing ditch and earthen embankments, which enclose the southern

Dolbadarn Castle

and eastern portions of the stone fortress, date from the Iron Age.

During the final two decades of its occupation, Dinas Bran belonged to the princes of Powys. In 1277, however, during King Edward's initial foray into Wales, the Earl of Lincoln, Henry de Lacy, besieged the castle. The Welsh lord of Dinas Bran was forced to submit to the invading army, which chose to set the castle on fire and destroy it rather than try to fortify it.

Placed high on its mountain top above the village of Llangollen, Dinas Bran has almost been its own character in the *After Cilmeri* series and has been featured throughout the books. After Math and Anna's marriage, Llywelyn gives them the castle and the surrounding area to oversee. In the subsequent books in the series, Dinas Bran remains the jumping off point for the characters' adventures, up to, and including, the most recent books, *Shades of Time* and *Champions of Time*, in which Math and Anna play important roles.

Dolbadarn Castle

Dolbadarn sits on a crest above a narrow valley in Snowdonia, overshadowed by the enormous mountains behind it. It is likely that a Roman road passed through the area, as traces remain of a temporary Roman camp further up the road, once it turns east to Betws-y-Coed.

According to Pettifer (2000), the keep at Dolbadarn, which is the most well preserved piece, "vies with the gatehouse at Criccieth as Llywelyn the Great's finest piece of castle architecture". All three floors had fireplaces and toilets, even the basement. The outer walls were high enough to shield the roof of the upper floor and protect it from being fired on by missiles.

Llywelyn ap Gruffydd kept his elder brother, Owain, imprisoned at Dolbadarn for 20 years. He was released in 1277 as part of the Treaty of Rhuddlan. Owain had by then had spent the majority of his life in prison, and Llywelyn gave him the cantref of Llyn, in which he died sometime before December 1282 (Smith 1998).

Dolwyddelan Castle

Dolwyddelan has been on a major thoroughfare through Wales for millennia. Before the present castle was built by Llywelyn Fawr early in the 13th century, an older castle sat on a knoll on the adjacent valley floor. Before *that* castle was built, a major Roman road through Snowdonia passed just to the east, connecting Tomen y Mur with the small fort of Bryn y Gefeilliau and the larger fort of Canovium (Caerhun).

Over the centuries, Gwynedd had often been the most powerful Welsh kingdom, and the expansion of Llywe-

Dolwyddelan Castle

lyn Fawr's domains gave him a greater ability to build castles than previous rulers. The newer Dolwyddelan Castle represented a major stronghold for both Llywelyns throughout the 13th century. Both of them improved its defenses, luxuries, and overall structure numerous times over the course of their reigns.

Dolwyddelan was one of the last castles that King Edward captured in the 1282 war, and that was only after it had been abandoned. The present Dolwyddelan Castle has been heavily restored.

Dolwyddelan is the base for Llywelyn's campaign against King Edward in *Footsteps in Time* and the castle to which Anna flees in *Crossroads in Time*.

Gwynedd

With the end of the Roman occupation of Britain, the land was left wide open to invaders of all types. While the Saxons and their ilk attacked from the north and east, the Irish invaded from the west, conquering large portions of Wales. Legend has it that, in desperation, the people of Wales invited Cunedda, a warlord from the territory of Manau Gododdin, the region around what is now modern Edinburgh in southeast Scotland, to Wales with the promise of kingship, provided he could wrest control of the region from Irish raiders.

Cunedda succeeded and proceeded to divvy up Wales amongst his sons, keeping only Gwynedd for himself. It is from him that Welsh nobility of all regions claimed their right

Llyn Padarn, in Gwynedd

Llangollen from Dinas Bran

On November 6, 1282, the Welsh achieved a great victory over the English, who had thought to surprise them by crossing the Menai Strait and driving down the coast to Aber, Prince Llywelyn's palace on the Welsh north coast.

The Menai Strait is a narrow body of water that separates Anglesey from the Gwynedd mainland, with a river-like flow that changes course according to the tide. The rising tide approaches from the southwest, causing the water in the Strait to flow north-eastwards as the level rises. It then flows counter-clockwise around Anglesey until, a few hours later, it shifts, and begins to flow the opposite way.

At that point, the water runs from Bangor (on the mainland) and Llanfaes (on Anglesey) through the Strait in a south-westerly direction. It was at Llanfaes where the English commander, Tany, held his troops, waiting to cross to attack Aber.

By the time the tide reverses course, the tidal flow from the Caernarfon end has weakened, even if the tide continues to rise in height throughout the Strait. Thus, slack water between Anglesey and Gwynedd tends to occur approximately one hour before high or low tide.

On the day of the attack, the English hoped to cross near high tide, when the water would be at its calmest. They began at noon, with high tide at 1 pm, but were surprised by a Welsh force that swept down from the heights above the mainland beach and held them trapped against the water. The ferocity of the Welsh at-

to rule for centuries afterwards. The name of Gwynedd probably comes from Cunedda (=Weneda =Gwynedd).

Llangollen

Llangollen is a village in Powys associated with Dinas Bran and Valle Crucis Abbey. It has guarded a bridge across the Dee since the medieval period. In the *After Cilmeri* series, the community grows over time, due to the patronage of Math and Anna. It is the first village to take in Jewish refugees, and it is where the twenty-firsters establish a hospital and university. It is from Llangollen that the twenty-firsters travel back to Avalon on the Cardiff bus in *Guardians of Time.*

Lyons (Holt) Castle

King Edward began Lyons Castle as part of the conquest of Wales in 1277. In 1282, he presented it to John de Warenne. The castle was built on a thirty-nine-foot promontory and had a moat fed by the River Dee. Like many of the castles that formed Edward's Iron Ring of Castles, the castle was built with the intent to subdue the populace of north Wales and included an adjacent English borough, in which the Welsh were not welcome. The castle is now entirely ruined.

In *Shades of Time,* John de Warenne participates in a rebellion led by Roger Mortimer and John Balliol, during the course of which he imprisons Ieuan and Math at Lyons.

Menai Strait

And he sent a fleet of ships to Anglesey, and they gained possession of Arfon. And then was made the bridge over the Menai; but the bridge broke and countless numbers of the English were drowned and others slain.
—*Brut y Twysogion*, Peniarth Manuscript 20 (*Chronicle of the Princes*)

Menai Strait

Montgomery Castle

tack forced the English soldiers back across the bridge, which then broke under the weight of men, horses, and equipment. By then, the tide was in full spate, moving west at 2.5 knots.

History records that 16 English knights, another 16 squires, and 300 footmen died that day.

Prince Llywelyn believed he could capitalize on this victory by leaving his brother, Dafydd, in charge of Gwynedd and going southeast to Powys to rally support among the other Welsh lords of Wales. Unfortunately, he was lured into a trap at Cilmeri and killed (an event averted by David and Anna in *Footsteps in Time*).

The Menai Strait plays a role in *Guardians of Time*, in that Cassie drives the Cardiff bus into one of the supporting pillars of the modern bridge across the Menai, in order to time travel back to Earth Two.

Montgomery Castle

After the Norman conquest of England, the Mortimers became one of the most powerful families in England. They were Marcher barons, meaning they controlled portions of the March, the borderlands between England and Wales, and did everything in their power to hold onto it. During the Second Barons' War, the Mortimers were loyal to the crown, but later, Roger Mortimer, son of Edmund, overthrew Edward II and ruled England for a time at the side of Queen Isabella.

While the seat of the Mortimers was at Wigmore Castle, Montgomery Castle was an outpost of their power. It was destroyed by the Welsh at least twice and was also besieged and captured by Simon de Montfort during the Second Barons' War.

Anna is held prisoner at Montgomery Castle with Edmund Mortimer in *Crossroads in Time*.

Rhuddlan Castle

Rhuddlan Castle was begun by King Edward in 1277, immediately after he defeated Llywelyn ap Gruffydd in the first Welsh war. In fact, Llywelyn made his submission to Edward in the bailey of the old castle, after which Edward had it torn down and the new one built several hundred yards to the north.

For centuries before that, Rhuddlan had been a fiercely contested location in eastern Gwynedd. The old castle, built in the eleventh century by Robert of Rhuddlan, was only the latest in a long line of strategically built command centers on the River Clwyd.

King Edward not only built a massive castle on the site, but, in order to keep his castle supplied from the sea, diverted the River Clwyd for over 2 miles to provide a deep-water channel for ships. The remains of a defended river gate still exists in the outer ring of the walls.

Rhuddlan Castle

What remains of Llys Conwy

Rhuddlan Castle acts as a base of operations for David and Llywelyn in *Footsteps in Time* and *Winds of Time* and is the backdrop for the arrival and death of Marty in *Ashes of Time*.

The Royal Llys

For the kings and princes of Gwynedd, their primary residence was the royal *llys* or palace. Beginning no later than the twelfth century, in order to maintain control of the country, Gwynedd's kings moved from one place to another, staying at what scholars believe to be twenty different llys. The only llys so far excavated is Llys Rhosyr, located in southwestern Anglesey. The complex was possibly as large as 450 feet by 300 feet, built in stone and wood, and surrounded by a stone wall.

Other llys included: Aber (Garth Celyn), Aberffraw, Deganwy, Aberconwy, Dolwyddelan, Criccieth, Llan-faes, and Dolbadarn. Many of these llys were converted into actual castles in the thirteenth century, although it is still possible that the larger, less well defended llys continued to be used. Llys Rhosyr, Aberconwy, Llanfaes, and Aber Garth Celyn were all deliberately destroyed by English forces after the conquest of Wales in 1282. Likely, the remaining eleven llys were destroyed as well, which is why we have no record of them or their location.

Saint Gwenffrewi's Well

Gwenffrewi, or Winifred in English, was a 7th century Christian saint, the daughter of a Welsh nobleman. When she decided to become a nun instead of marrying a suitor, he decapitated her. A healing well sprang up where her head came to rest. Her uncle, Saint Bueno, restored her head to her body, and she eventually became an abbess. Her bones were ultimately interred in Shrewsbury at the Abbey of St. Peter and St. Paul.

In *Champions of Time,* Bronwen's friend Margaret has gone to the well to pray for the ability to conceive a child.

Saint Gwenffrewi's Well

Snowdon (Yr Wyddfa)

Snowdon is the highest mountain in Wales at 3560 feet (1085 meters). For millennia, it has been linked with mysticism and aspects of Welsh mythology, primarily King Arthur, but before that, it was the domain of the Welsh gods, goddesses, and fairies. In the introduction to Llywelyn in *Daughter of Time*, it is to Snowdon he is looking: "It was as if my boots had been planted in the soil of Wales, and no power in heaven or earth could move me from this spot." Snowdon is even included in Llywelyn's title, which is officially *Prince of Wales and Lord of Snowdon.*

In *Shades of Time*, Anna's plane flies into Snowdon in order to escape pursuit by MI-5.

Mount Snowdon, summit in the clouds

Tesco (Bangor and Caernarfon)

Tesco is a British grocery and general merchandise store that has outlets throughout Wales and England. Both the Caernarfon and Bangor Tescos are featured in *Guardians of Time*. In *Champions of Time*, it is in the Bangor Tesco produce section where David meets with the director of MI-5.

Valle Crucis Abbey

Valle Crucis Abbey (Valley of the Cross) takes its name from Eliseg's Pillar nearby, which would already have stood for nearly four centuries when the abbey was founded in 1201. It was a monastery of the Cistercian Order, established in a valley north of Dinas Bran, under the patronage of Madog ap Gruffydd, King of Powys. Traditionally, the Cistercian monks were supportive of the Welsh kings and princes and, in some cases, refused to abide by orders of excommunication and interdict

Bangor Tesco

handed down by the English Church. By the time of the Reformation, the Abbey had fallen into disuse and disrepair.

David and Anna meet with Humphrey de Bohun in the nave of Valle Crucis Abbey in *Crossroads in Time*.

Ysbyty Gwynedd

Ysbyty Gwynedd is a hospital both in Bangor, Gwynedd in Avalon and at Dinas Bran in Earth Two. The Avalon version is a setting in *Guardians of Time* and *Champions of Time*.

Valle Crucis Abbey

Powys
Deheubarth
Healing Waters
Buellt
Cilmeri
Painscastle
Brecon
Offa's Dyke
The March
Chepstow
Caerphilly
England

South Wales

South Wales

Abbey Cwm Hir

After the assassination of Llywelyn ap Gruffydd, Roger Mortimer took Llywelyn's head to the king, and it was placed on a pike at the Tower of London, but tradition states that his body was buried at Abbey Cwm Hir, a remote abbey north of Cilmeri. Today the abbey stands in ruins, with a modern memorial slab in the grassy field where the nave used to be. What may or may not be the original coffin lid, inscribed with a longsword, is preserved inside the current church.

The abbey appears to have been founded by Cadwallon ap Madog in 1176. The complex was further augmented by Llywelyn Fawr in the thirteenth century, though that building program appears to have been left unfinished. After the conquest of Wales, Abbey Cwm Hir came into the possession of the Mortimers, who neglected it in favor of Wigmore Abbey.

Llywelyn's memorial at Abbey Cwm Hir

Brecon Castle

Brecon Castle was begun in 1093 by the Norman conqueror Bernard de Newmarch, as he carved out the lordship of Brecon. The Normans had come to Britain only in 1066, and the March was just being established. *The Chronicle of the Princes* (Red Book of Hergest version) says (for 1093) "the French devastated Gower, Cydweli, and the Vale of Tywi; and the countries remained a desert."

Because it sat at a crossroads between England and Wales, Brecon played a continual role in the power struggles not only between the two countries but between rival Marcher lords, and it changed hands many times. After Newmarch, the castle passed to the Braose dynasty. In 1207 King John seized it from William de Braose, who was in rebellion, but then William's son Reginald recaptured it. In 1241, it passed to the Bohuns as earls of Hereford (Pettifer 2000), though they lost it during the Baron's war to Gilbert de Clare and then

Llywelyn ap Gruffydd (Smith 1990). With the treaty of 1277, Llywelyn lost control of Brecon, and it returned to the Bohuns.

In the modern world, part of the castle has been turned into a hotel. The castle is featured in *Daughter of Time* in both Avalon and Earth Two.

Buellt Castle

Buellt Castle (Builth Wells) was the seat from which the Mortimers lured Llywelyn ap Gruffydd to his death near Cilmeri on December 11, 1282. It was a major Edwardian castle in its time, but all of the stone work has disappeared. In the *After Cilmeri* series, this region of the Wye comes under the control of Ieuan ap Cynan and Bronwen.

Caerphilly Castle

Begun in 1268 by Gilbert de Clare, Caerphilly Castle is the largest castle in Wales. As described in *Daughter of Time*, Llywelyn ap Gruffydd, ruler of Gwynedd and most of Wales, saw the building of the castle as a threat to his dominance of the region. He burned it shortly after it was begun, but Llywelyn could not maintain control of the area, and Clare eventually completed it.

Carew Castle

Carew Castle, located in southwestern Wales near Pembroke, was built on a site that has been occupied for two thousand years. The name 'Carew', *Caeriw* in

Carew Castle

Welsh, is an anglicized combination of, "caer" meaning fortress, and "rhiw" meaning hill—not that the area on which the castle stands is hilly. The name also might come from 'Caerau', simply the plural, 'forts'.

Tradition states that the original castle was built by Gerald de Windsor, a Norman who came to Wales with Arnulph de Montgomery, the first Norman Earl of Pembroke. Gerald married Princess Nest, a daughter of Prince Rhys ap Tudur of Deheubarth. Her daughter, Angharad, was the mother of Gerald of Wales, whose quote begins this book. William, the eldest son of Gerald de Windsor, was the first to adopt the title 'de Carew' ('from Carew'), according to the Norman tradition. His descendant, Nicholas de Carew, is a friend and confident of David throughout the *After Cilmeri* series.

Chepstow Castle

William the Bastard (William the Conqueror, William the Norman) won his first battle for the conquest of England at Hastings in 1066, and Chepstow Castle was begun in 1067, giving the Normans their first foothold in south Wales. Built on a cliff on the western side of the River Wye, the castle could be supplied from England, and the Welsh never managed to take it. Chepstow Castle itself was controlled initially by William Fitz Osbern, passing next to William Marshal and then to Roger Bigod.

In the beginning of *Children of Time*, Meg, Llywelyn, and Goronwy jump from a balcony at Chepstow Castle in order to time travel to Avalon and then again at the end of the book, traveling from Avalon to Earth Two, this time accompanied by Alexander Callum.

The infamous balcony at Chepstow Castle

Cilmeri

Located west of Buellt or Builth Wells, Cilmeri is where Llywelyn ap Gruffydd met his death on December 11, 1282, lured into an ambush by Roger and Edmund Mortimer. It is here, in *Footsteps in Time*, that Anna and David save Llywelyn's life by driving their aunt's minivan from Radnor, Pennsylvania into medieval Wales. The town gives the series title its name because the story begins *after* the events at Cilmeri.

Deheubarth

Deheubarth was a southern Welsh kingdom, arising from the former kingdoms of Dyfed and Seisyllwg in 920 AD, under the rule of Hywel Dda. At various times, the kingdom fell under the auspices of Gwynedd, specifically during the rule of Gruffydd ap Llywelyn in 1055 and again in 1137 under Owain Gwynedd, who annexed a portion of it called Ceredigion.

At other times, the Normans controlled the kingdom, accepting a client rule in certain instances. With the help of his brother-in-law, Owain Gwynedd, King Gruffydd led a successful revolt in 1136. The king was killed in battle in 1137, but his son Anarawd went on to rule Deheubarth until he was murdered by Owain Gwynedd's brother, Cadwaladr, in 1143. The kingdom was passed from brother to brother until reaching Rhys (the Lord Rhys), who ruled from 1155 to 1197, one of the strongest Welsh monarchs of the era.

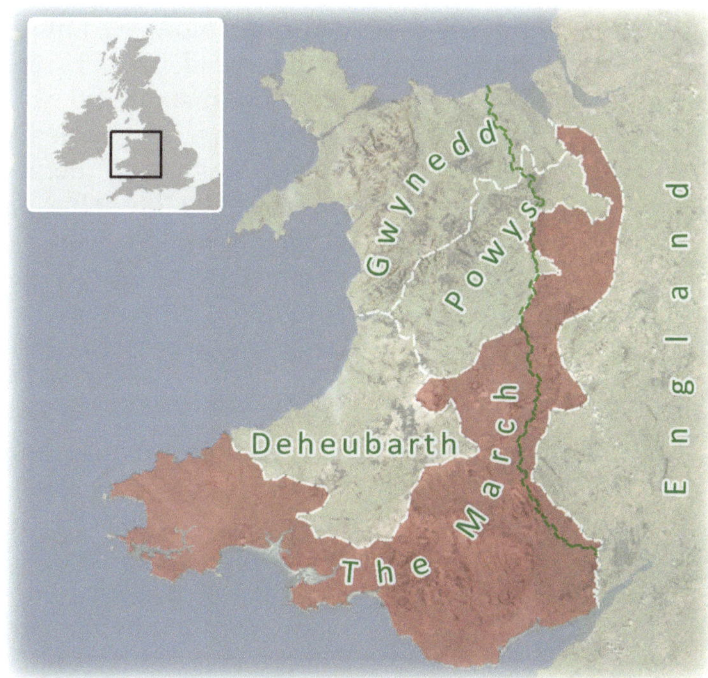

The March

The well at Cilmeri

Healing Waters Spa

In *Children of Time*, Meg, Goronwy, and Llywelyn time travel from the medieval Chepstow Castle to the Healing Waters Spa, located to the east of Aberystwyth.

The March

The March was the region of Britain that marked the border between England and Wales. Because the kings of England had been unable to conquer Wales, they gave their vassals land in the March, with the promise that if they could conquer it, they could keep it. The March acted as a buffer zone between what the Normans perceived as the rebellious and lawless Welsh and civilized England. The earldoms included in the March were those of Chester, Shrewsbury, Hereford, Gloucester, and Pembroke.

More than simply ruling the March, however, Marcher lords were afforded wide-ranging powers not given to their counterparts in England. They were, in effect, kings in their own right, which is one reason they supported Simon de Montfort during the Second Barons' War, hoping to curtail the power of the king and maintain or bolster their own.

Lords of the March were allowed to raise their own armies, exact taxes, build castles without the king's consent, and enlarge their dominions at the expense of Welsh nobility. This process took the form of taking possession, by force or by marriage, of lands held by Welsh royal families, and adding them to their own estates.

Marcher families in the *After Cilmeri* series include the Bohuns, the Clares, and the Mortimers.

Offa's Dyke

In 780 AD, King Offa, who ruled Mercia, a Saxon kingdom adjacent to the Welsh kingdom of Powys, was at the height of his authority. Prior to his rule, in 750 AD, King

Eliseg (immortalized by Eliseg's Pillar near Llangollen) had swept the Saxons out of the plains of Powys. Offa, in turn, attacked Powys in 778 and 784, and tradition states that he built the dyke sometime during this period. Prior to this, Aelthelbald, King of Mercia, had built 'Wat's Dyke', which extends from the Severn Valley northwards towards the estuary of the River Dee (Davies 2007).

George Borrow, writing in 1907, states, "it was customary for the English to cut off the ears of every Welshman who was found to the east of the dyke, and for the Welsh to hang every Englishman whom they found to the west of it." This is most likely apocryphal, but indicates the significance of this man-made border between the two countries.

One of the biggest mysteries about Offa's Dyke is why it was built. It was a huge undertaking to construct the earthwork, 150 miles in length, up to 65 feet wide and 8 feet high in places, along the entire length of the border between what is now England and Wales. Since it was never defended, it doesn't seem to have been built to keep the Welsh out of England or to protect the Saxons.

Both English and Welsh kingdoms appear to have had a hand in determining where to build it too, since it runs to the east of Wat's Dyke when the two constructions are parallel, and, in Gwent in particular, leaves the lowlands to Wales to the east of natural features it might normally have followed. The dyke was dug by piling displaced soil into a bank on the Mercian (eastern) side. In places where the dyke runs along the top of a hill, it was built on the western slope in order to provide an uninterrupted view of Wales.

The prevailing opinion is that Offa built his dyke as a sign of his authority and power—as a means of saying, *beyond this wall, here be dragons.*

Offa's Dyke acts as the political boundary between England and Wales in *Prince of Time*. David and Lili also are pursued across it with Gilbert de Clare and William de Bohun in *Crossroads in Time*.

Painscastle

Located in the March, the borderlands between England and Wales, the land upon which Painscastle was built changed hands many times over the course of its history. First built shortly after 1066 by Pain FitzJohn, the castle was destroyed and rebuilt four times, with Ralph de Tosny rebuilding it the final time in 1277.

The castle plays a role in *Prince of Time*, where it is once again destroyed by the forces of David and Llywelyn.

Powys

Powys was one of the most powerful medieval kingdoms of Wales. Because of its location on the border with England, its rulers tended to be more accommodating to the Saxons and Norman invaders than were the more distant and protected kings of Gwynedd. Powys was ruled before the death of Llywelyn ap Gruffydd by Gruffydd ap Gwenwynwyn, whose descendants, because of their willingness to work with their Norman masters, were among the few Welsh nobility to maintain power after the conquest. Gruffydd's son, Owain (who plotted to assassinate Llywelyn in 1274), became a true Marcher lord under the name 'de la Pole' or 'Poole'.

Offa's Dyke

Scotland and Northern England

Scotland and Northern England

Carlisle Castle

Carlisle Castle

Prior to the coming of the Normans, during the Roman period, Carlisle was one of the western anchors of Hadrian's Wall. The castle itself was begun in 1092, shortly after the Norman conquest of England, and for five hundred years played an important role in the conflicts between Scotland and England. After the death of Margaret of Scotland, during the initial outbreak of hostilities between the two countries, Robert Bruce had command of the castle. The castle itself is enormous, its twelfth century curtain walls encompassing four acres.

In *Winds of Time,* Meg rescues Thomas Hartley, nephew of Carlisle's castellan, John de Falkes. In *Prince of Time,* Falkes imprisons David and Ieuan in the outer ward, after which they are set free by Thomas. Callum also travels to Carlisle in *Exiles in Time.*

Hadrian's Wall

Hadrian's Wall was begun in 122 AD, during the reign of the Roman emperor Hadrian, as a defensive fortification to keep out the northern tribes. The wall ran from the banks of the River Tyne near the North Sea to the Solway Firth on the Irish Sea. The very fact of building it was an admission that there was a limit to Rome's power, but Hadrian decided that it would be a waste of resources to continue to attempt to control the lands north of the wall.

The wall was built in stone, with milecastles every mile (naturally) and a fort about every five miles. From north to south, the defensive works consisted of a ditch in front of the wall, the wall, a military road, and then the 'vallum', which was basically a rampart/ditch/rampart structure that demarcated the southern side of the militarized zone.

In *Winds of Time*, Meg finds herself abandoned at the wall not far from the western end at Carlisle. It is here that she rescues Thomas Hartley.

Hadrian's Wall

Skipton Castle

Skipton Castle

The original motte and bailey castle of Skipton was built on a cliff on the southern side of the Eller Beck in 1090 by the Norman conquerors of England. Because of the threat of Scottish invasion, it was rebuilt in stone shortly afterwards. The castle is featured in *Champions of Time*.

Mugdock Castle

Located in Stirlingshire, Mugdock Castle was the stronghold of Clan Graham from the mid-thirteenth century, though the remains of the current castle date from at least a hundred years later. The Grahams are Norman in origin, having arrived in Britain with William the Conqueror. They were given land after the crowning of King David I. Later, the Grahams were followers of William Wallace in his battles against King Edward of England.

In *Exiles in Time,* Cassie is befriended by the clan chief, Patrick Graham, and she and Callum rescue his son John from the MacDougalls.

Stirling Castle

Mugdock Castle

Stirling Castle

Although few of the castle's current structures date to the medieval period, Stirling Castle was an important castle throughout Scottish history, due in large part to its location on a rocky crag above the last downstream crossing of the River Forth. Stirling Castle has been a royal seat since at least the rule of King Alexander I in 1110 AD. In *Exiles in Time,* after Cassie and Callum rescue James Stewart, they travel to Stirling to meet the Guardians of Scotland.

Southeast England

Southeast England

Dover Castle

Situated on the clifftop above the English Channel, Dover Castle was begun in the 1180s by Henry II, though the Saxons, the Romans before them, and the native Britons before them built at the site, recognizing its strategic location and importance in the defense of the island. It was besieged by France during the reign of King John.

Dover Castle is an important royal seat in *Warden of Time*.

Hythe

In the medieval period, Hythe was in the confederation of Cinque Ports, five towns given autonomy and authority to defend England from invasion. The other towns were Dover, Hastings, New Romney, and Sandwich. In 1293, according to Hasted (1797), a French fleet landed at Hythe, but "the townsmen came upon them and slew every one of them: upon which the rest of the fleet hoisted sail and made no further attempt." These events are adapted in *Warden of Time*.

Westminster Palace

Today, Westminster Palace is the seat of the British government and bears no resemblance to what it looked like in the Middle Ages. The Old Palace was destroyed by fire in 1834 and, unfortunately, no floor plans of what Westminster Palace looked like in the Middle Ages exist. We do know that William Rufus, who came to the throne in 1087, wanted to build a palace that would rival the size and splendor of Westminster Abbey. While his vision was never fully realized, his Westminster Hall still exists, and by the end of the thirteenth century, it was the site of the Courts of Kings Bench, Chancery, and Common Pleas.

Westminster Palace is one seat from which David rules England, and the palace plays a significant role in *Masters of Time*.

Windsor Castle

William the Conqueror chose the site of Windsor Castle after his conquest as part of his program of castle building. It was one of a ring of castles built twenty miles, roughly a day's march, from central London. Windsor had been one of the seats of the Saxon rulers of England. Establishing his own castle in the same place implied that William was the rightful claimant to that lineage. It has been a royal seat for the Kings of England ever since.

Meg, Llywelyn, Goronwy, and Callum appear at Windsor Castle after being in Avalon in *Children of Time*.

Westminster Palace

Castle Roche
Roscommon Castle
Drogheda
The Pale
Bective Abbey
Trim
Hill of Tara
River Boyne
Dublin
Ireland

Ireland

Ireland

Bective Abbey

Bective Abbey

Founded in 1147 by the Irish lord of Meath, Bective Abbey was the second Cistercian abbey in Ireland. After the Normans conquered portions of eastern Ireland in 1171, the Abbey fell under their auspices, and its abbot sat in Parliament. Hugh de Lacy was briefly buried there before his grave was removed to Dublin.

In *Outpost in Time*, David, Llywelyn, Meg, and friends retreat to the abbey to regroup after the rebellion at Trim Castle.

Boyne River

Bective Abbey, Drogheda, Trim Castle, and the Hill of Tara are all found along the course of the Boyne River, which in places also demarcated the extent of The Pale. The Normans recognized its significance as a waterway and as a barrier in their rule of the country, but its importance dates back to prehistoric times, with the megalithic World Heritage site of *Bru na Boinne* also along it, and the river was important to Irish mythology.

In *Outpost in Time*, David and his companions escape from Trim Castle into the Boyne, and a significant portion of the book takes place along its course.

Drogheda

Drogheda appears to have begun as a Norman walled town that spanned both sides of the River Boyne. In Gaelic, Drogheda means *bridge of the ford*, logical since there is an ancient ford there, but the Normans built a bridge to connect the two sides of the town they built. The little that remains of the medieval city includes a piece of the original city wall and the St. Lawrence Gate, both dating to the thirteenth century, and a tower at St. Mary Magdalene Friary from the fourteenth.

James Stewart and Robbie Bruce confront Red Comyn in Drogheda on the south side of the River Boyne in *Outpost in Time*.

St. Laurence's Gate, Drogheda

Castle Roche

Dublin

The Danes came *a-Viking* to Ireland in the 8th and 9th centuries, ultimately settling on the south bank of the River Liffey, where they established a fortified town over the ruins of a monastery they'd sacked. By the twelfth century, Dublin was home to four thousand people and was the foremost trading center for the whole region. In 1171, Dublin was conquered by the Normans, and the Danish residents were moved to Oxmantown on the north bank of the Liffey.

The Pale

Beyond the Pale is a commonly used English phrase meaning outside the safe boundary or the limits of proper behavior, but its source is less well-known. In medieval Ireland, the Pale referred to the area around Dublin that had been conquered by Norman forces after 1171. In the fourteenth and fifteenth centuries, parts of the perimeter that encompassed some or all of the counties of Louth, Meath, Dublin, and Kildare were actually fenced or ditched. The word 'pale' derives from the Latin 'palus' meaning *stake* for a *fence*. Thus the phrase *beyond the Pale*.

Roche (Castle Roche)

Built by the Verdun family in the thirteenth century, Roche held a strategic position guarding the South Armagh pass between the Pale and Gaelic Ulster. In *Outpost in Time,* Robbie and James Stewart travel to Roche to muster support for David.

Roscommon Castle

The area around Roscommon Castle is the homeland of the Connachta dynasty of High Kings. Archaeological evidence points to the land being occupied since at least 1800 BC. Roscommon Castle itself was begun in 1169 by the Normans, on lands taken from the local Augustinian friary. The O'Connors took it by 1172, and possession went back and forth throughout the thirteenth and fourteenth centuries. The castle was built on a large lake, which in the modern era has almost entirely disappeared.

In *Outpost in Time*, Christopher and Aine travel to Roscommon Castle to ask for the help of the O'Connor clan in defeating the rebellion against David.

Tara (Hill of Tara)

Since the Iron Age, Tara has been the seat of the High King of Ireland. On the hilltop today, the remains include an iron age enclosure, known as the *Ráith na Ríogh* (the Fort of the Kings or the Royal Enclosure); a barrow; a Neolithic passage tomb; and a standing stone, the *Lia Fáil* (Stone of Destiny), upon which the High Kings were crowned. According to legend, the stone would scream when the king stood or sat upon it.

In keeping with this tradition, David is crowned High King of Ireland at Tara in *Shades of Time*.

Trim Castle

Hugh de Lacy built Trim Castle, the largest castle in Ireland, as part of the Norman conquest. It was built on the south bank of the River Boyne, a part of which was diverted to form a moat around the castle. The castle overlooks a ford on the river, which was navigable in the medieval period all the way to Trim, twenty-five miles from the sea. In the later thirteenth century, Geoffrey de Geneville was its castellan. Upon his death, the castle was inherited by the Mortimers.

Trim Castle provides the backdrop for much of the events in *Outpost in Time*.

Roscommon Castle

Trim Castle reflected in the River Boyne

Additional Places

Avalon

The twenty-firsters chose to refer to the modern world as 'Avalon' because the term plays off the idea that David is the return of King Arthur, a story that is well known in thirteenth-century Britain.

Château Niort

Located in the French town of Niort, the castle overlooks the River Sèvre. Begun by King Henry II of England as part of his consolidation of the region, after his marriage to Eleanor of Aquitaine, the castle was built on a massive scale with ten towers and two donjons nearly one hundred feet high.

In *Masters of Time*, David and King Philip of France meet here and fall from the battlement when Gilbert de Clare's men attempt to assassinate them.

Earth Two

Earth Two is another way of speaking of the medieval alternate universe. It was first suggested as a term by Chad Treadman, CEO of Treadman Global, in *Shades of Time*.

Land of Madoc

The Land of Madoc is the first term used in *Footsteps in Time* to refer to the modern world. The son of King Owain Gwynedd, Madoc was a twelfth century explorer, who legend says sailed from Wales to the new world. The kings of Gwynedd had close relations with the Dublin Danes and would have known about the Viking explorations to Newfoundland. The fact that Madoc's brother Dafydd had embarked on an ambitious plan to murder all of his brothers (possibly as many as eighteen), makes the idea that Madoc would escape by sailing west not as far-fetched as it might seem at first.

Radnor, Pennsylvania

Radnor is home to Meg's family, and Meg and Anna time travel to and from Radnor in *Daughter of Time*. David and Anna time travel from Radnor in *Footsteps in Time* to save the life of Llywelyn at Cilmeri, and David, Ieuan, and Bronwen drive from State College to Radnor in *Prince of Time* to visit David's aunt, Elisa.

Umatilla Indian Reservation

Located in northeastern Oregon, the Umatilla Indian Reservation came into being in 1855 as part of a treaty between the Umatilla, Cayuse, and Walla Walla Indian tribes and the United States government. Cassie McKay Callum is a member of the CTUIR (Confederated Tribes of the Umatilla Indian Reservation), and it is to the reservation that Meg and Anna time travel in *Ashes of Time*.

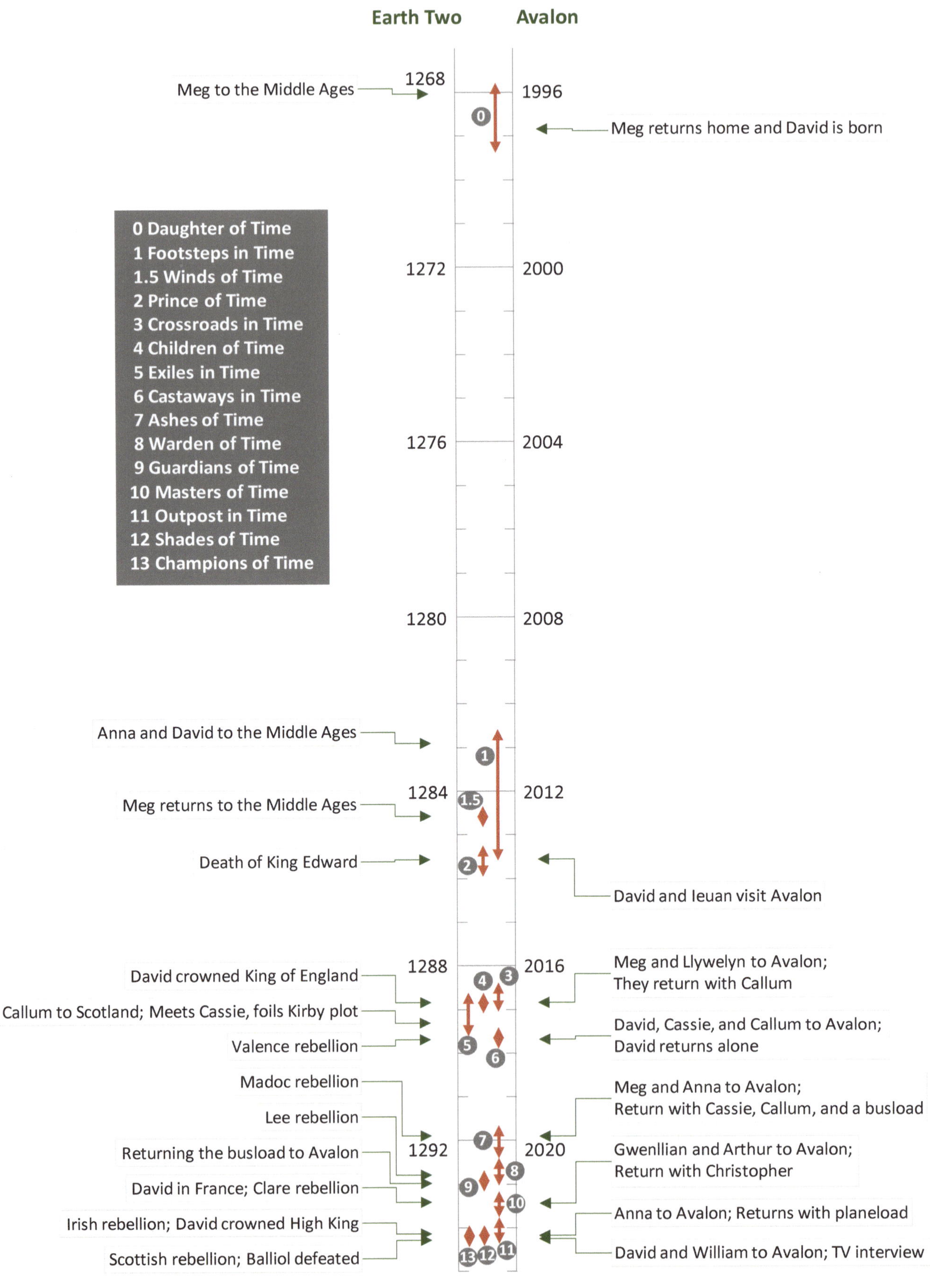

Timeline: The After Cilmeri Series

Chapter Six: Fifteen Journeys

At their very essence, each of the books in the *After Cilmeri* series is a journey—for the characters, for the reader, and for me as an author. The following pages contain timelines for the first fifteen books in the series and maps of the journeys the characters undertake. Because journeys are so important to the progression of the story, each book entry includes at least one map—and sometimes many maps. Rather than recapping the plot of the novels, which are much better when read in their entirety, I have included just a brief outline to provide context for the journeys, as well as a description of when and how the book was written.

To date, the *After Cilmeri* series encompasses a period of time from 1996 to 2022 in Avalon and from 1268 to 1294 in Earth Two, with the events of the two worlds occurring 728 years apart. In the comprehensive timeline, the red arrows indicate timespans for the novels, which are expanded upon in each individual book's timeline, included in the subsequent pages.

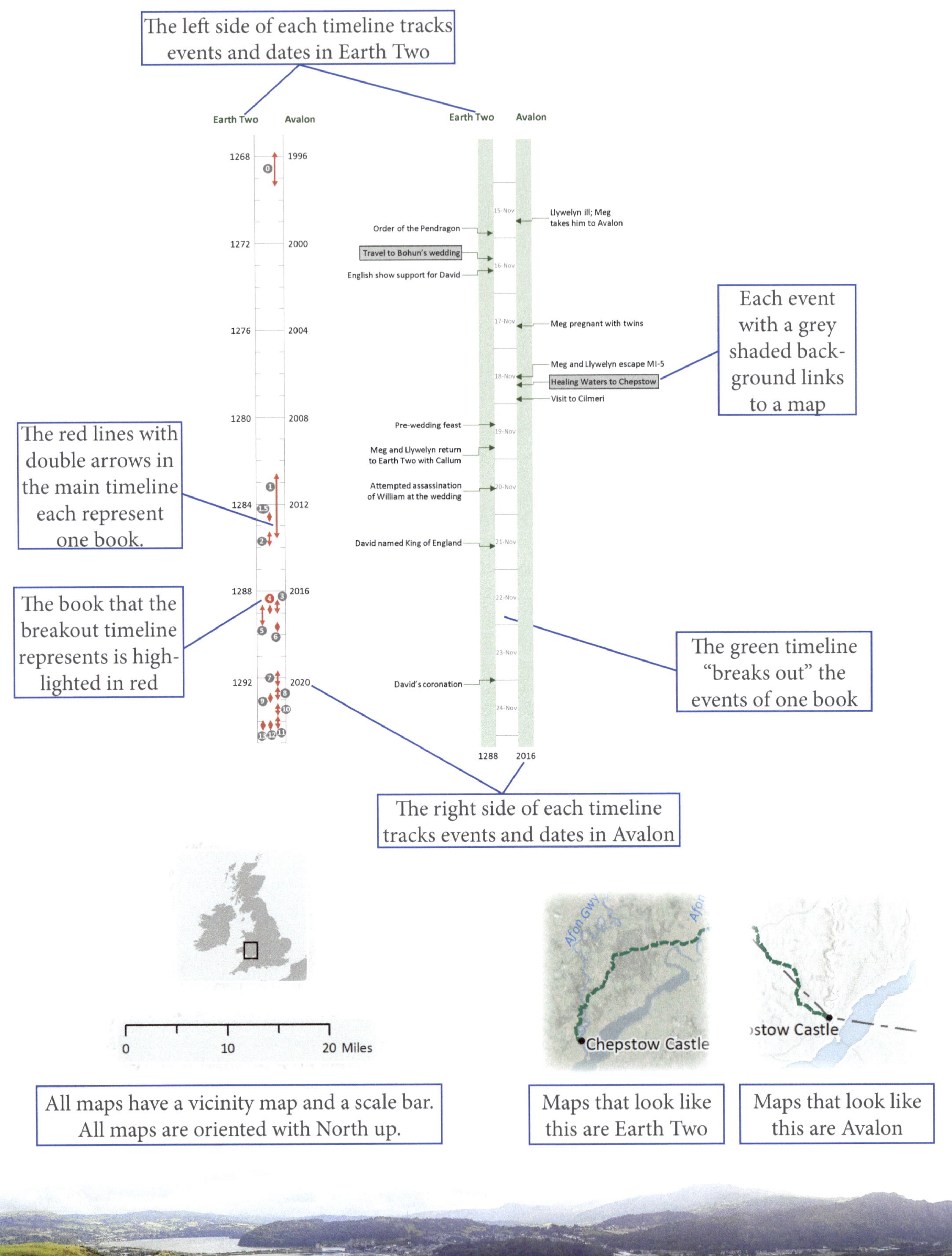
The left side of each timeline tracks events and dates in Earth Two

Earth Two
Avalon
Earth Two
Avalon

1268
1996
0

15-Nov
Llywelyn ill; Meg takes him to Avalon

Order of the Pendragon
1272
2000
Travel to Bohun's wedding
16-Nov
English show support for David

17-Nov
Meg pregnant with twins
1276
2004

Meg and Llywelyn escape MI-5
18-Nov
Healing Waters to Chepstow
Visit to Cilmeri

1280
2008
Pre-wedding feast
19-Nov
Meg and Llywelyn return to Earth Two with Callum

Attempted assassination of William at the wedding
20-Nov
1284
15
2012
1

2

David named King of England
21-Nov

1288
2016
22-Nov

23-Nov

1292
2020
David's coronation
24-Nov

1288
2016

Each event with a grey shaded background links to a map

The red lines with double arrows in the main timeline each represent one book.

The book that the breakout timeline represents is highlighted in red

The green timeline "breaks out" the events of one book

The right side of each timeline tracks events and dates in Avalon

0   10   20 Miles

All maps have a vicinity map and a scale bar. All maps are oriented with North up.

Afon Gwy
Chepstow Castle
Maps that look like this are Earth Two

stow Castle
Maps that look like this are Avalon

Making Sense of the Timelines and Maps

This section of the book is full of timelines and maps. Hopefully they are intuitive and informative, but just in case some aspects remain confusing, here's some information that should make them a little more useful.

Timelines

To the left you can see a diagram of a sample timeline, and how it relates to the maps. There are timelines for each book, but they are not necessarily comprehensive. Each timeline is designed to be used with the full text of the book and includes useful benchmarks so you can orient yourself. The timelines are also designed to focus on the most action-filled sections of each book, so there may be a prologue or an epilogue that is not represented in the timeline. One of the most useful aspects of the timelines is that they have highlighted events that relate directly to the maps in this book. Those should allow you to get a better feel for where the characters are at specific points in the books.

Maps

Like the timelines, the maps in this section are designed to be used with the books. When you are reading a section in one of the books, hopefully the maps have enough information for you to orient yourself using places discussed in the full text.

While the maps strive to invoke the feel of the Middle Ages, they are not trying to be perfectly accurate. It is important to remember that landscapes change significantly over time. There are man-made changes, such as the growth of urban areas and transportation networks that connect them. Forests are cut down and re-planted. Rivers are straightened, and dams are built to create reservoirs.

Roscommon Castle and former lake

There are also many natural changes to the landscape. The mountains are unlikely to have changed too much in the seven hundred years or so since Llywelyn's time, but there will be landslides and rockfalls, and the vegetation will change relatively rapidly. The most obvious natural changes, however, revolve around bodies of water. Rivers meander through their floodplains. Shorelines change radically year-to-year, and the areas around the mouth of a river can change significantly with a single storm.

One example of this sort of change is the lake around Roscommon Castle, described in *Outpost in Time*. Over time, sedimentation will fill a lake, and eventually it will turn into a marsh, a meadow, and finally farmland.

The bottom line: please let the maps enhance your imagination of the stories, but don't get too hung up on the details.

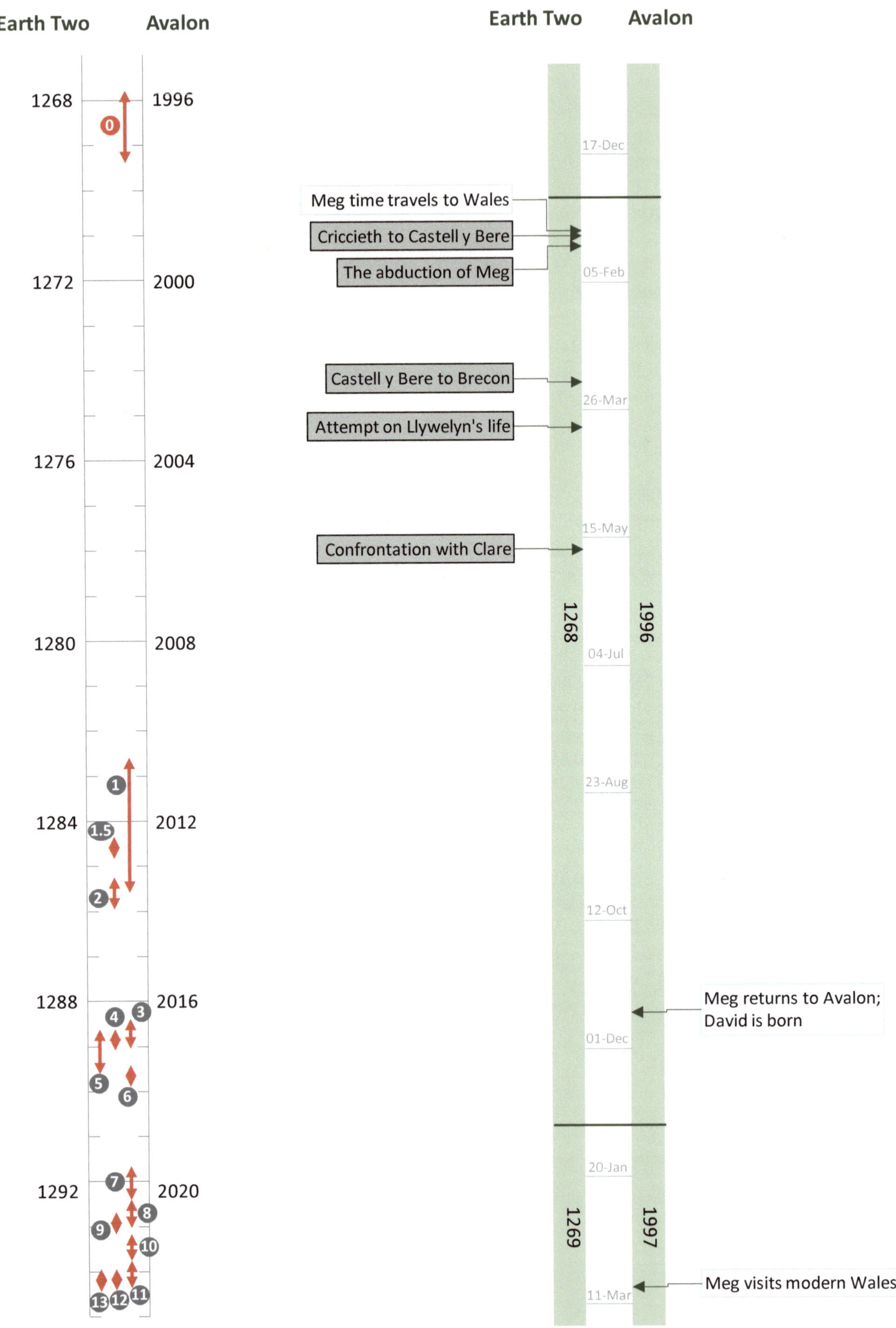

Timeline: Daughter of Time

Prequel: Daughter of Time

Even though it is the prequel, *Daughter of Time* is actually the fourth book I wrote in the *After Cilmeri* series. Book One, *Footsteps in Time*, came first, followed by *Winds of Time* and *Prince of Time*. In late 2007, after my agent at the time failed to sell *Footsteps* to any publisher, I decided it was absurd to continue to write sequels to a book I couldn't sell. I could have started a new series (which I ultimately did, once *Daughter of Time* failed to sell as well), but instead decided to take a reader's advice and tell Meg's story.

The book opens as Meg is visiting the body of her late husband in the morgue. Their relationship was abusive, and she is relieved that she is no longer with him, but she still feels guilt at the fact that he is dead. Later, as she is driving to take her daughter, Anna, out for ice cream, her car skids on an icy road in the exact spot where her husband died, and she loses control of the vehicle. It slides into an embankment at high-speed, but instead of experiencing a fatal impact, she time travels to medieval Wales, where she is rescued by Llywelyn, the Prince of Wales.

Llywelyn is drawn to her, despite her attempt to stab him with a stolen knife, and he decides to bring her and Anna with him as he rides to confront Gilbert de Clare (a Marcher lord encroaching on his lands), rather than leave them behind where they would be at the mercy of his brother Dafydd.

Criccieth to Castell y Bere

Llywelyn's company leaves Castell Criccieth, intending to confront Gilbert de Clare over the building of a new castle at Caerphilly on Welsh land. On the way to Cas-

tell y Bere, the party is ambushed at the Coedwig Gap by men sent by Dafydd, who later attempts to abduct Meg at the ford of a river.

Criccieth to Castell y Bere

The Abduction of Meg

The Abduction of Meg

Llywelyn and his men pursue Dafydd towards the sea. After Dafydd loads Meg into a boat, she jumps overboard, and Bevyn swims to rescue her.

Castell y Bere to Brecon

The party travels south and then east. On the way they stop at a Roman fort called Bremia (it isn't named in the book).

Attempt on Llywelyn's Life

At Brecon Castle, an archer infiltrates the keep and attempts to assassinate Llywelyn. Meg and Llywelyn jump from the window into the river below and come ashore a half-mile downstream. They stop at a villager's hut for clothes before returning to Brecon to find the guards drugged and the gate open. After Meg and Llywelyn secure the castle, closing the gates and portcullises, Roger Mortimer arrives.

Llywelyn's Confrontation with Clare

Llywelyn leaves Brecon with an army with the intent of destroying Caerphilly and taking back Castell Morgraig.

Castell y Bere to Brecon

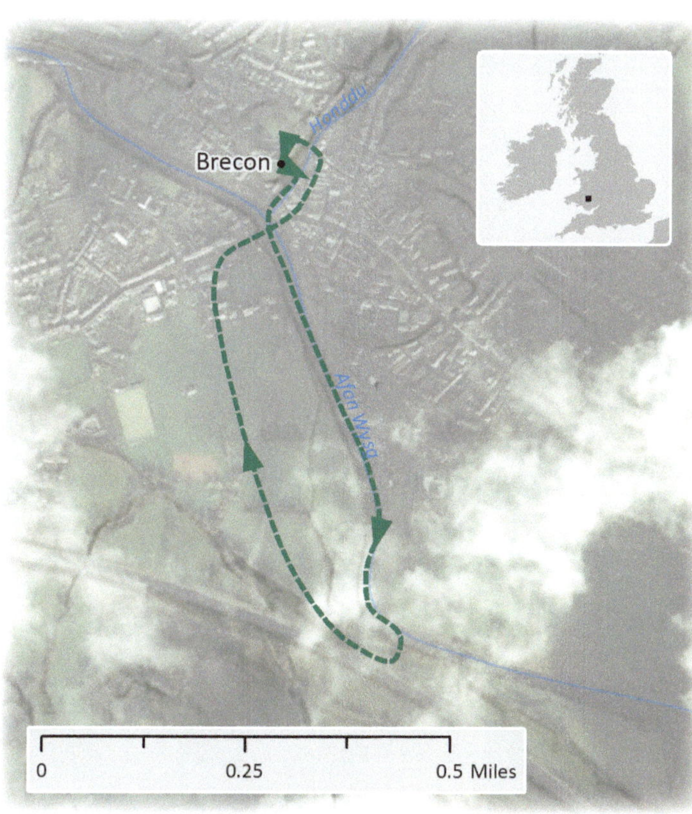

Llywelyn's Confrontation with Clare

Attempt on Llywelyn's Life

Afterwards, Clare asks for a meeting—which turns out to be an ambush—at Bwlch, south of Brecon. Prince Edward of England is there.

Although many Welshmen die, Llywelyn survives the ambush, thanks to a warning from Humphrey de Bohun. Llywelyn returns to Brecon, but shortly afterwards, Meg goes into labor and, with Anna, time travels back to the modern world where she gives birth to their son, David.

The standing stone at Bwlch

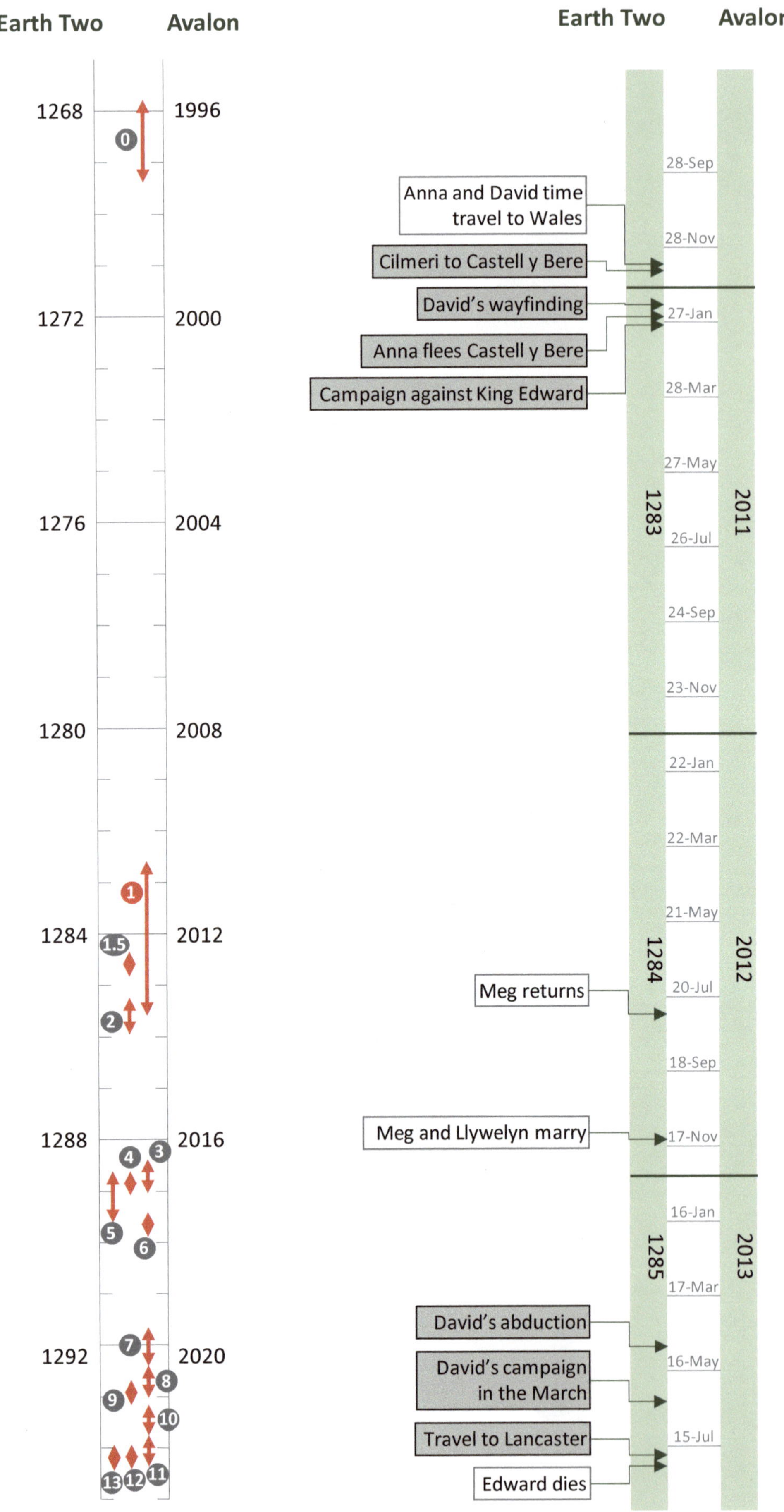

Timeline: Footsteps in Time

Book 1: Footsteps in Time

Footsteps in Time was the first book I wrote that I considered worthy of publication. I began it in the summer of 2006, after dreaming that I drove my minivan into medieval Wales. As I started playing around with the idea, I realized immediately that the protagonists of the story had to be David and Anna, rather than anyone resembling me. They still drove my minivan, however, a Toyota, the unique blue-green color of glacial melt.

Meg's story, which became *Winds of Time,* was originally part of this book, but I removed it once I realized that it didn't fit the story I was telling. I wrote *Footsteps in Time* over the course of five years, three times deleting a full one-third of the story from the book and rewriting it, until I finally published it in January 2011.

Footsteps in Time begins with the central premise of the entire series: despite Meg's warnings against it, Llywelyn travels south to meet the Mortimers. While driving their aunt's minivan to pick up their cousin, Anna and David crash their car through a temporal snowbank and are transported to medieval Wales. The van arrives in a field at Cilmeri and rolls into the men attacking Llywelyn. Thus, Anna and David save his life.

Cilmeri to Castell y Bere

Llywelyn's men take Anna, and David back to their camp where David and Anna are summoned to see Llywelyn, and he tells them who he is and what year it is. Over the next few days, they attempt to come to terms with their new reality.

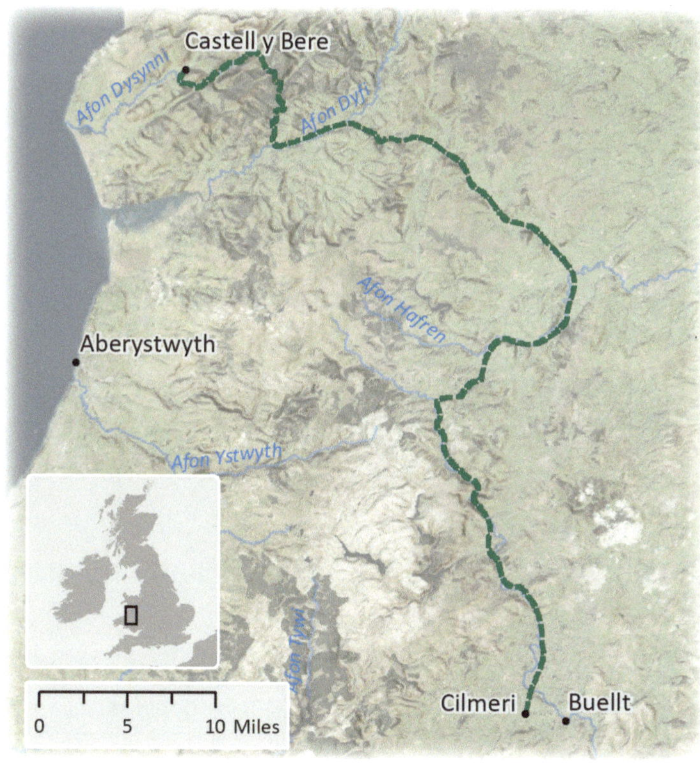

Cilmeri to Castell y Bere

David's Wayfinding

Shortly after their arrival at Castell y Bere, as part of David's training, Bevyn leads an expedition of the young men from the castle, with the intent of having them find their own way home. Math accompanies David and Owain, and they are the last to return. Llywelyn is surprised and upset that he was so worried about them.

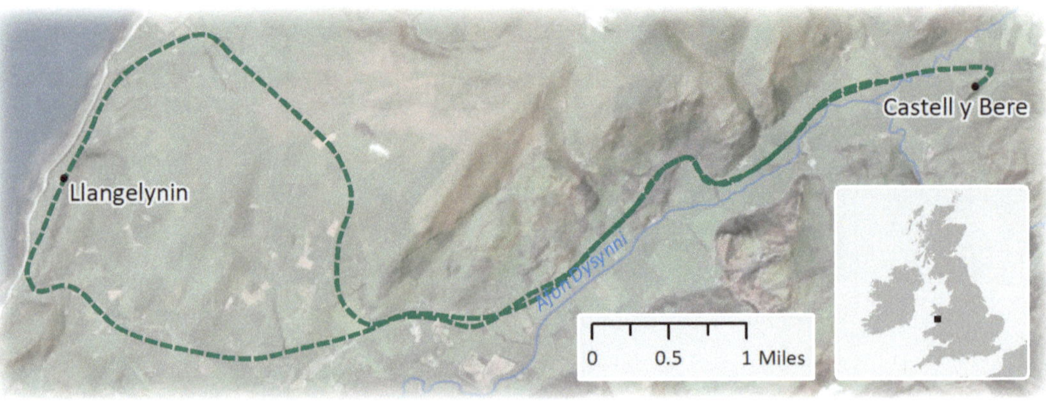

David's Wayfinding

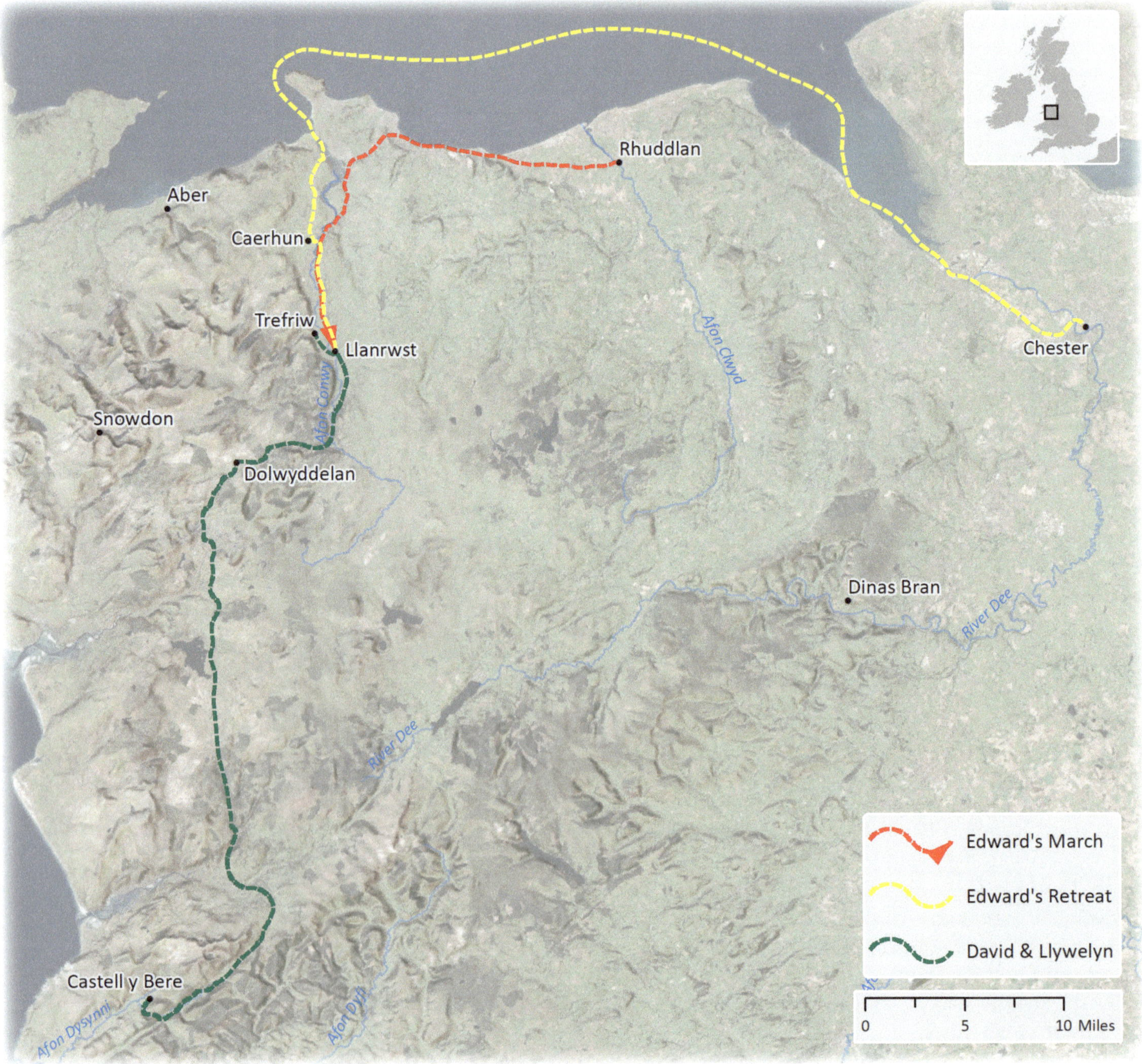

Llywelyn's Campaign against King Edward

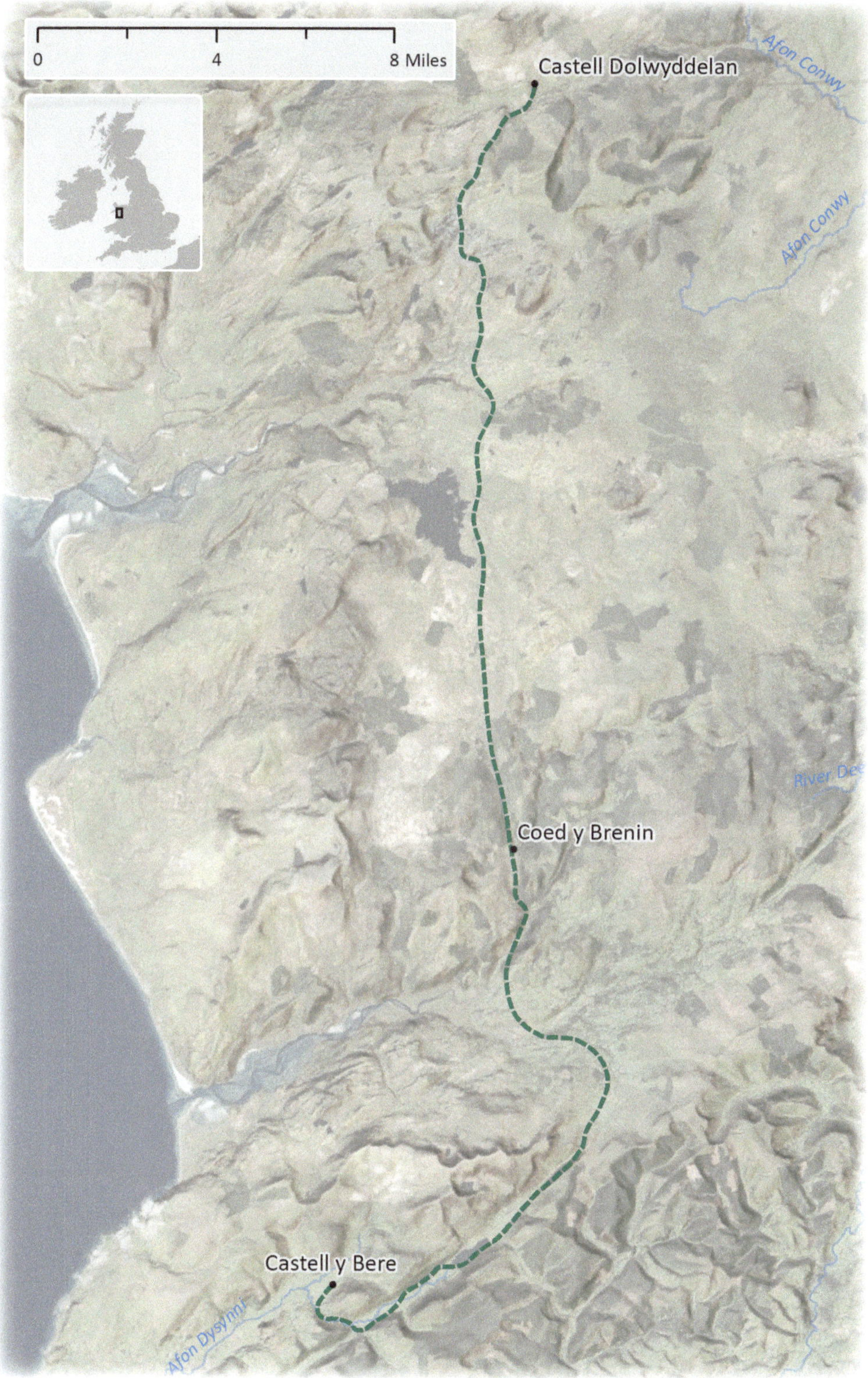

Llywelyn's Campaign against King Edward

Eventually, Llywelyn tells David and Anna that he loved their mother and that David is his son. David's arrival, in fact, has breathed new life into Llywelyn's world. Now that he has a son and heir, Llywelyn is driven to ensure that, no matter how much time he has left, David will be prepared to succeed him.

To that end, David and Llywelyn march north to engage Edward's forces, ultimately ambushing the English in the Conwy River Valley between Llanrwst and Llansanffraid. Following their successful role in the battle, David's party safely reaches Llywelyn's hunting lodge at Trefriw. The next day, Welsh archers continue to pick off English soldiers from the ridge on the west side of the river as Edward slowly retreats up the Conwy Valley, commandeers boats, and sails back to Chester.

Anna flees Castell y Bere

Anna flees Castell y Bere

After the army marches away, Anna and Hywel discover a camp of English soldiers and overhear a plot to take the castle. They flee north with Gwenllian, Llywelyn's infant daughter, and Heledd, the baby's wet nurse, under the cover of night. Ultimately, Math finds them and takes them to Dolwyddelan, and, after the victory in the Conwy Valley, he asks Anna to marry him.

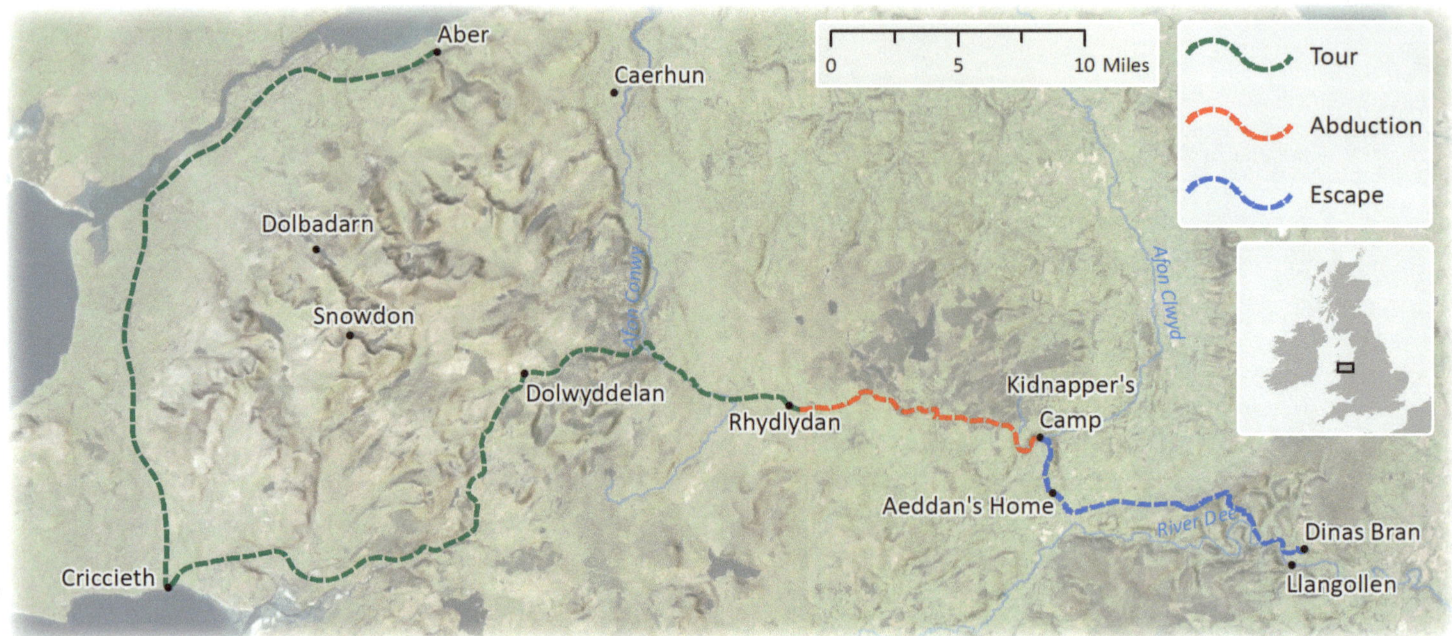

David's Abduction

David's Abduction

Meg returns to Earth Two in 1284 (related in *Winds of Time*), and, after her marriage to Llywelyn, David, Anna, Aaron, and Meg travel from Aber to Dinas Bran, via Dolwyddelan, rallying goodwill throughout the countryside. Near the village of Rhydlydan, David is abducted by a group of traitors within his own men. Eventually, he escapes and finds a small village where he is recognized by the inhabitants, given shelter, and escorted to Dinas Bran.

David's Campaign in the Marches

David and his men harass Humphrey de Bohun's men at Brecon, Bronllys, and Hay.

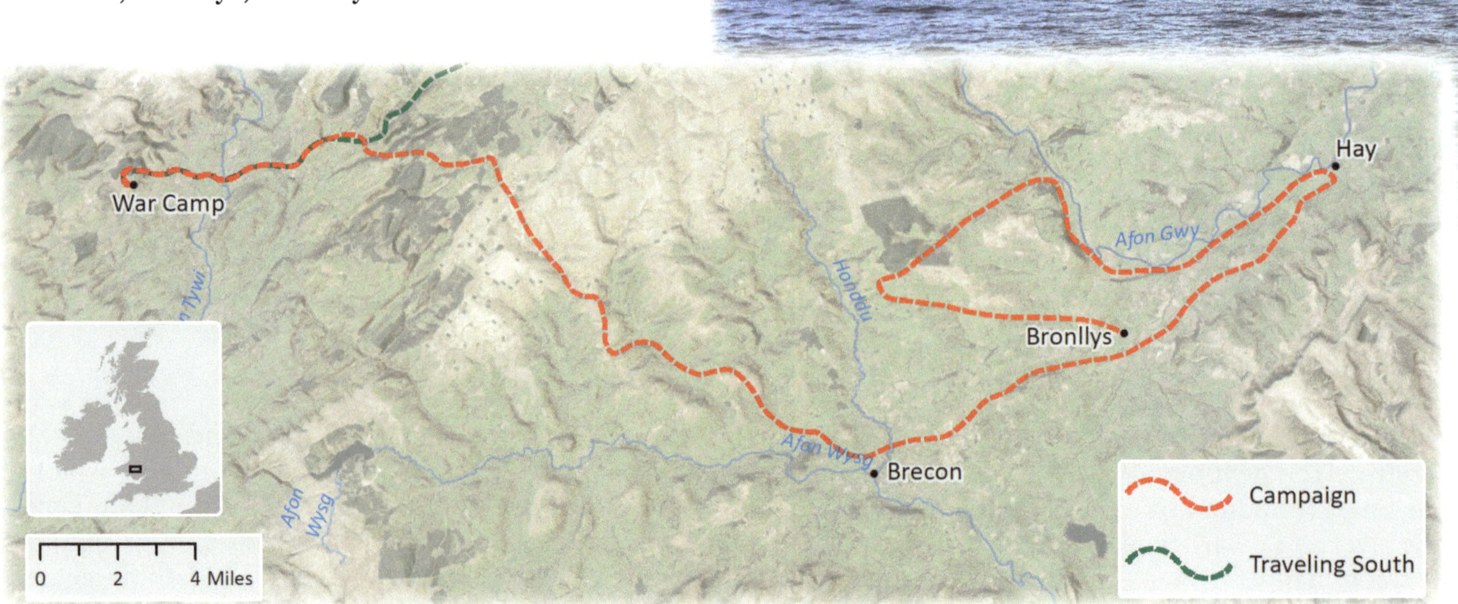

David's Campaign in the Marches

<u>Travel to Lancaster</u>

Accompanied by Nicholas de Carew, David travels by sea from Rhuddlan to Lancaster in order to attend King Edward's peace summit. However, unbeknownst to David, in retaliation for Edward's pogrom against the Jews, Aaron's brother has poisoned everyone in the camp. King Edward, Llywelyn's brother Dafydd, and many other English barons are killed, and David and his party flee the scene unharmed.

Welsh coast from the Irish Sea

Travel to Lancaster

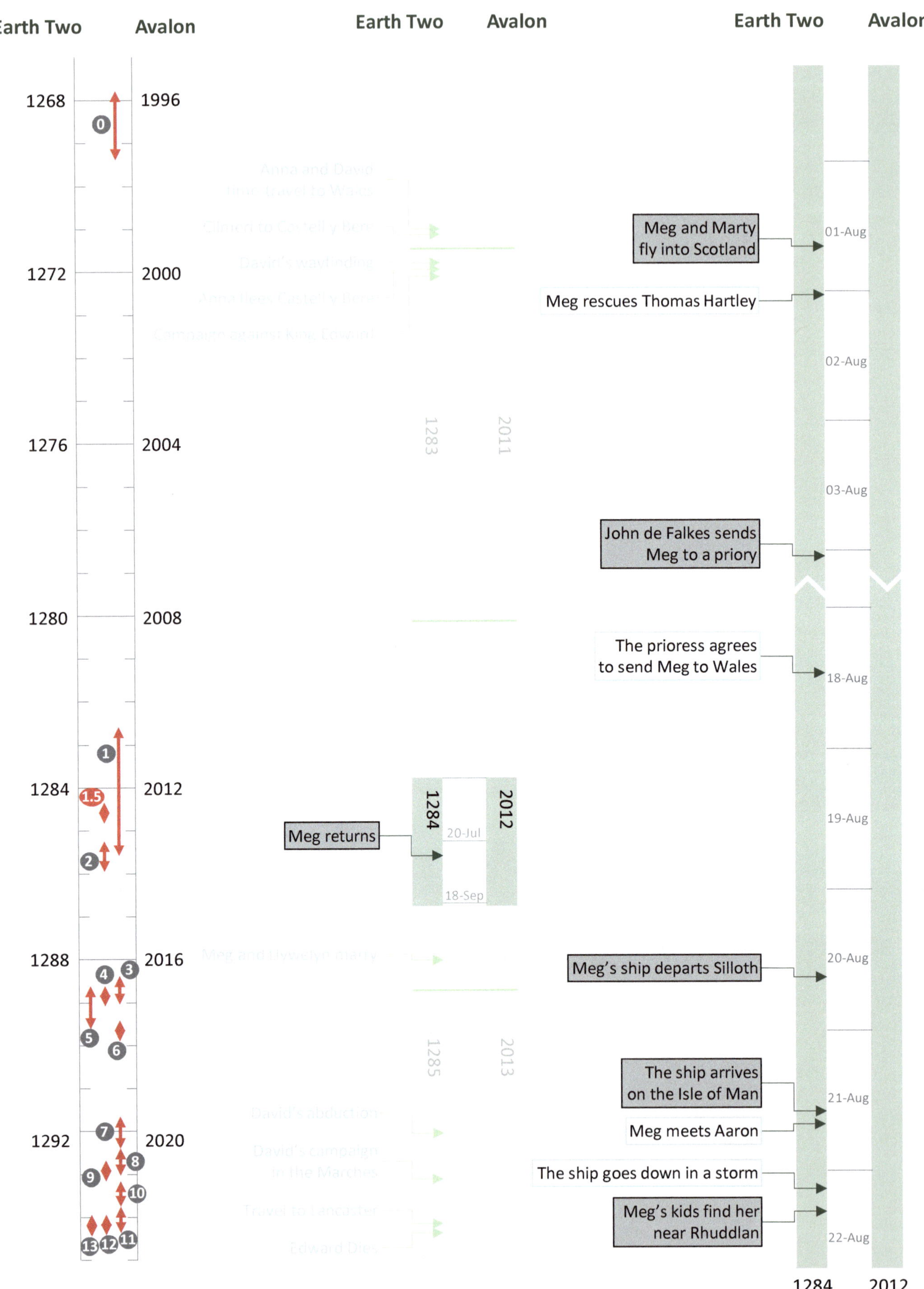

Timeline: Winds of Time

Book 1.5: Winds of Time

The novella, *Winds of Time*, started out as the middle third of *Footsteps in Time*. I soon realized, however, that *Footsteps in Time* was really David and Anna's journey, and it further became clear to me over many rewrites that Meg needed her own book to properly tell the story of her return to Earth Two and Llywelyn.

The book opens with Meg flying from Pasco, Washington to Boise, Idaho. The flight goes awry, and she ends up in the year 1284 in the borderlands between Scotland and England. Marty, the pilot, flies away, leaving her behind.

Meg walks along Hadrian's Wall until she encounters Thomas Hartley, the nephew of John de Falkes, castellan of Carlisle Castle. Falkes arranges for Meg first to stay at a convent, and then to travel by boat back to Wales, where she is ultimately reunited with her children and Llywelyn.

Near Marty's landing site

Meg's Return to the Middle Ages

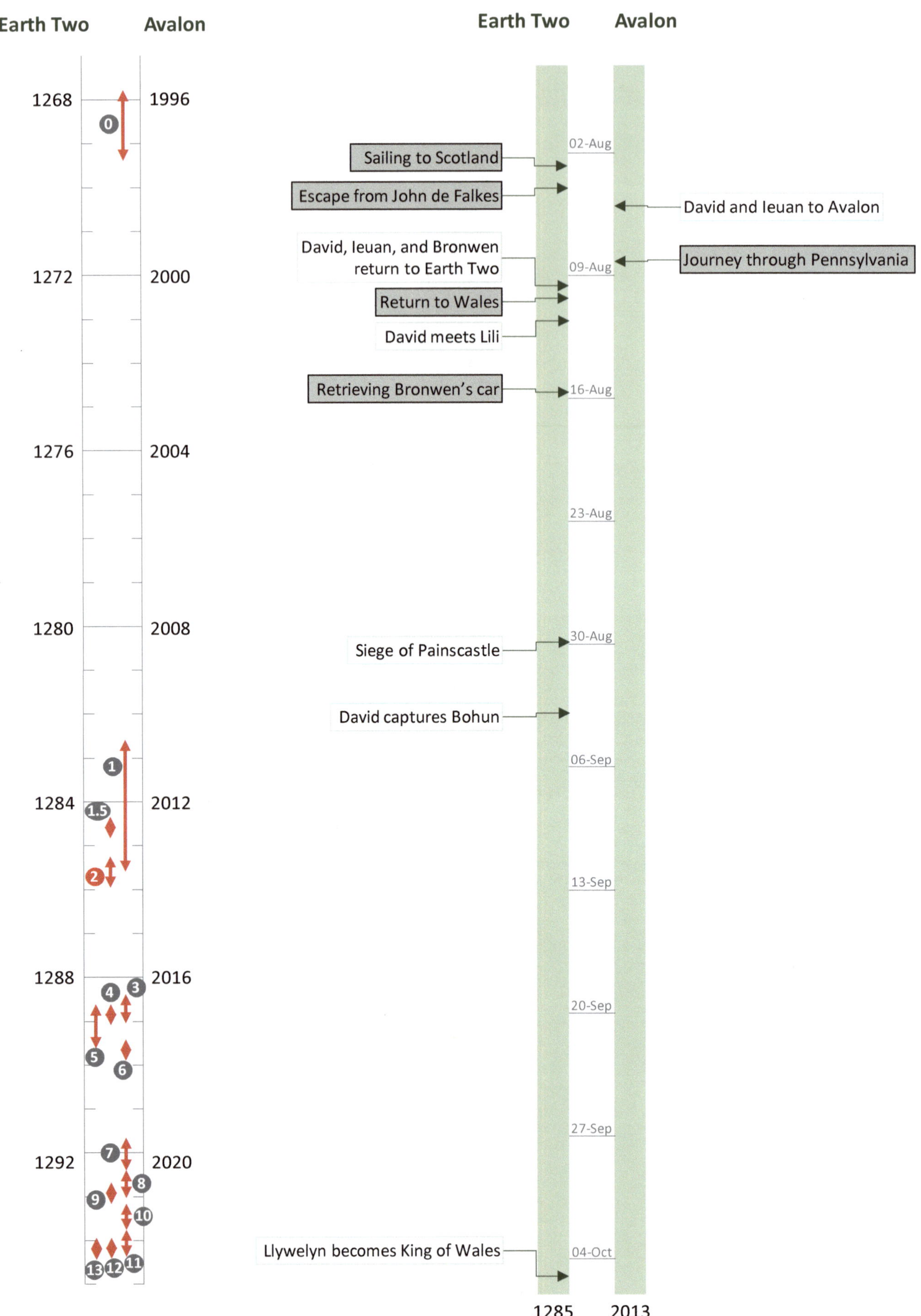

Timeline: Prince of Time

Book 2: Prince of Time

By the spring of 2007, my first agent had begun querying publishers about *Footsteps in Time,* freeing me to stop editing it and finally begin writing a new book. My father was also diagnosed with cancer in January of that year, and writing *Prince of Time* was a refuge from what was going on with him, as well as something for me to do during long hours in the hospital. Some elements of Ieuan's experience with the hospital in State College are from my memories of my father's hospital stay.

Prince of Time is also structurally different from *Footsteps* and *Daughter*, in that it takes place over a relatively short period of time, giving it momentum and urgency. I published it along with *Footsteps in Time* in January 2011.

The story itself picks up immediately after the end of *Footsteps in Time*, with David and his men sailing away from Lancaster, where King Edward has died. Rather than returning immediately to Wales, David decides to retrieve his mother's suitcase and backpack from where she left them on Hadrian's Wall.

Sailing to Scotland

On their return trip from the debacle with Edward in Lancaster, David's party docks in Annan, Scotland, located somewhat to the west of Annan in our world.

Sailing to Scotland

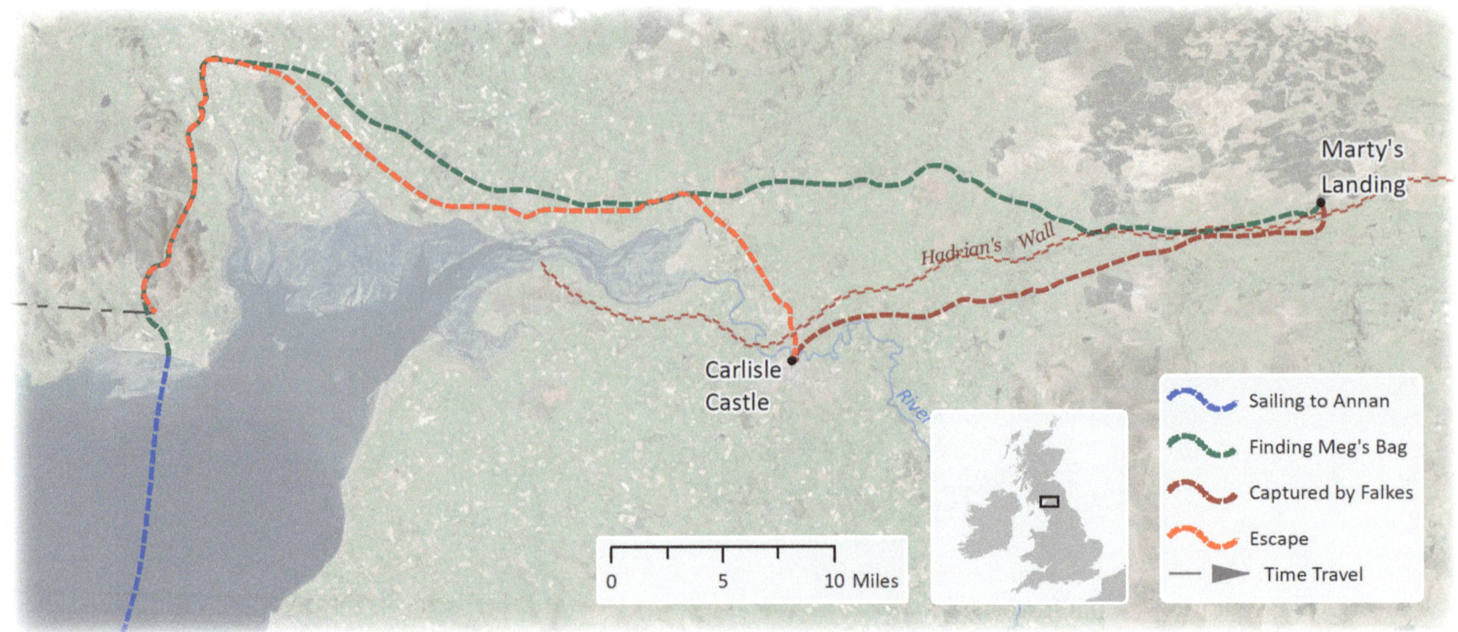

David and Ieuan in Scotland

Retrieving Meg's Belongings

David hopes to retrieve the gear Meg left behind during her return journey from Avalon. Although he manages to recover her things, he and Ieuan, his captain, are captured by John de Falkes. Aaron, who'd accompanied them on the trip, gets away. Falkes takes David and Ieuan back to Carlisle Castle, and they've just arrived when a messenger informs Falkes that King Edward is dead and the Welsh may be involved.

David and Ieuan realize that, with so many lords dead in Edward's encampment, Humphrey de Bohun is likely to rise up and attempt to take as much land in Wales as he can, as well as seek the Regency of England.

Escape from Carlisle Castle

Thomas Hartley, having fond memories of how Meg saved him, frees David and Ieuan, but in the course of finding their way back to their ship, Ieuan is shot by an English bowman. To save his life, David jumps off a cliff, transporting himself and Ieuan to the 21st century.

Hadrian's Wall

Carlisle Castle

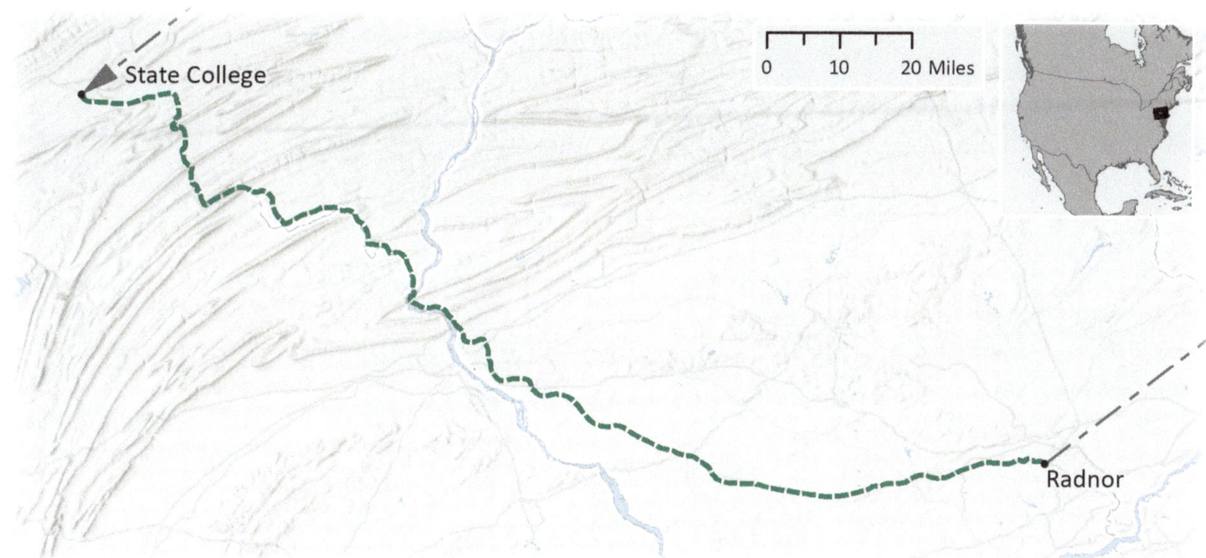

Journey through Pennsylvania

Journey through Pennsylvania

David and Ieuan arrive at the Penn State campus in State College, Pennsylvania where they meet Bronwen, an archeology graduate student, who calls an ambulance for Ieuan. Once she becomes convinced that David and Ieuan are from an alternate universe, Bronwen agrees to drive them to David's aunt's house.

Return to Wales

David, Ieuan, and Bronwen return to Earth Two and find themselves east of Offa's Dyke near Huntington Castle. David negotiates with a villager for a horse and cart as well as clothes. After they encounter some of Humphrey's men, they abandon the cart and head for Ieuan's holdings on foot.

Shenanigans ensue, David and Llywelyn are reunited, and a plan to attack Painscastle is implemented. In the course of the battle, Humphrey de Bohun is captured, and Llywelyn trades Humphrey's freedom for Welsh independence.

Twyn y Garth

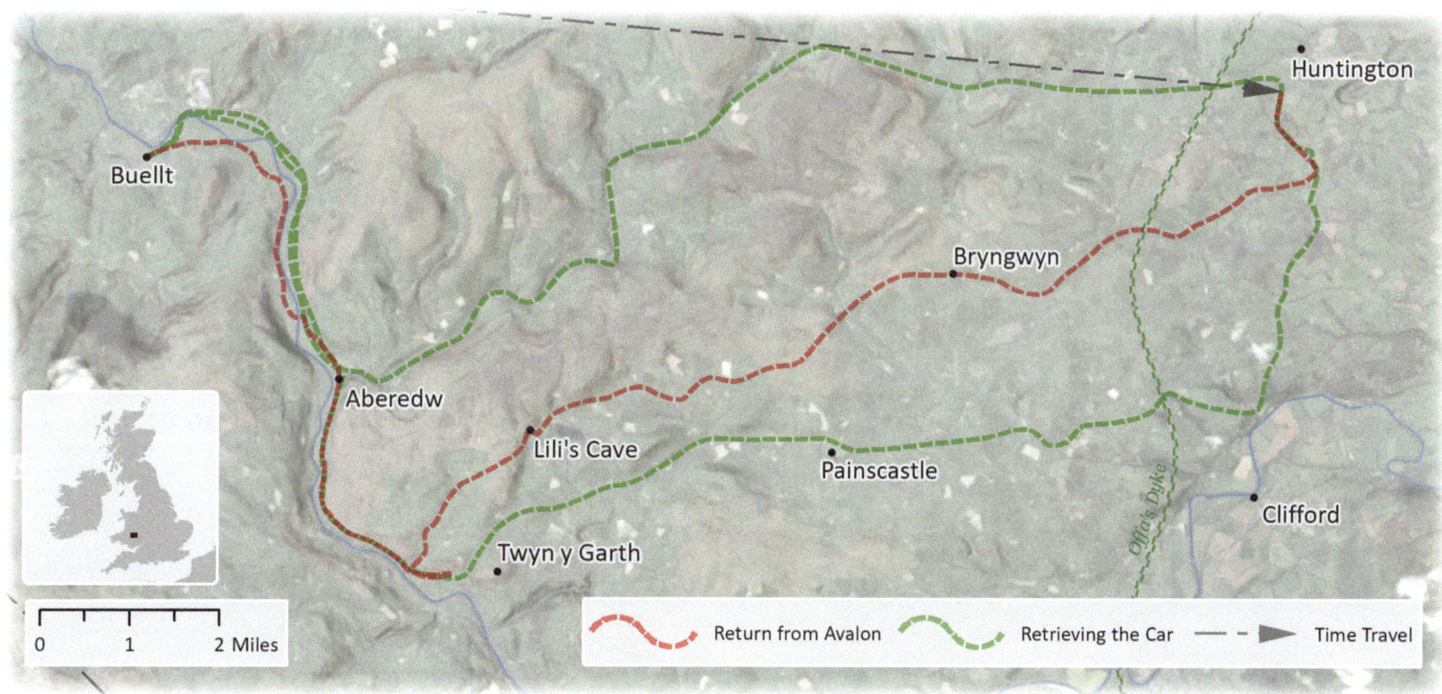

Return to Wales

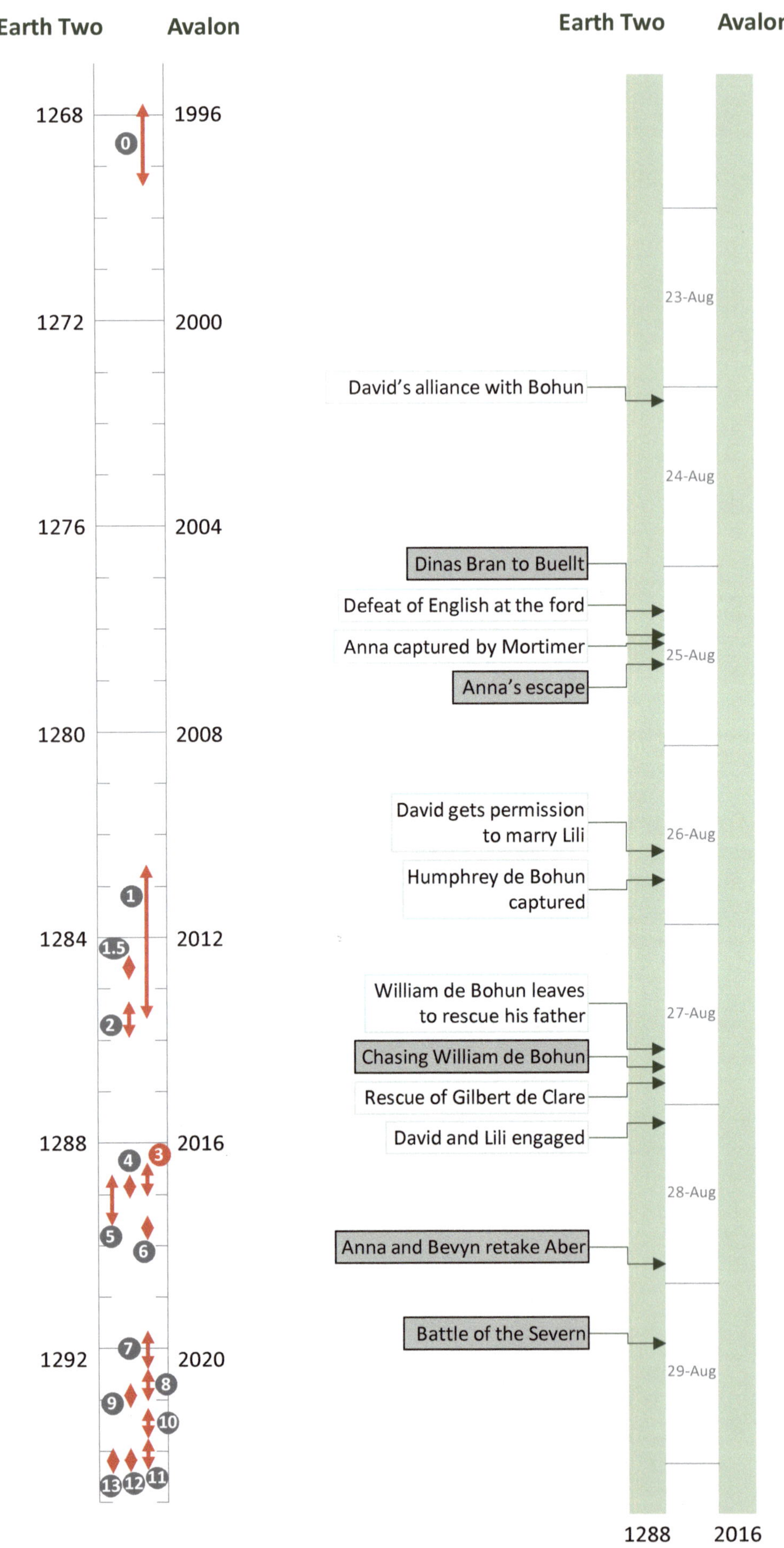

Timeline: Crossroads in Time

Book 3: Crossroads in Time

Crossroads in Time is not a book I ever intended to write. I had written the ending of *Prince of Time* in such a way that it could have been the *end* of the series. At the time, I had been thinking of the needs of a traditional publisher instead of my own or those of future readers. I had been told that publishers liked trilogies and were wary of long series.

Once I published *Daughter, Footsteps,* and *Prince* in 2011, however, I began looking at the series completely differently, since I was now publishing the books myself. In the fall of 2011, I realized I had a much bigger story to tell and now that I was on my own, I was free to tell it.

Crossroads in Time became, then, the third book in a four book story arc, that begins with David and Anna's arrival in Wales to save Llywelyn's life in *Footsteps in Time*, and ends with David's crowning as King of England in *Children of Time*. By the time I began *Crossroads*, I had the full sweep of that story in my head. The book is also the beginning of the redemption of Humphrey de Bohun, a process which doesn't come to full fruition until book thirteen, *Champions of Time.*

Thus, the book opens with David, Math and Anna meeting Humphrey de Bohun at Valle Crucis Abbey near Llangollen to make an alliance against the barons of England. Humphrey is seeking to set up his son, William, to become king of England if King Edward's son, also named Edward, dies of smallpox. While they are meeting, the group is ambushed by men dressed in Mortimer colors. It is the first step by Humphrey towards making amends for the events of *Prince of Time.*

Looking west from Dinas Bran

Dinas Bran to Buellt

Knowing that David is coming to Buellt, Lili goes out to practice her archery. She hears an arriving company of horsemen and is surprised that they are wearing Mortimer colors. They are let into the castle, and Lili heads north to intercept David and warn him that the castle is now a trap for him. David's company assumes they will be ambushed, but sees no danger until they reach the ford of the river. The English attack, only to discover that David's men are ambushing them instead, and the English are soundly defeated.

Anna's Capture and Escape

On the road not far from Dolforwyn, Anna's party is ambushed by men claiming to be working for Gilbert de Clare. Anna and her three-year-old son, Cadell, are taken to Montgomery castle and imprisoned with Edmund Mortimer. They manage to escape the castle with Humphrey de Bohun's wife and younger son in tow. They head to Aber to warn Bevyn of what is coming.

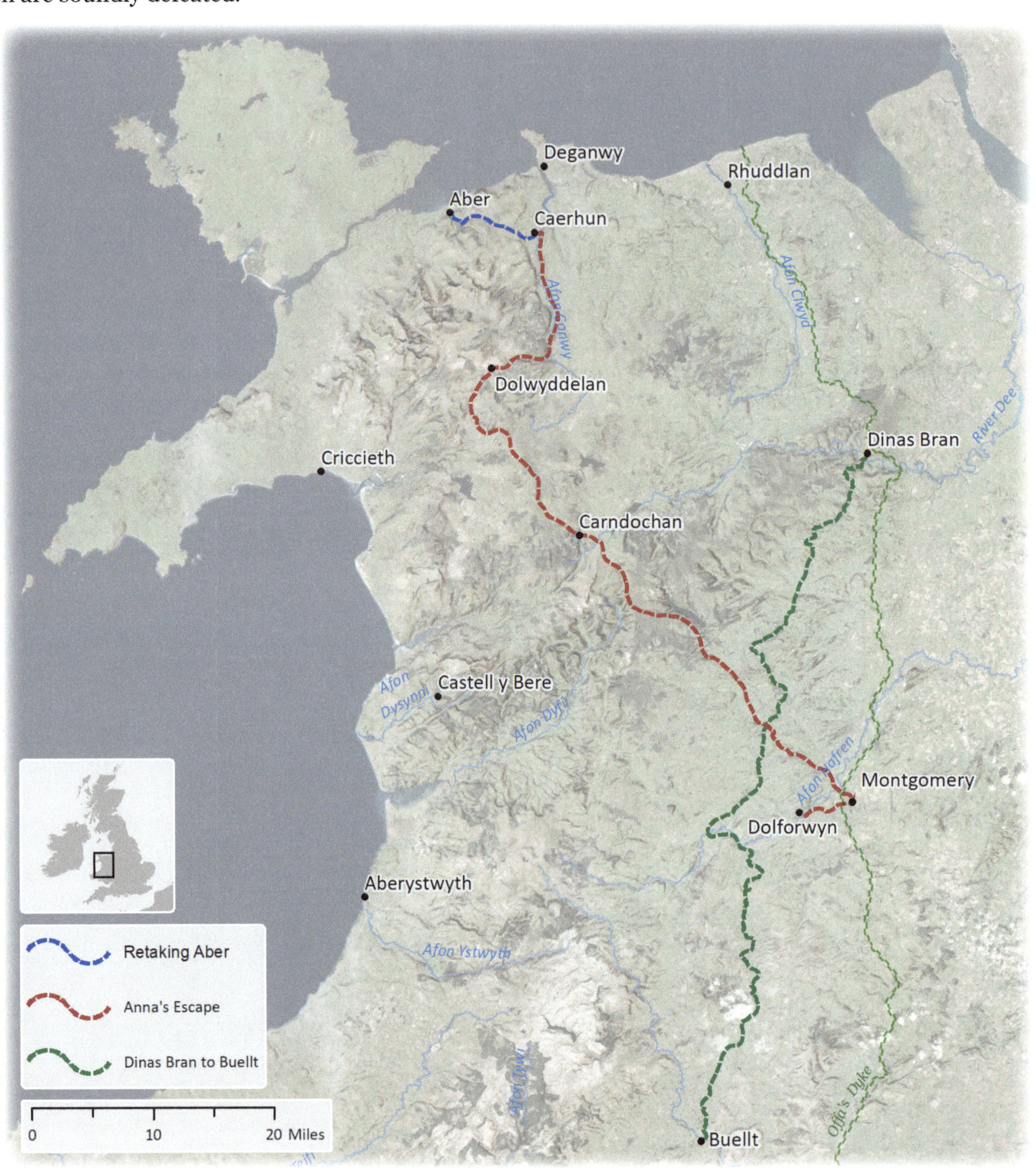

Dinas Bran to Buellt and Anna's escape

Chasing William de Bohun

William is overwhelmed by fear for his father and rides to England to save him. David and Lili give chase. William crosses the border near Hay and leads Lili and David to Clifford Castle, which appears to have been stolen from Bohun through treachery. Gilbert de Clare is imprisoned in the tower, and David helps him escape.

The group goes over Offa's Dyke with the Normans in pursuit, arriving at Painscastle only to find that Gilbert's men have taken it—without his knowledge—but since the soldiers think they are working for Gilbert, they let him in. When David and his company free the castle's prisoners, they discover that Humphrey de Bohun has been imprisoned too.

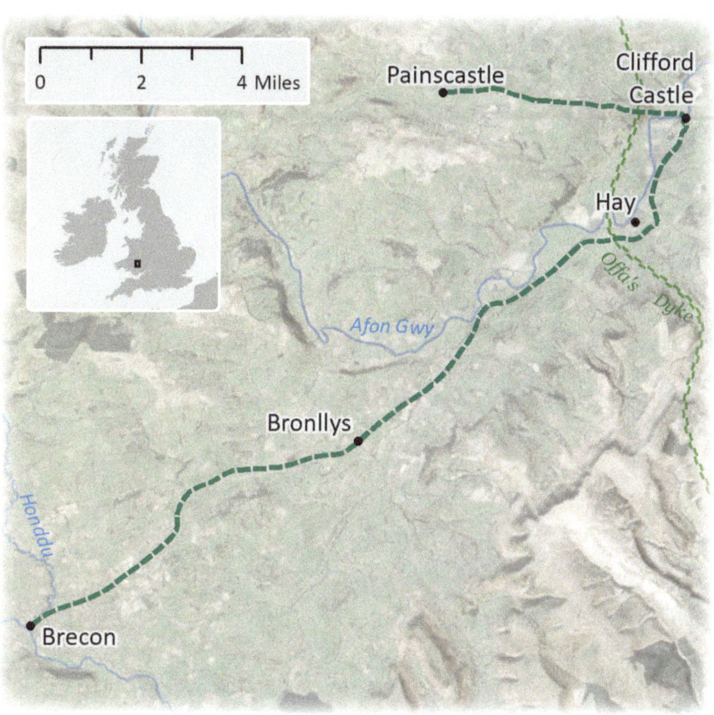

Chasing William de Bohun

The Severn Estuary

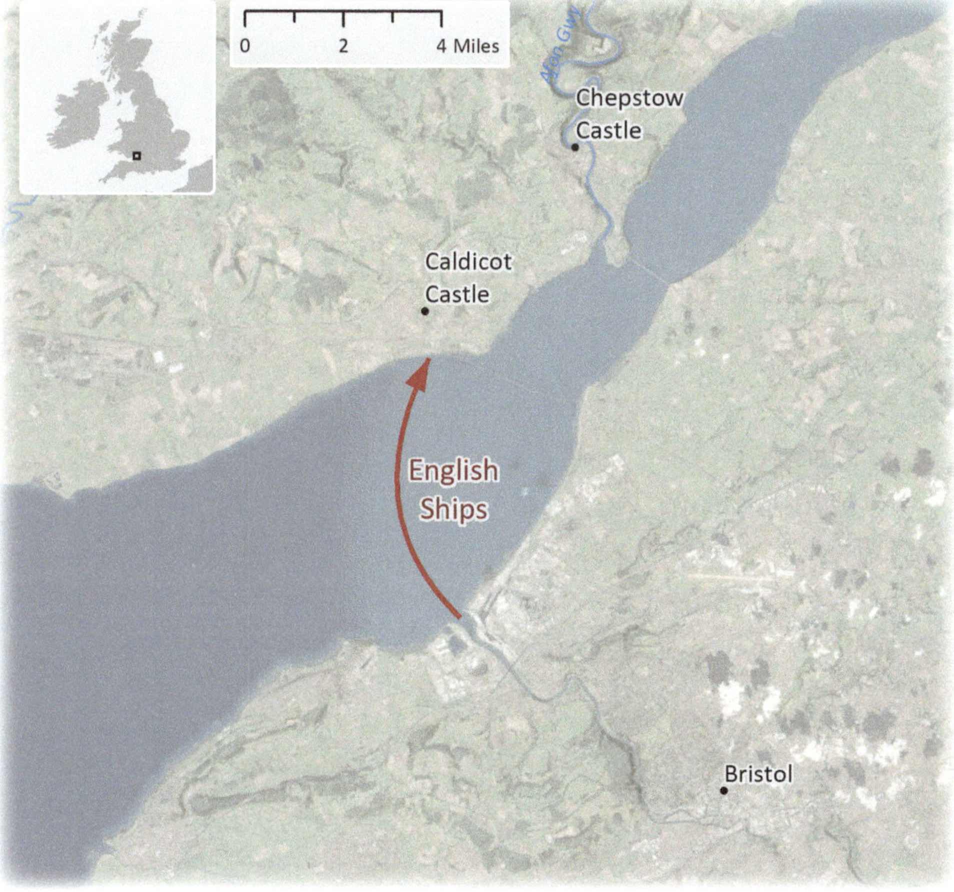

Battle of the Severn

Battle of the Severn

Llywelyn and Math receive word that their fireboats have been sabotaged and have foundered off the dock. A mist hides the approaching English fleet, but they can hear the ships in the Severn Estuary. Then the wind shifts, the fog disappears, and over two hundred English ships are seen. However, it is also clear that a storm is coming fast. Math reveals his archers on the dunes to force the English to choose between facing the army on the beach and the coming storm.

The storm hits, and Llywelyn is swept up in the flash flood that follows, but David arrives in time pull him from the sea.

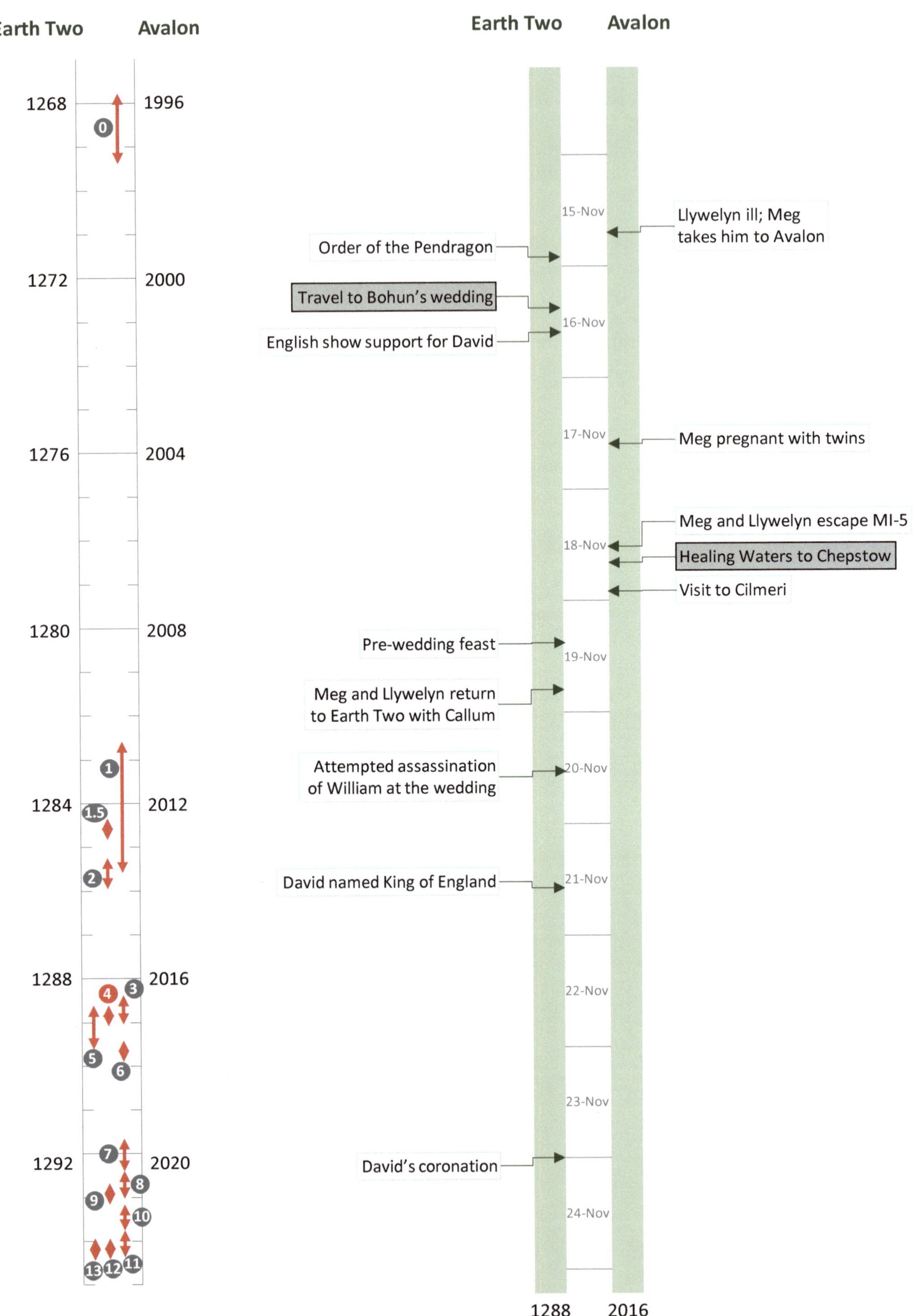

Timeline: Children of Time

Book 4: Children of Time

When I started writing *Children of Time*, I had a plan for how I wanted the story to go, but I genuinely didn't know if I had the ability to write it. I love many aspects of writing, but perhaps the one I love the most is the magic of sitting down at my computer not knowing what I'm going to write that day, and, once I get going, having the words pour through my fingers, almost outside my control. For some books, I experience that only intermittently, but with *Children of Time* it was every day.

The story opens with Llywelyn urging David to make a bid for the English throne, invoking the myth of Arthur. David resists, but then, towards the end of the conversation, Llywelyn feels ill, and David runs to get Aaron. Just as he returns, Goronwy, Meg, and Llywelyn jump from the balcony and are transported to Avalon, where they arrive at a private health clinic near present-day Aberystwyth. Llywelyn's health has been on Meg's mind, and she has sewn her passport, driver's license, credit card, and $400 into the hem of her skirt. It turns out, Llywelyn has pericarditis, which can be treated with antibiotics.

Meanwhile, back in the medieval world, Bevyn reveals to David that, in order to better protect him, he has created an extensive spy network called the Order of the Pendragon, and members are concerned that the trip to London for the wedding of William de Bohun is a trap. Of course, they are right.

Chepstow Castle

AFTER ACTION REPORT

28 November 2016

From: Natasha Clark, acting director, Cardiff Station

RE: Search for Director Alexander Callum

On the morning of 19 November 2016, Alexander Callum, Director of the Security Service's Cardiff Office, attempted to apprehend three individuals wanted for questioning regarding an incursion into the Healing Waters Spa, near Aberystwyth. In the course of the pursuit, Director Callum is presumed to have fallen from the balcony at Chepstow Castle (ancient monument in the care of CADW) into the River Wye. While witnesses reported the above events, none have been able to corroborate that Director Callum landed in the water. Regardless, the subsequent search for the director and the fugitives was unproductive.

In the course of our investigation into the incident, the fugitives were identified as Margaret Lloyd (American), Llywelyn ap Gruffydd (Welsh), and Goronwy ap Heilin (Welsh). The current location of the fugitives and Agent Callum is at this time unknown.

It is the recommendation of the investigators and this office that, unless more information is forthcoming, the investigation be suspended.

MI-5 Memo: Callum's disappearance

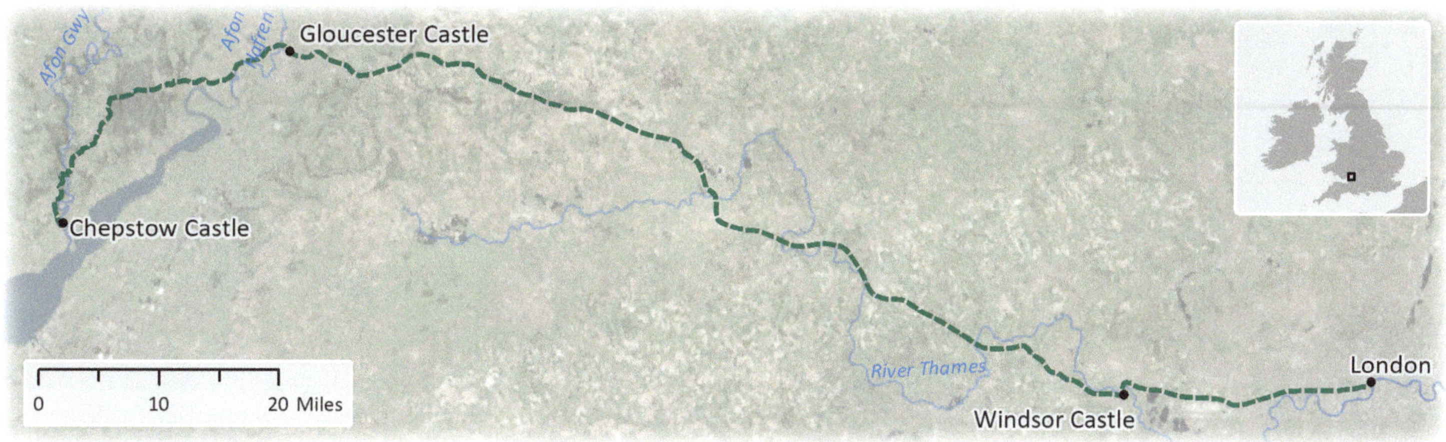

Travel to the Bohun Wedding

Travel to the Bohun Wedding

On the way to Gloucester, Gilbert de Clare's stronghold, David's company meets Edmund Mortimer, who has just broken up an ambush meant for David. At Gloucester, David is honored with a birthday dinner, and Lili learns that Joan, William de Bohun's prospective bride, had wished to join the church rather than marry. From there, the company continues on to London.

From Healing Waters to Chepstow

In Avalon, Meg calls Ted, her brother-in-law, who buys a plane ticket and plans to arrive in Wales the next day. When government agents arrive too, Meg, Llywelyn, and Goronwy are forced to flee. At Llywelyn's request, Meg drives to Cilmeri, and Llywelyn finally realizes why David feels so much pressure about their possible future.

MI-5 agents track the trio to Chepstow. Rather than surrender, however, and hoping to return to Earth Two, Meg, Llywelyn, and Goronwy jump off the balcony once again. The head MI-5 agent, Alexander Callum, falls with them. The group arrives at Westminster Palace in time to witness William's aborted wedding and to participate in the events that follow, ultimately leading to the crowning of David as King of England.

From Healing Waters to Chepstow

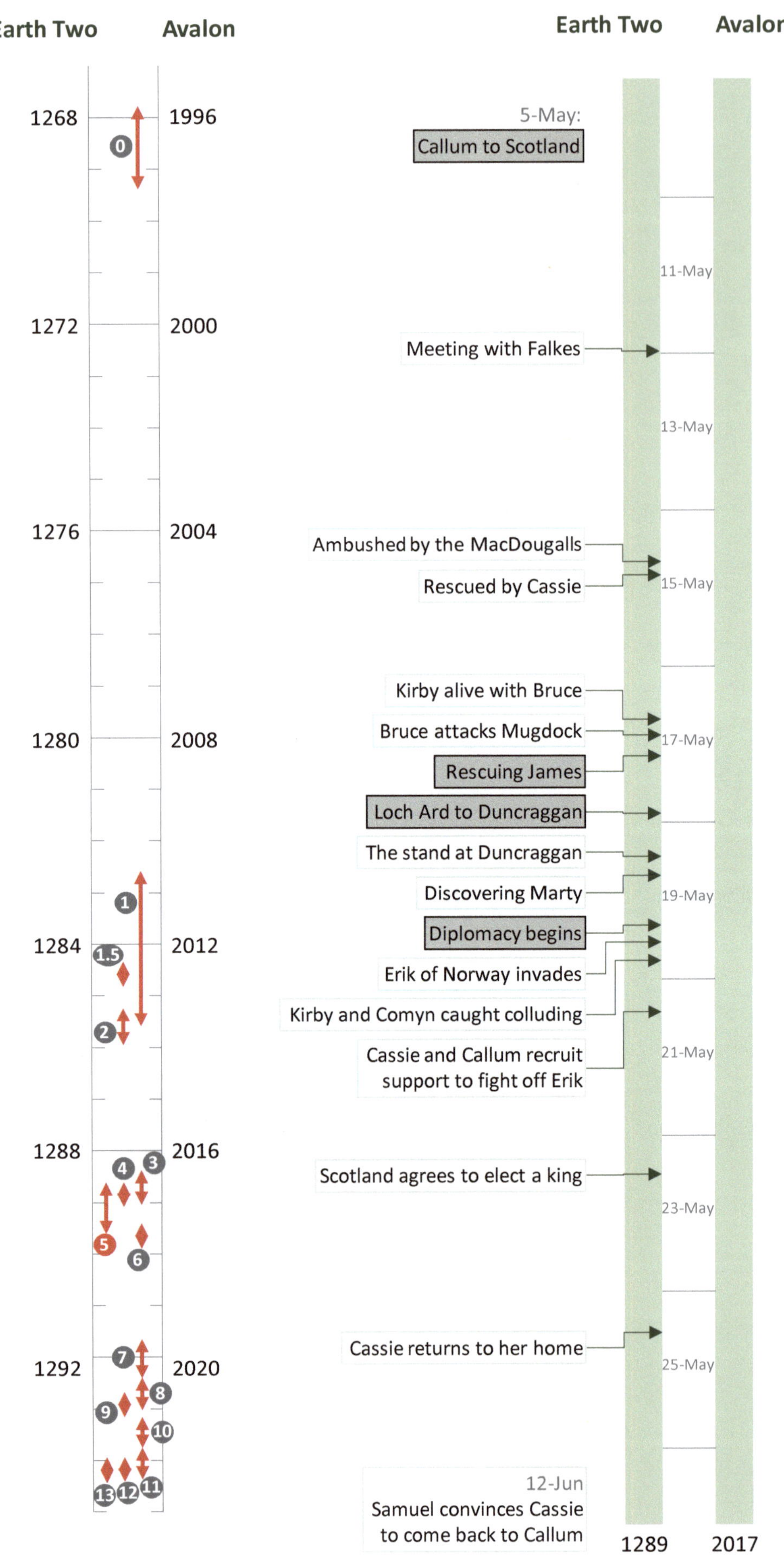

Timeline: Exiles in Time

Book 5: Exiles in Time

When one of my editors (who also happens to be my mother-in-law) read a draft of *Children of Time*, she questioned the presence of Callum, seeing no point to him traveling to Earth Two with Meg, Llywelyn, and Goronwy. I told her to wait, that I knew what I was doing, and that he was going to be important. It was the publication of *Exiles in Time* that most clearly sent the message to my readers that this was going to be a long-running series, and that just because David didn't play a role beyond the first chapter, didn't mean I'd forgotten him.

Exiles in Time also, for the first time, takes us to Scotland, which is experiencing unrest over the succession to the crown. As in Avalon's history, the sides are divided into two factions: those who support the Bruces and those who support the Comyns. David asks Callum to go to Scotland as his emissary, appointing him Earl of Shrewsbury in order to give him the status he will need to complete his task successfully.

Callum to Scotland

Callum travels first to Skipton Castle, where he meets James Stewart and Robert "Baby" Bruce (Robbie),

Callum to Scotland

Ambush site, south of Kilsyth

and then travels with them to Carlisle Castle. There, Callum reveals to John de Falkes who David really is. Falkes is horrified, and struggles to believe that David bears him no ill will.

<u>Callum and Cassie in Scotland</u>

Callum's party is ambushed on the road to Stirling Castle. The majority of the travelers are killed and the rest abducted. Archbishop Kirby appears to have been killed, and Callum, who is knocked unconscious, is left for dead. Cassie rescues him and takes him back to her hut, where she discovers that he is carrying a gun.

Looking west and south from Stirling Castle

From Cassie, Callum learns that the MacDougalls took prisoners from the ambush and marched them west. The pair decide to go to Mugdock Castle to talk to Lord

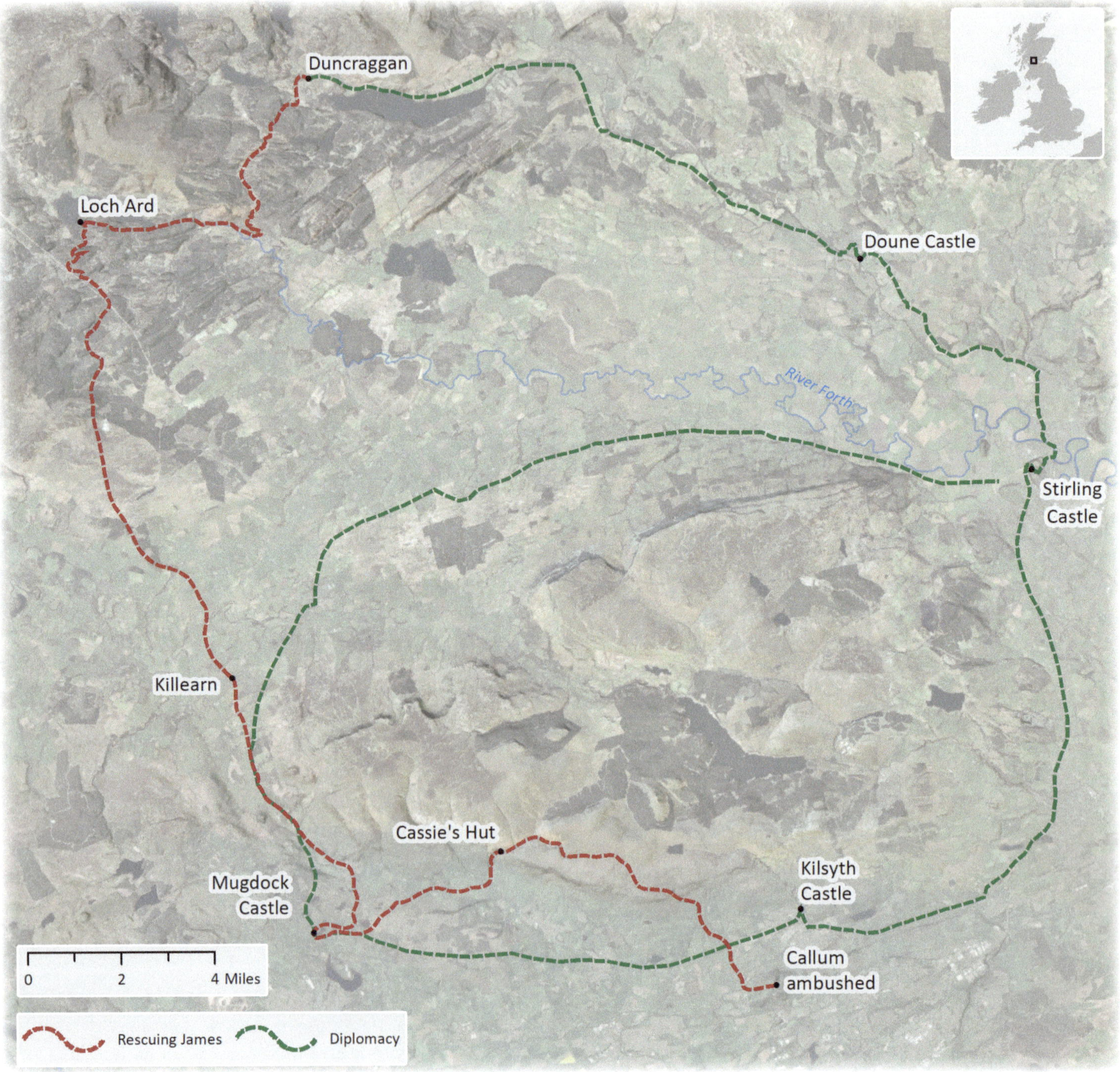

Callum and Cassie in Scotland

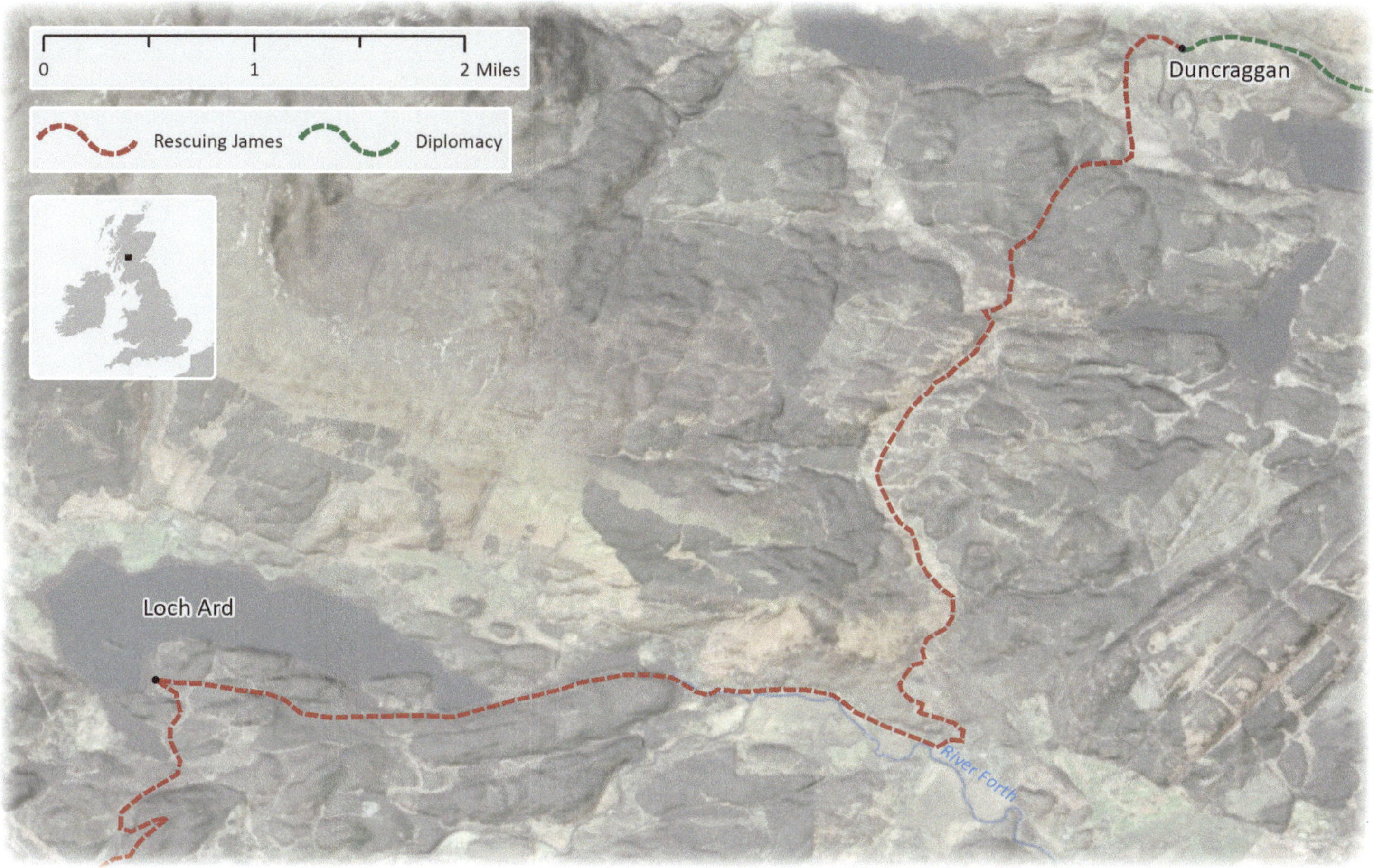

The map shows labeled routes and places.

Loch Ard to Duncraggan

Patrick, but Robert "Daddy" Bruce thinks Patrick is involved in the ambush and arrives with an army. As it turns out, the MacDougalls took all but one of the prisoners north. Liam, the man they left behind, helps Cassie and Callum leave the castle undetected. Cassie and Callum send Liam to Stirling to tell the Guardians of Scotland what has happened.

Loch Ard to Duncraggan

Meanwhile, Cassie and Callum seek the MacDougall's prisoners at Loch Ard, a hunting lodge. While Cassie sets everything on fire, Callum sneaks into the fort and frees the captives, including James Stewart, Samuel, and John Graham.

The current bridge at Duncraggan

Fleeing Loch Ard, the group arrives in the little village of Duncraggan, where they discover that the headman is the pilot, Marty, who left Meg at Hadrian's Wall years ago. The MacDougalls arrive with a hostage, but they demand John Graham rather than James. Callum shoots their leader.

The entire party travels to Stirling Castle, where they learn that Kirby has conspired with William de Valence to place Black Comyn on the throne. The barons of Scotland agree instead to an election—and Cassie and Callum decide to get married.

Loch Ard

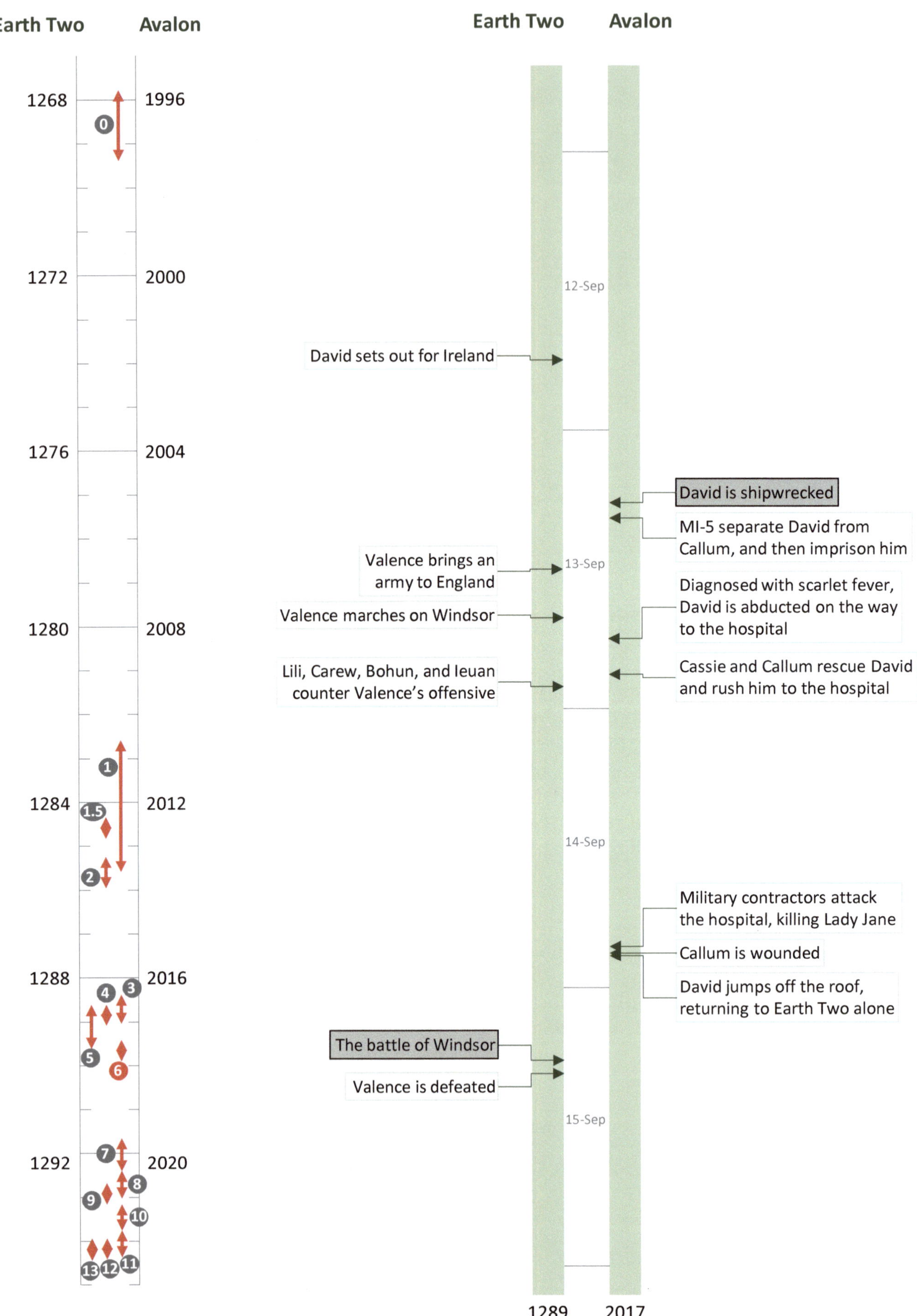

Timeline: Castaways in Time

Book 6: Castaways in Time

Castaways in Time opens with Cassie, Bronwen, and Lili pressuring David to improve women's standing in society. As with David, it wasn't as if I, the author, had in the previous books forgotten about the importance of the status and role of women, but it was definitely taking a back seat to the broader political situation.

David's Shipwreck

David, however, is headed to Ireland to finally deal with the unrest there, now that Scotland is somewhat settled. Unfortunately, his ship doesn't travel far before the ship's captain discovers that the rudder has been sabotaged. When the ship goes down, David, Callum, and Cassie time travel, and they arrive in modern-day Cardiff, where David is immediately taken into custody by MI-5.

Callum is angry at what is happening to David, but then Jane Cooke (Lady Jane), the director of MI-5, explains that she fears they have a traitor within the agency. David figures out that he has scarlet fever and is quarantined, but rather than taking him to a hospital, the ambulance goes to an apartment. With the help of Mark Jones, Cassie and Callum follow and rescue him.

Once David finally reaches the hospital, Lady Jane tells Callum that she has information proving a military contractor is behind David's abduction and probably has corrupted MI-5 agents. When Lady Jane is shot and killed through a hospital room window, David, Cassie, and Callum make for the roof, but Agent Driscoll follows them and shoots Callum. Knowing that Callum needs medical attention and can't come with him, David jumps off the roof by himself.

David's Shipwreck

Windsor Castle

The Battle of Windsor

When Valence lands a flotilla of ships in Southampton, Ieuan marches to intercept him, but Valence moves faster than expected. He reaches Windsor, which is defended by Lili, Bronwen, Anna, and Math. David appears in Earth Two near Maidenhead, where he finds loyal citizens. Soon after, William de Bohun, who'd left Windsor two days earlier to find reinforcements, arrives in Maidenhead with an army of five hundred men. While William marches to meet Ieuan west of Windsor, David floats down the Thames to Windsor Castle, where he reunites with Lili.

Realizing he is outnumbered and outmaneuvered, Valence flies a white flag, but David distrusts his motives, for good reason. An assassin's arrow fails to pierce David's Kevlar, and his men take Valence prisoner.

Back in Avalon, Callum becomes head of a newly formed division within MI-5 called The Time Travel Initiative.

Bridge over the Thames in Windsor

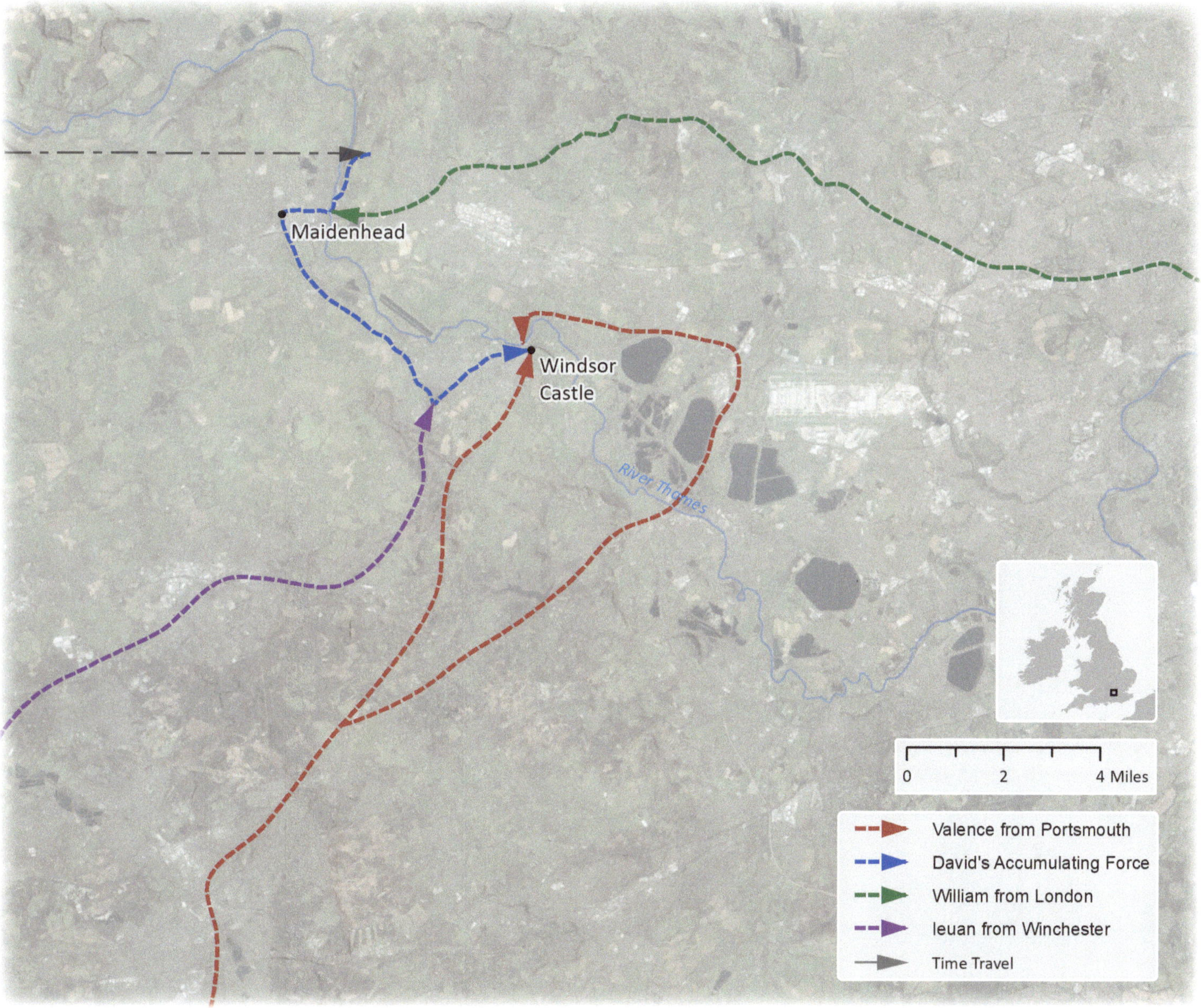

The Battle of Windsor

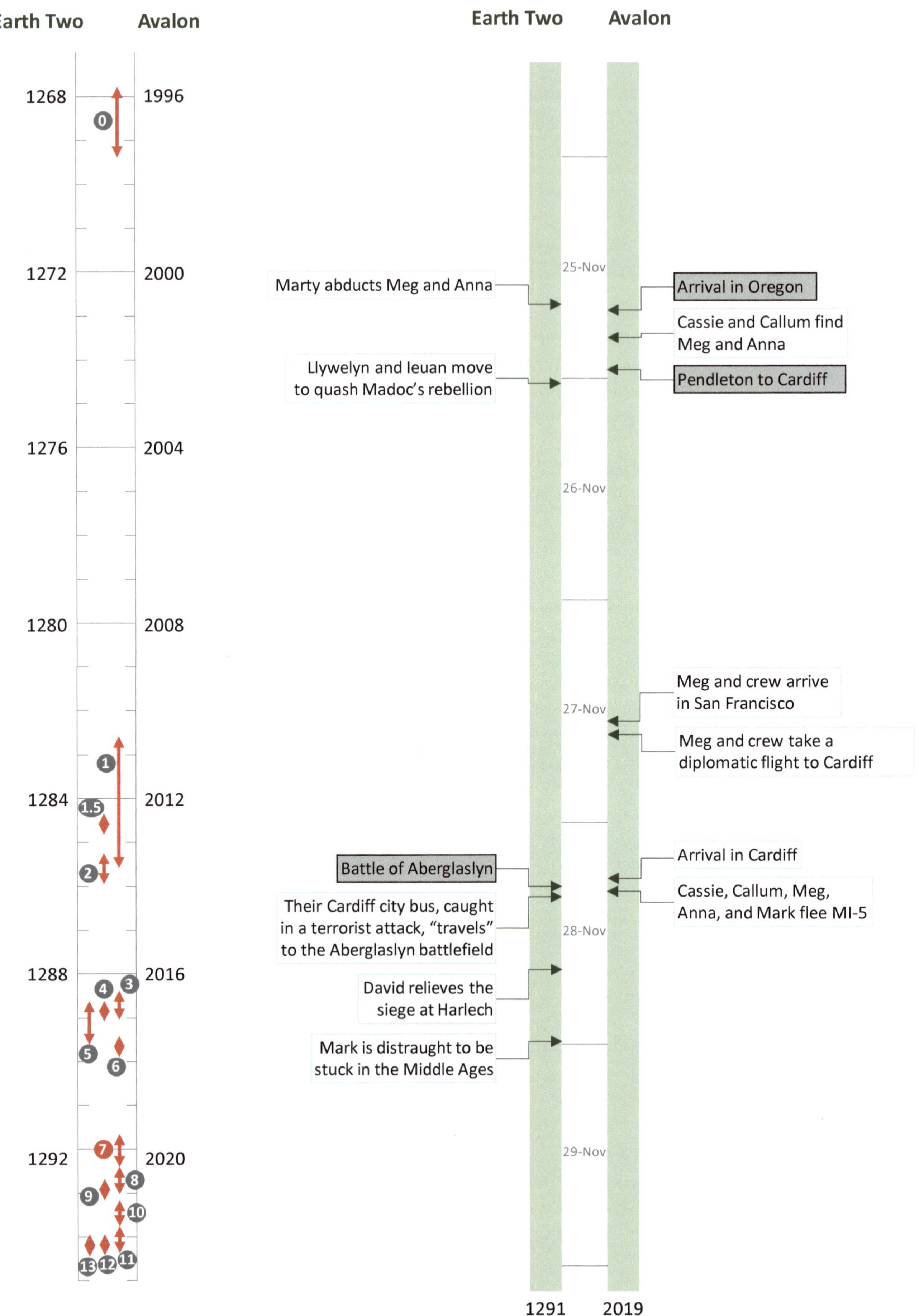

Timeline: Ashes of Time

Book 7: Ashes of Time

Ashes of Time has one of the most fun scenes I have ever written, which is the crashing of the Cardiff bus into Earth Two. I giggled as I wrote it. That we would ever get there, however, wasn't a given. I have a whole posse of readers who edit my books after they're written, but my first reader, my husband, is the one to tell me if I've lost my mind or gone down a rabbit hole. I feared that the Cardiff bus would be one of those moments, but he liked it as much as I did, so it stayed.

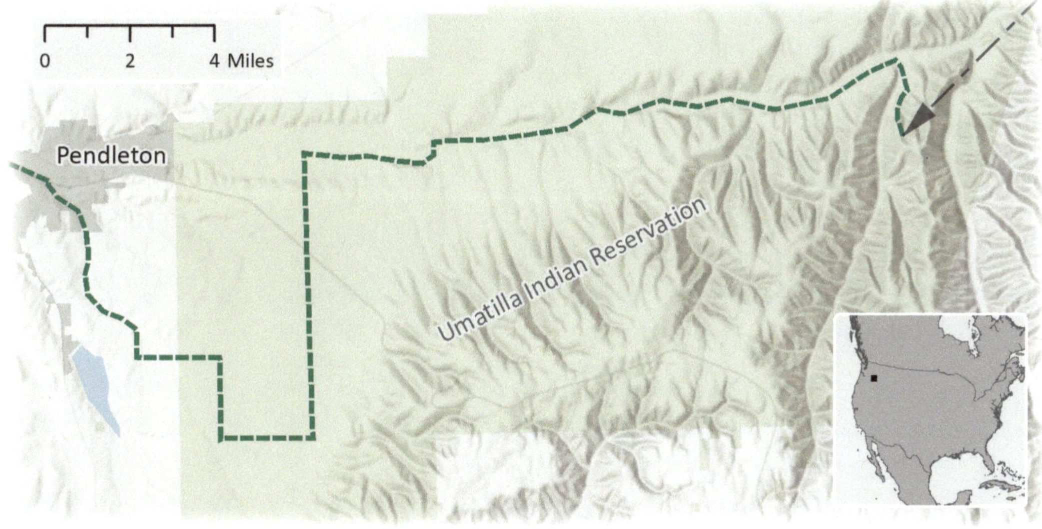

Arrival in Oregon

That scene is at the end of the book. *Ashes of Time* begins with Thanksgiving dinner at Rhuddlan Castle, where the family discusses how they might implement a modern democracy in the medieval world. The party is broken up by Marty, who takes Anna and Meg to a tower at knife point. He forces them to jump with him because he wants to go home. Anna manages to wrestle free of him at the last second, so she and Meg travel to Avalon while Marty falls to his death.

Near Pendleton, Oregon

Arrival in Oregon

Meg and Anna arrive in what appears to be a remote location in Avalon. They hike to a paved road, and a man, who says they are near Pendleton, Oregon, takes them to a gas station. The man knows Cassie and her grandfather, Art, whom Cassie and Callum happen to be visiting for Thanksgiving.

Meanwhile, Mark Jones calls Callum to tell him that someone has come through from Earth Two and that there has been a terrorist bombing in the UK targeting GCHQ (a government communications facility).

Having borrowed Art's truck, Cassie, Callum, Meg, and Anna drive west and south, trying to put as much distance as possible between them and where Anna and Meg arrived. They stop at a Wal-Mart in western Oregon to pick up supplies, hoping ultimately to take them back to Earth Two. When they exit the store, however, they find a police officer closely examining Art's truck. They decide to hop on a bus to southern Oregon rather than trying to get the truck back from the police. Mark arranges for them to pick up a rental car in Medford.

A British diplomat picks them up at a Six Flags parking lot in northern California to shuttle them to the Oakland airport. Though an arrest warrant has been issued for them, the group makes it to the airport and takes off for England.

Travel from Oregon to Cardiff

<u>Battle of Aberglaslyn</u>

David and Llywelyn receive word of a rebellion in western Wales. They split up, with Llywelyn openly riding south from Beddgelert, hoping to fool Madog's men into thinking they are all coming from the same direction. As Llywelyn's force attacks from the front, David's and Ieuan's forces assault the rebels' flank. Madog has held his cavalry in reserve and attacks from the south, but David and Llywelyn manage to rally their men and push the enemy back until Math's troops arrive. David kills Madog when he refuses to surrender.

Meanwhile, back in Avalon, Meg, Anna, and Cassie leave Callum and Darren, another MI-5 agent, and head to Cassie and Callum's safehouse. Callum and Darren intend to speak to the director, but they distrust MI-5's motives and go on the run. All the companions ultimately meet on a Cardiff city bus, and just as the bus is passing a large government complex, a building explodes. The bus travels to Earth Two, plowing right through the middle of the battle at Aberglaslyn.

Ieuan's route to Aberglaslyn

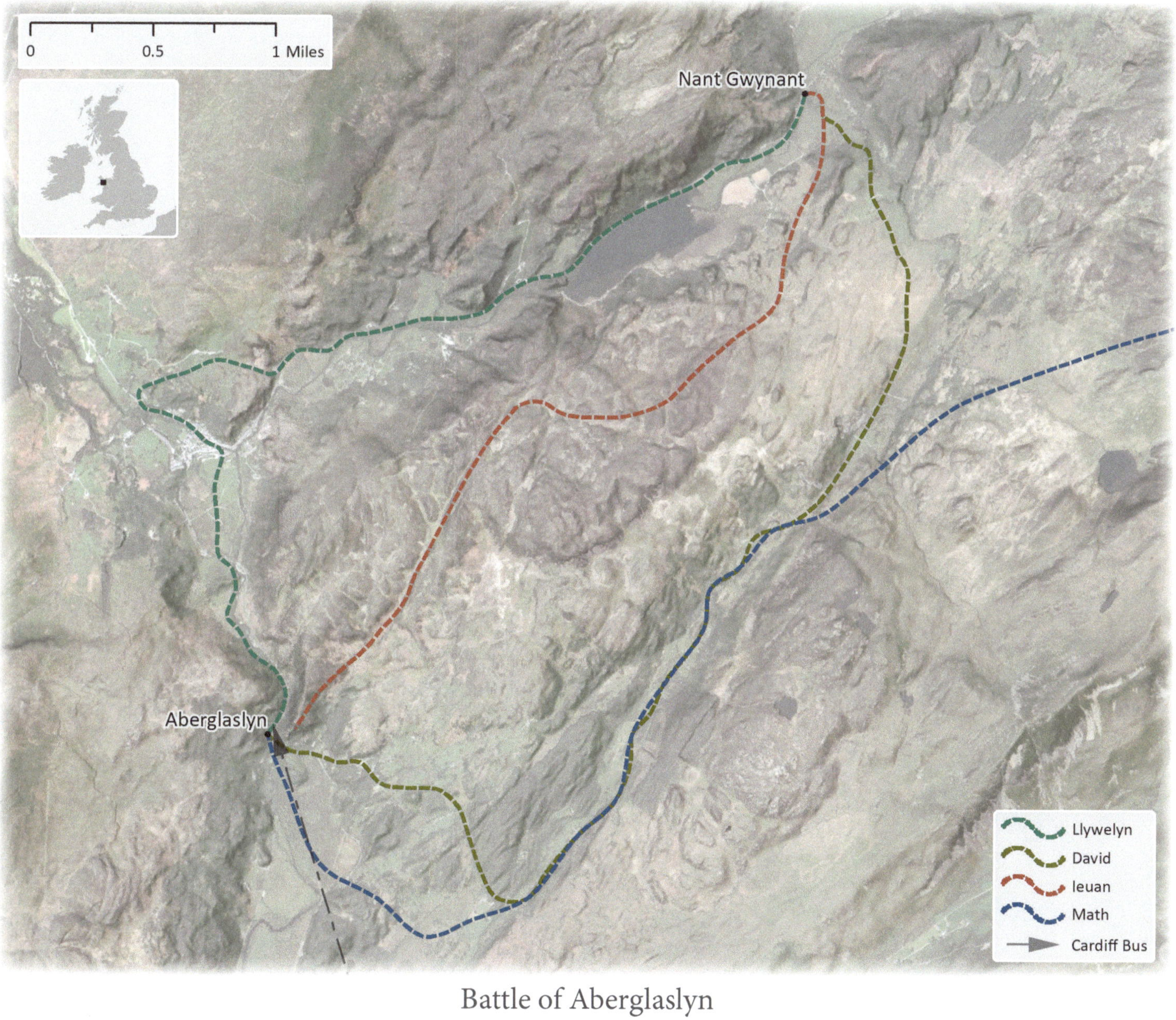

Battle of Aberglaslyn

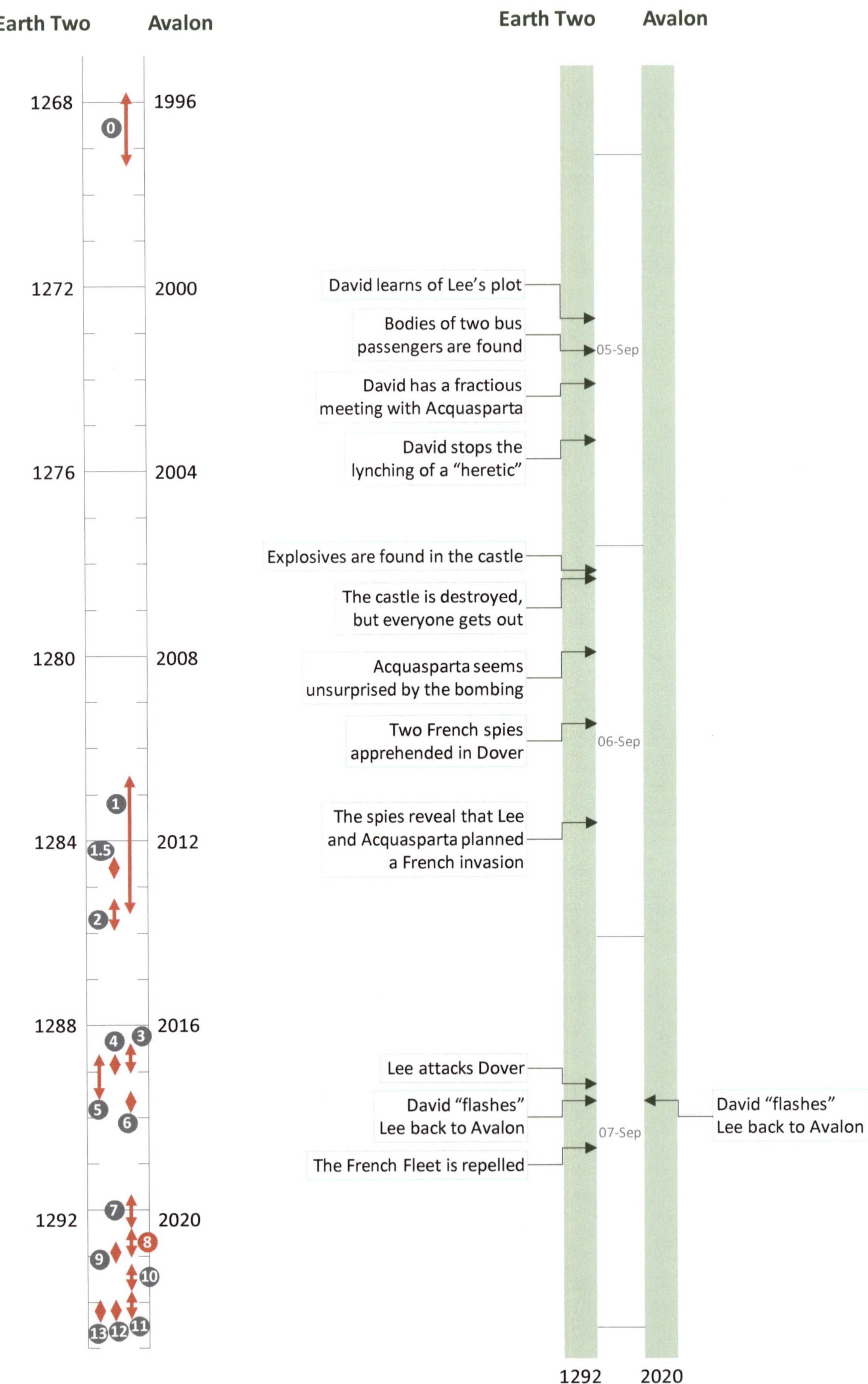

Timeline: Warden of Time

Book 8: Warden of Time

One of the positive benefits, out of many, of being an independent author, is that I get to do what I want. Sometimes that can lead me astray, if what I want really isn't a good idea. At other times, it means that if I want to write a book in the first person, one that is all in David's voice, all the time, I can.

One of the themes of *Warden of Time* is unintended consequences. Anna and Meg brought the Cardiff bus to Earth Two, and in so doing, inadvertently brought a whole host of other people with them. Some of those people were a huge net benefit, and others not so much. Lee and his friends, two of whom he murders, are definitely in the latter category. When Lee allies with the Papal Legate and the King of France, there are unintended consequences for them as well.

Dover Castle

Canterbury: from Castle to Cathedral

<u>Conflict in Southeast England</u>

The Papal Legate (Acquasparta) comes for an audience at the behest of the new pope (Boniface VIII), who has three demands for David: 1) Eliminate religious freedom in England. 2) Abrogate the agreement between the crown and the English Church, ceding 10% of donations to the state. 3) Withdraw his claim to Aquitaine. The Pope offers nothing in return, and Acquasparta threatens England with interdict and David's possible excommunication if he does not accede to these demands.

Shortly afterwards, a modern explosive device is discovered in one of the latrines in the keep of Canterbury Castle. Callum disarms the bomb, and David and Callum manage to evacuate the castle just before the rest of the bombs explode, utterly destroying the keep and other parts of the castle.

David sends Lili away for safety, and later follows her to Dover in pursuit of two French spies, who were caught trying to slip out of the country. Geoffrey de Geneville arrives at Dover Castle and interrogates the spies, who reveal they have been working with Lee and Acquasparta. In addition, believing David may be dead, King Philip of France sends a force of two thousand men to invade England in hopes of taking the throne.

The next morning, after Lee engineers an explosion in the outer ward of Dover Castle, David confronts him on the wall-walk. Lee tells David that unless he's taken back to Avalon, he will blow up Dover like he did Canterbury. David falls from the wall with Lee, and they struggle with one another, time traveling in the process. But immediately upon arrival in Avalon, David releases Lee, who fires his gun at David, sending him right back to 13th century Dover.

Having learned where the French forces are headed, David marches for Hythe at the head of Clare's army, only to find that the local militia has already driven the French back. Ultimately, David meets with Acquasparta and informs him that he will not accede to any of the Pope's demands and that he knows of his role in the plot to help Philip take the English throne.

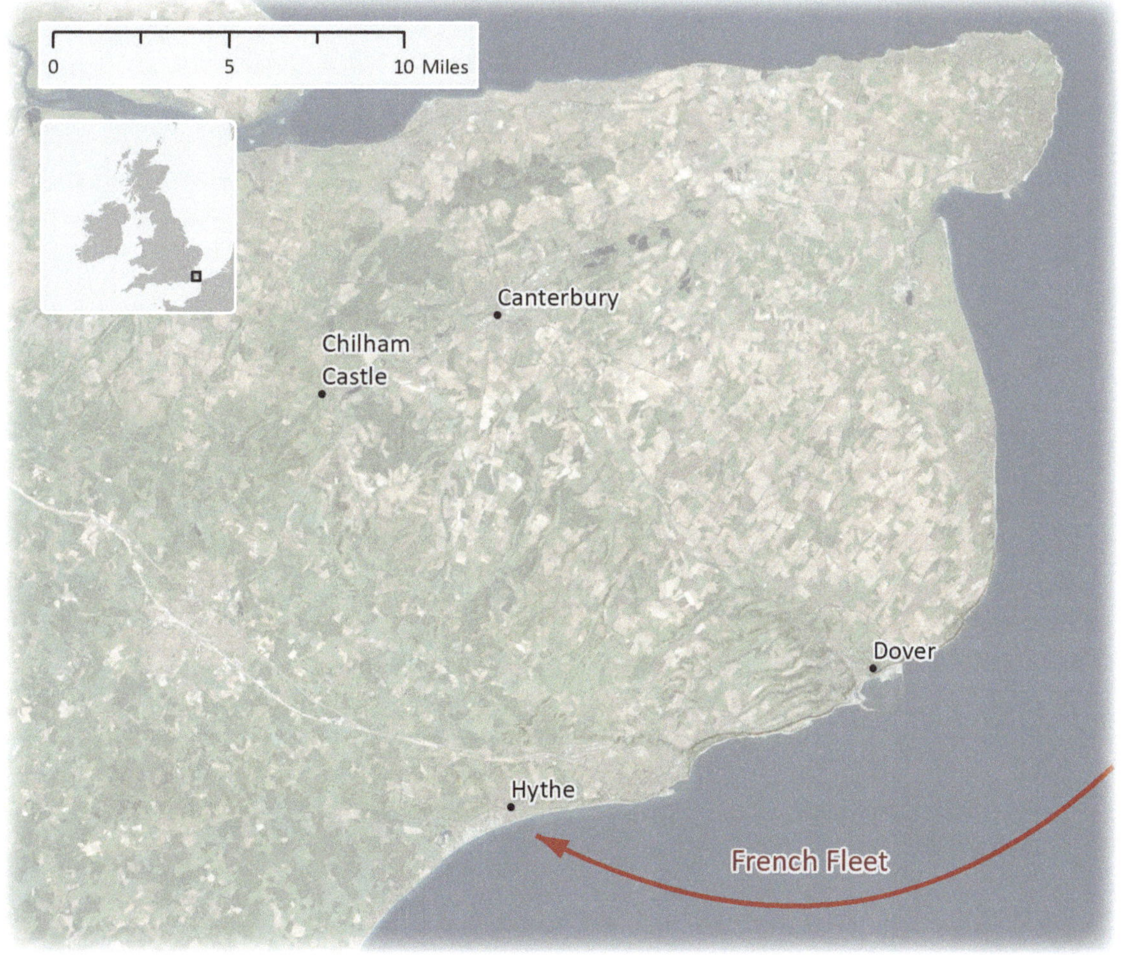

Conflict in Southeast England

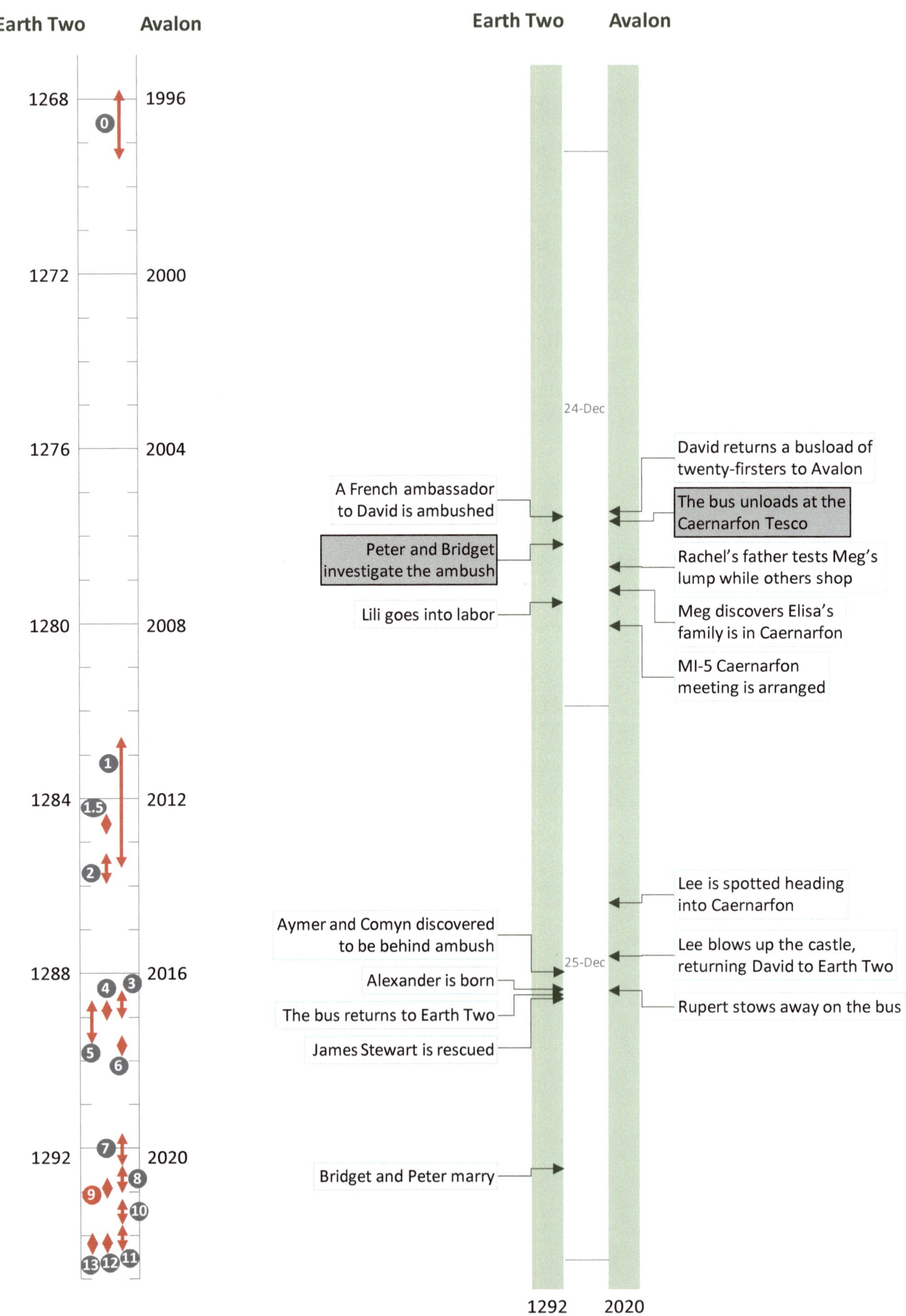

Timeline: Guardians of Time

Book 9: Guardians of Time

One of the wonderful things about having such familiar characters is that sometimes, when I'm not sure what needs to happen next, I put my characters in a room together and let them talk among themselves. And by doing so, they figure it out for me. That happened when David decided he needed to take back to Avalon everyone who wanted to go.

The beginning of *Guardians of Time* marks the second time that David makes a deliberate trip to Avalon, the first being when he saves Ieuan's life in *Prince of Time*. David decides to travel on Christmas Eve so fewer people will notice he's gone. There is some last-minute shuffling when they are ready to drive the bus into a cliff: Math refuses to be left behind in Earth Two without Anna, and then Bridget realizes that Peter Cobb doesn't intend to stay in Avalon. She kisses Peter and tells him she too wants to remain in Earth Two. David agrees that they should stay behind, and they get off the bus together.

The attempt to return to Avalon is successful, despite arriving headed the wrong way down a highway, and they pull into a Tesco parking lot in Caernarfon. Callum arranges for the passengers to stay at the Black Boar Inn there, and David and Rachel plan for the medical treatments needed for Meg, who has a breast lump, and Shane, a young boy with childhood leukemia. Rachel's father, Abraham, is a doctor in Bangor.

Caernarfon Castle latrine

Whittington Castle

Caernarfon and Bangor

Menai Bridge from Anglesey

Caernarfon and Bangor

Having dropped Shane and his parents off at Ysbyty Gwynedd and Meg at Abraham's clinic, David, Callum, and Cassie go to the Bangor Tesco to get supplies and then to Bangor University to use the internet connectivity. It turns out that Meg's sister, Elisa, and her family are also staying at the Black Boar, and while Elisa is on the phone with Meg, MI-5 shows up at the inn. The companions drive to Caernarfon to meet with Elisa's family and then take everyone to Abraham's house, which turns out to be the remains of Aber Castle. Along the way, Christopher reveals that Ted has done some genealogy work, and Meg *is* actually descended from King Henry III, who had an affair with a daughter of King Alexander of Scotland.

The next morning, Abraham discovers that MI-5 has surrounded his clinic, and the travelers and MI-5 negotiate a meeting outside Caernarfon Castle, where the Prince of Wales (contemporary) is scheduled to give a Christmas Day address. They plan to hide in the crowds and make use of the swing bridge across Afon Seiont.

David and his team get into the castle without a problem but encounter Lee wearing a maintenance uniform. Although they are able to overpower him and call for help, Lee has already left a bomb in the latrine. Although they can't prevent the explosion that follows, David links arms with Llywelyn and Darren and returns with them to Earth Two.

The companions left behind in Avalon are followed by Rupert, a reporter. He sees them retrieve the bus, and, as they return the rental van, he slips inside the bus and hides on the upper deck where he, quite literally, has a front-row view of Cassie driving the bus, at full speed, into one of the pillars on the Menai Bridge.

Peter and Bridget's Investigation

Geoffrey de Geneville is traveling with James Stewart to Dinas Bran to speak to David when they are ambushed. Peter is tasked with investigating the incident. Acting as his assistant, Bridget tells Peter that she has heard chatter in recent weeks that King Philip might have an alliance with Gilbert de Clare.

In the course of their investigation, they speak to an innkeeper at Chirk, who tells Peter that Fulk Fitzwarin has a group of Scots as his guests. They have been on the road in *hunting parties*.

Peter and Bridget head to Whittington where they find that Fitzwarin's guests, Red Comyn and Aymer de Valence, have captured James Stewart. The bus arrives and crashes into the tower where Stewart is being held. Aymer and Comyn come out of the castle with their men, but when Comyn discovers who Callum is, he turns on Aymer. In addition, the Whittington guard closes ranks against them, and Samuel arrives with a host of men, ending any chance of danger.

Callum's company returns to Dinas Bran to find that David and Llywelyn have arrived safely too, and Lili has given birth to her second son, Alexander.

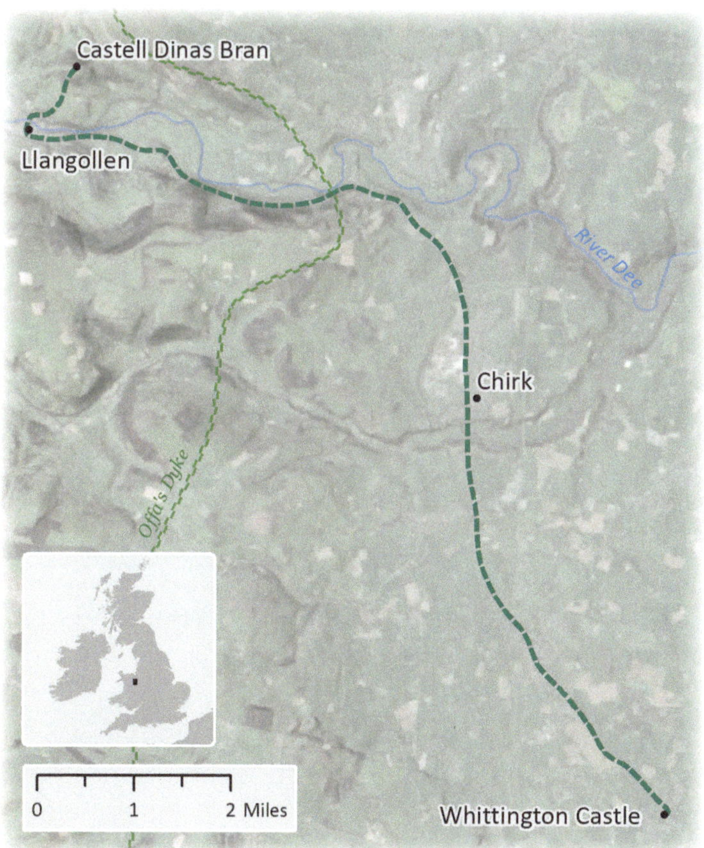

Peter and Bridget's Investigation

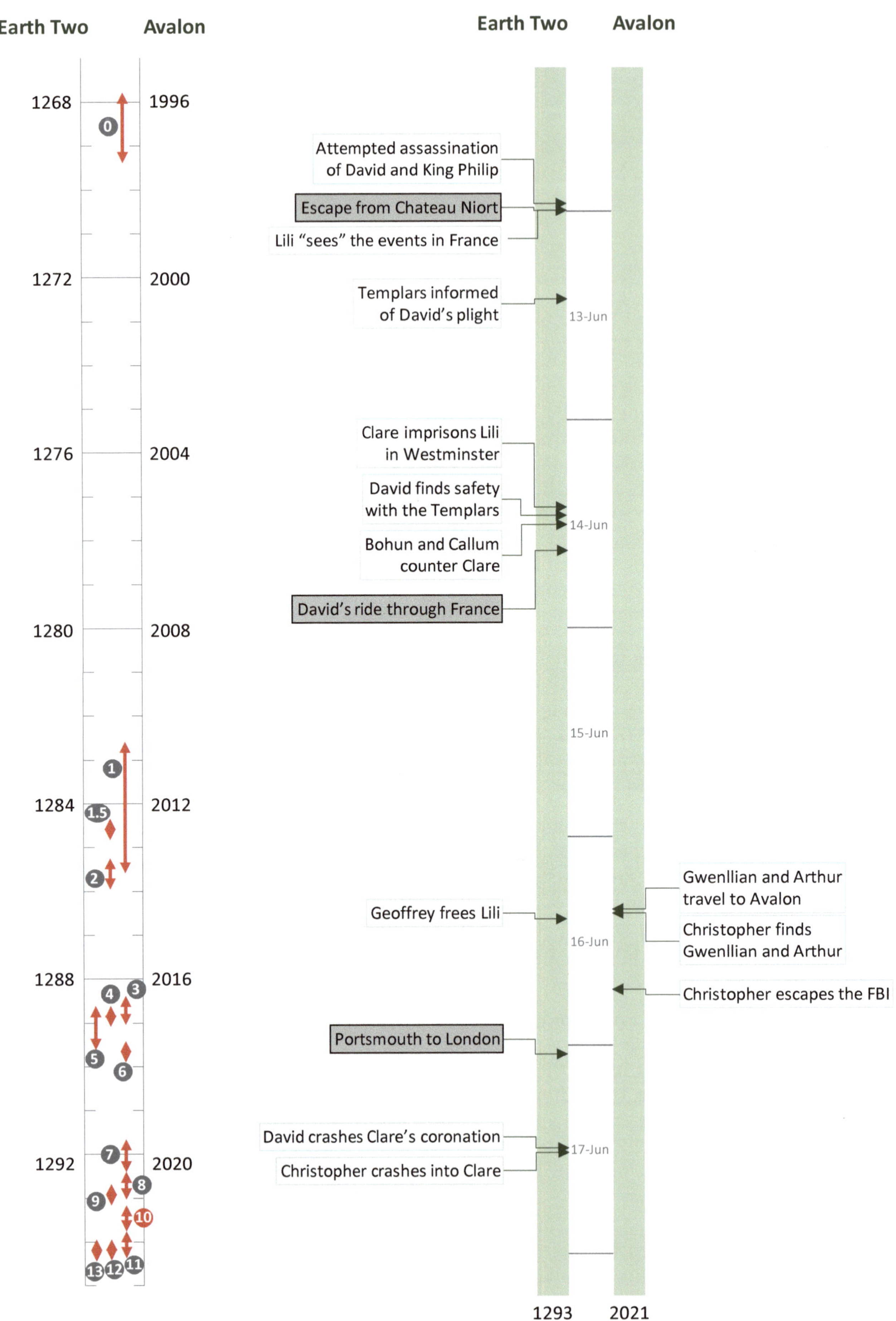

Timeline: Masters of Time

Book 10: Masters of Time

When I first related the plot of *Masters of Time* to my eldest son, explaining that it was Gilbert de Clare who was the antagonist of the story, his response was *of course it is*. In our history, Gilbert de Clare distinguished himself by being one of the most opportunistic and ruthless of the Marcher lords, which is saying something, since the Marcher lords were known for both qualities. But while his rebellion was inevitable, like David, I was sorry to see him go. As Callum says in *Champions of Time*, "It was an open question how to properly mourn a friend who'd tried to kill you."

As *Masters of Time* opens, David and King Philip are meeting at Chateau Niort for negotiations regarding Aquitaine. Supposedly, Gilbert de Clare has been working as an intermediary, but he does not arrive, so midnight finds both David and Philip on the battlement, unable to sleep. Suddenly, all the torches in the bailey are doused except those highlighting David and Philip, and Philip is shot in the shoulder. David then positions himself between Philip and the attackers and takes two arrows in his Kevlar armor before Philip grabs him

from behind and flings them both off the parapet and into the river.

Back at Westminster Castle, Lili wakes with a vision of these events and tells Bridget, Peter, and Nicholas de Carew what she saw. They decide to send Bridget and Peter to warn Callum (in Shrewsbury) while Carew tries to enlist his half-brother (Godfrid de Windsor) who is the head of the Templars in London.

Escape from Chateau Niort

David and Philip float down the river to get as far from Chateau Niort as possible, eventually fetching up on the south bank, where David dresses Philip's wound. Once Philip is able to walk, David seeks help at a village but overhears Clare's men telling the villagers that David and Philip are dead and they are seeking the assassins. Philip believes his brother, Charles, is the one plotting with Clare to assassinate them.

Escape from Chateau Niort

Road Trip through France

Back in England, Carew meets with Godfrid, who agrees to send word to the Templars on the Continent that David may be in need of aid, which, of course, he is. As expected, Clare comes to Westminster and informs Lili of David's "death." His men take control of Westminster and imprison Lili, the children, and Carew in the tower.

Eventually, David and Philip make it to the Aquitaine coast and the city of La Rochelle, where they find refuge at a Templar commanderie. After insuring that Philip is going to be cared for, David meets with Pierre, the master of the commanderie, who recognizes him. Pierre tells David that the fastest way for him to get home is to ride north to Le Havre and then sail the English Channel. However, he will need to change horses every ten miles to make it in a timely fashion. Fortunately, the Templars can help him to accomplish this, and David departs from the commanderie with Henri, the Templar who was manning the gate when David and Philip arrived.

Meanwhile, back in England, Clare has imprisoned the royal family, so Gwenllian clasps Arthur to her chest and jumps from the window of the tower. The two of them travel to Avalon, and Christopher inadvertently meets them at a train station just outside of Radnor.

Portsmouth to London

When Clare returns after unsuccessfully searching the Thames for Arthur and Gwenllian, Lili tells him that the boy has gone to Avalon, and, for the first time, she sees a hint of fear in Clare's eyes. Later, while Clare is addressing Parliament, Geoffrey de Geneville arrives at the tower to free Lili and Carew, shepherding them to a small boat on the castle dock where Huw is waiting to take them to safety.

After crossing the Thames, they walk to Kingston. In the middle of the night, David arrives at Portsmouth and goes to the Templar commanderie to try to get a horse. The commander does not recognize him, but when he removes his helmet, Thomas Hartley, who is the commander's assistant and knows David from Carlisle, recognizes him. Thomas and Henri accompany David on another marathon ride to London because they must arrive before the coronation of Clare at noon.

Lili and Carew are only a few miles out of Kingston when they meet David on the road. David and his companions continue to London to stop Clare, while Lili, Huw, and Carew take over the London radio station so they can inform the country that David lives. David and his companions get into the castle, and, with his helmet concealing his identity, David approaches the crowning ceremony. Across the river, Rupert helps Carew and Huw subdue the final guard at the radio station so Lili can begin the broadcast. As David, still incognito, is working his way towards the coronation platform, Lili comes on the radio to tell the crowd that David is alive and likely among them.

Back in Avalon, Christopher is trying to protect Gwenllian and Arthur from government (and possibly rogue) agents. When seemingly friendly FBI agents call for backup, Christopher takes the opportunity to slip out the back with door Gwenllian and Arthur, but as they enter the main road in his car, he pulls into the path of a speeding fire truck.

David reveals himself and the crowd chants his name. As he stands on the dais, Clare protests his innocence of any wrongdoing—and then Christopher's car arrives out of thin air, striking and killing Clare.

Temple Church in London

Portsmouth to London

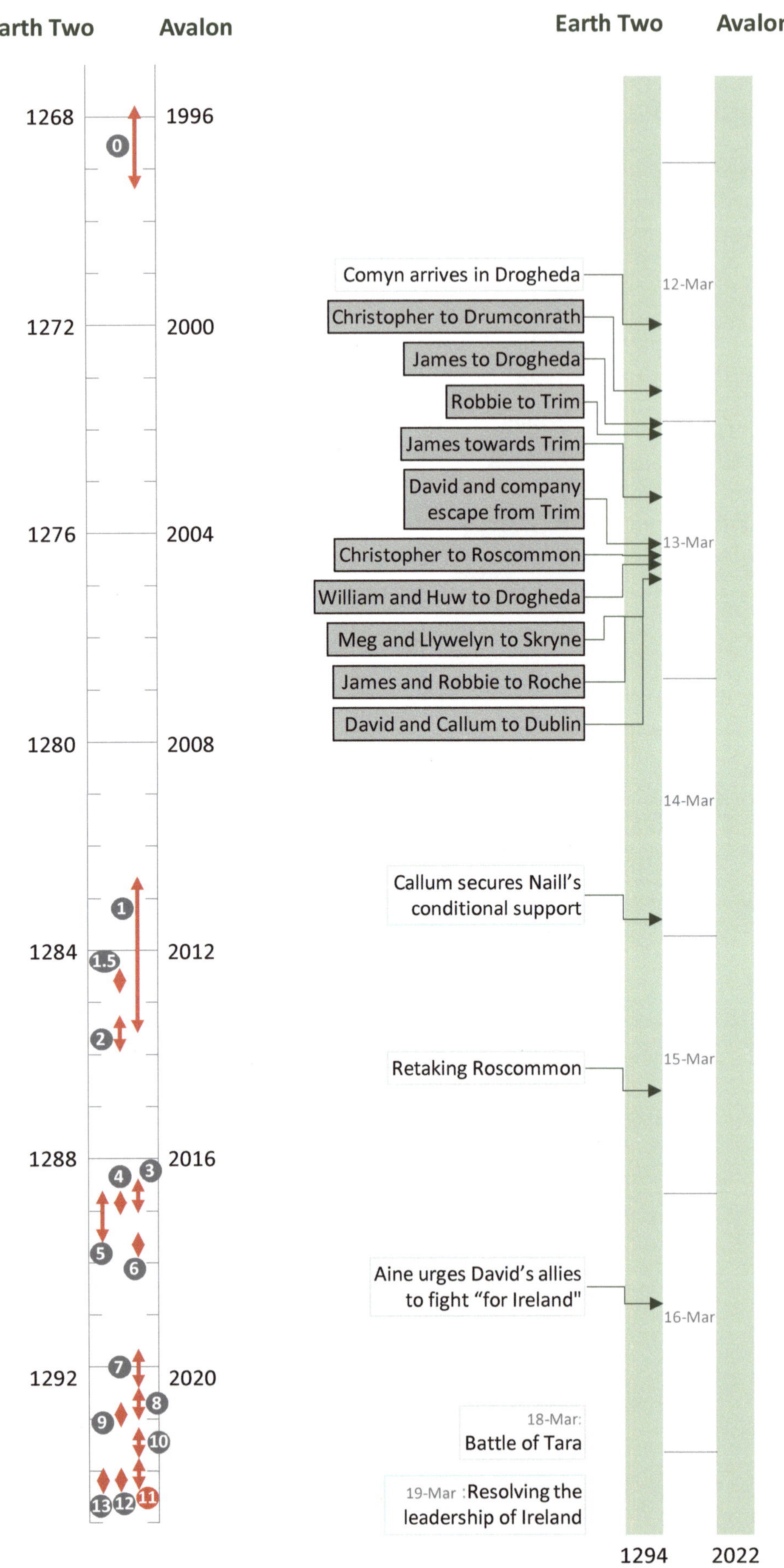

Timeline: Outpost in Time

Book 11: Outpost in Time

Although I was the only one who knew it when it was initially published, *Outpost in Time* is the first book in a trilogy about a rebellion led by John Balliol, King of Scots. To my mind, the need to tell this story was inevitable, given the way the conquest of Scotland and Ireland went in our world. The maps on the following pages relate the various journeys the characters undertake in the book.

As you may recall, David was making his way to Ireland at the beginning of *Castaways in Time,* hoping at that time to address the issue of Ireland's independence. His plan was derailed by a storm and the machinations of William de Valence.

This time, David makes it to Ireland, but out of fear that he will give their lands to the Irish, Norman lords have conspired with John Balliol and Red Comyn to kill him. Christopher and his friends witness

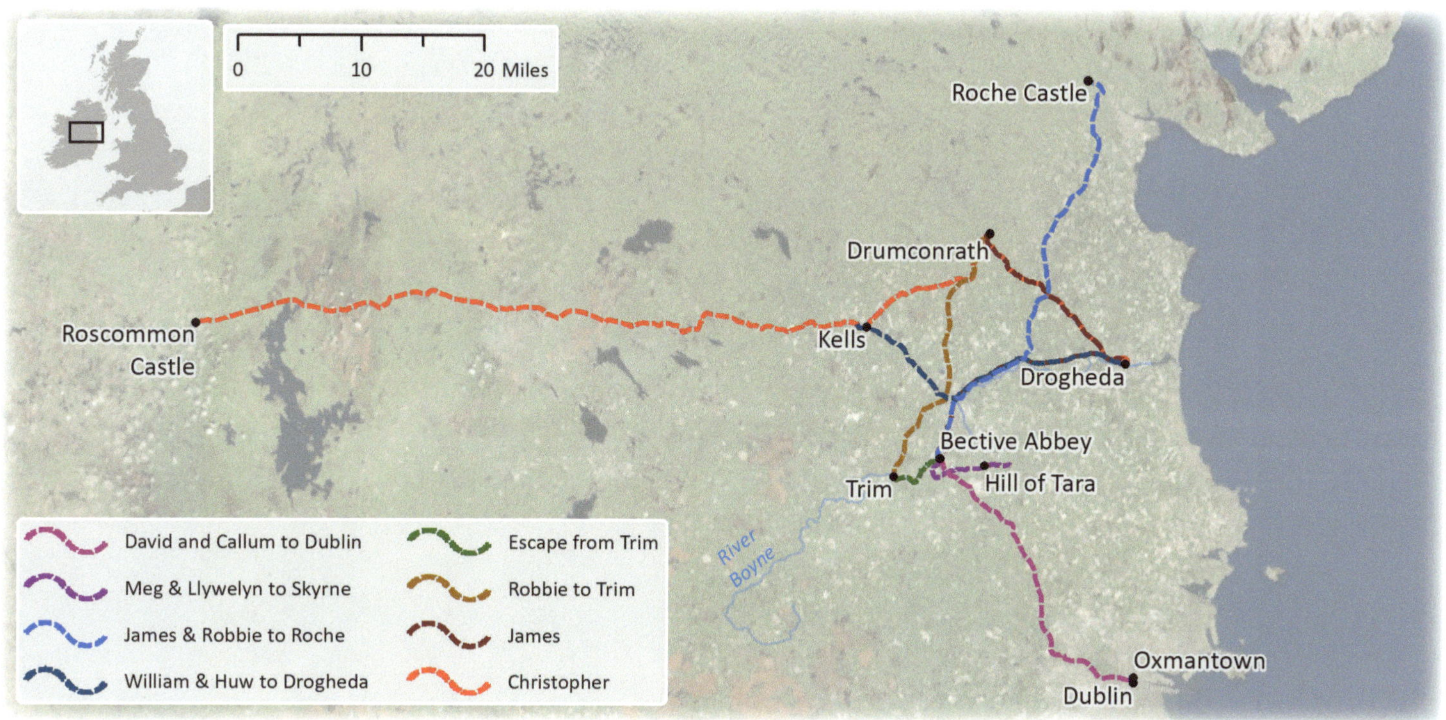

All Travels in Ireland

Christopher

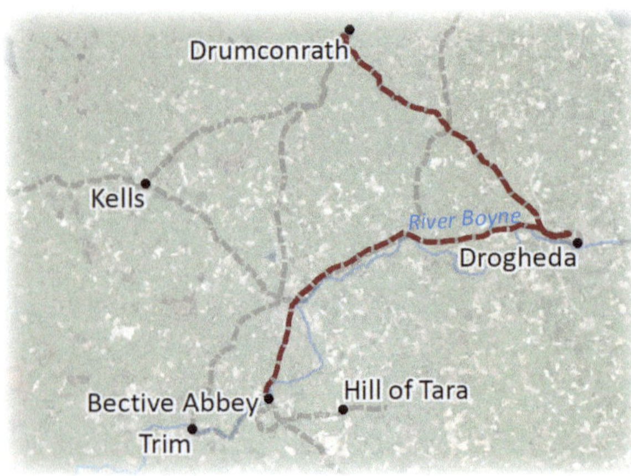

James

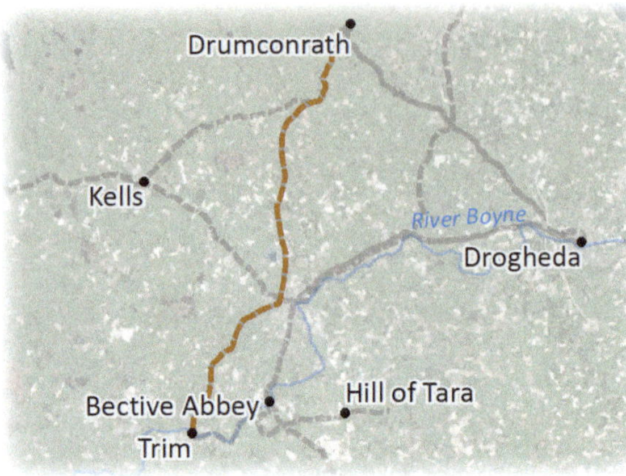

Robbie to Trim

Escape from Trim

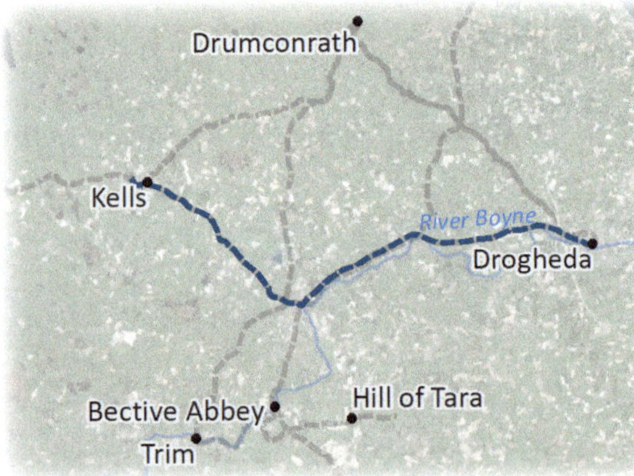

William and Huw to Drogheda

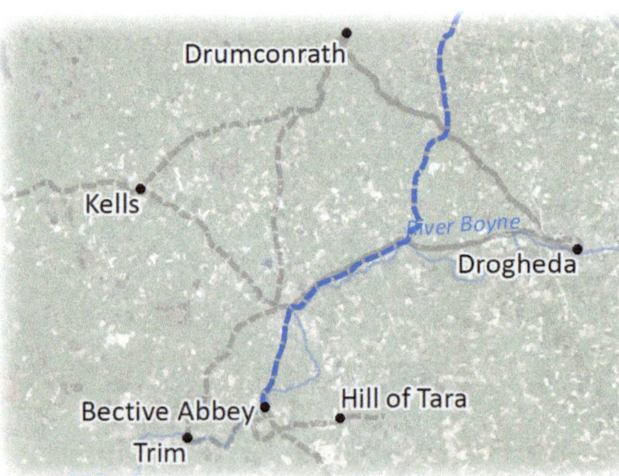

James and Robbie to Roche

Meg and Llywelyn to Skyrne

David and Callum to Dublin

ships bearing the colors of Red Comyn (who has been promised the High Kingship) sailing into Drogheda. James Stewart, the young men's chaperone, decides they should split up to find out what is happening, with Christopher staying back to guard the horses. Unfortunately, the result is that Christopher is abducted by Irish partisans working for Gilla O'Reilly, a minor lord, and taken to his manor near Drumconrath, which Thomas de Clare, Gilbert's very angry brother, then attacks.

Back at Trim Castle, the insurrection Christopher learns of at Gilla's manor breaks out, with half the participants of the peace talks launching a surprise attack on the other half. Callum and Llywelyn escape from the great hall and make for the battlement wall, where they meet Robbie, whom Christopher has sent to Trim to tell David of the plot against him.

Ultimately, Christopher's party splinters entirely, with James riding to Drogheda, Robbie to Trim, Christopher and Gilla's daughter, Aine, to Roscommon to recruit help from the O'Connor clan, and Huw and William riding to Castle Roche. These latter two are captured by Aine's brother, Matha, who appears to have aligned himself with Red Comyn and Thomas de Clare. Matha takes Huw and William to Drogheda.

Meanwhile, David finds himself in a boat on the Boyne River, fleeing Trim Castle.

> The Dane, Magnus, clambered in next, followed by Callum. He hardly needed any assistance, which prompted a sour look and comment from Dad. "You would show me up."
>
> "It's because I practice climbing into boats all the time." Callum pushed back his hair and huffed a breath as he sat beside David on the seat. He picked up one of the oars, as if rowing a boat was something he did every day too, and set to work.
>
> David laughed at their exchange, more relieved than he knew how to express that his father and Callum had gotten out of the castle in one piece.
> —*Outpost in Time*, Chapter 14

The companions take refuge in Bective Abbey, downriver from Trim. James, who had also left Christopher's original party, arrives at Bective Abbey just as the river boats loaded with Comyn's men are going past. David decides he has no choice now but to take up the High Kingship of Ireland. The companions split up and set out, with the intent to gather forces from all directions and meet at Tara, where they defeat the rebels in battle.

The Round Tower of Kells

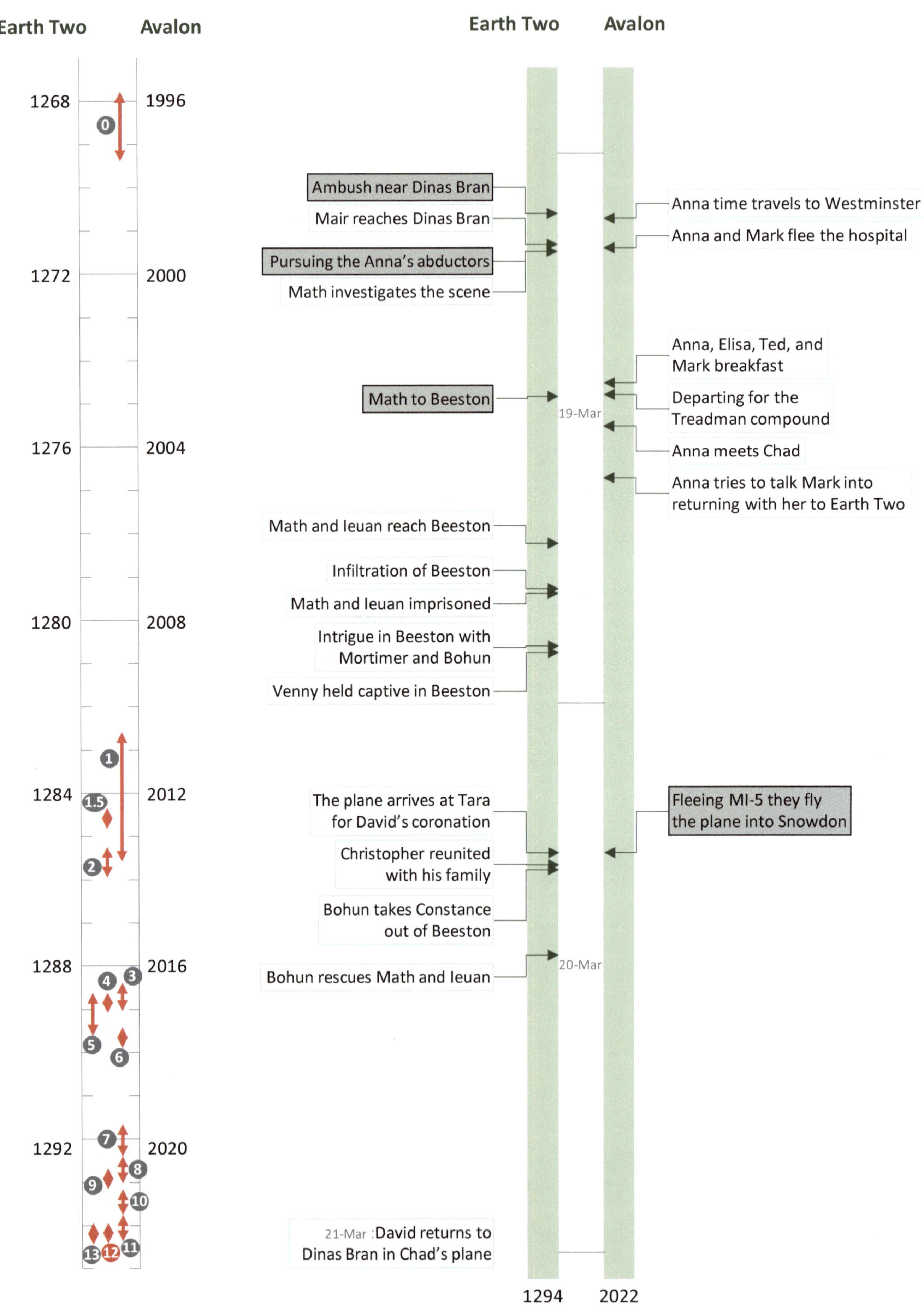

Timeline: Shades of Time

Book 12: Shades of Time

Book Two in the trilogy, *Shades of Time*, takes place at the same time as *Outpost in Time*, opening with Anna returning from a birth near Glyn Ceiriog. It is rare for Anna to travel in the middle of the night, but the birth she was attending was for Heledd, Gwenllian's wet nurse in *Footsteps in Time*.

Ambush near Dinas Bran

Unfortunately, Anna is unaware of the plot to assassinate David in Ireland or its larger aims, and thus, she and her party are completely surprised by the men sent to abduct her. She tries to outrun them, and when her horse leaps a hedge on the rim of a ravine, instead of falling to her death, she travels to Avalon, arriving inside Westminster Palace.

Dinas Bran from the south

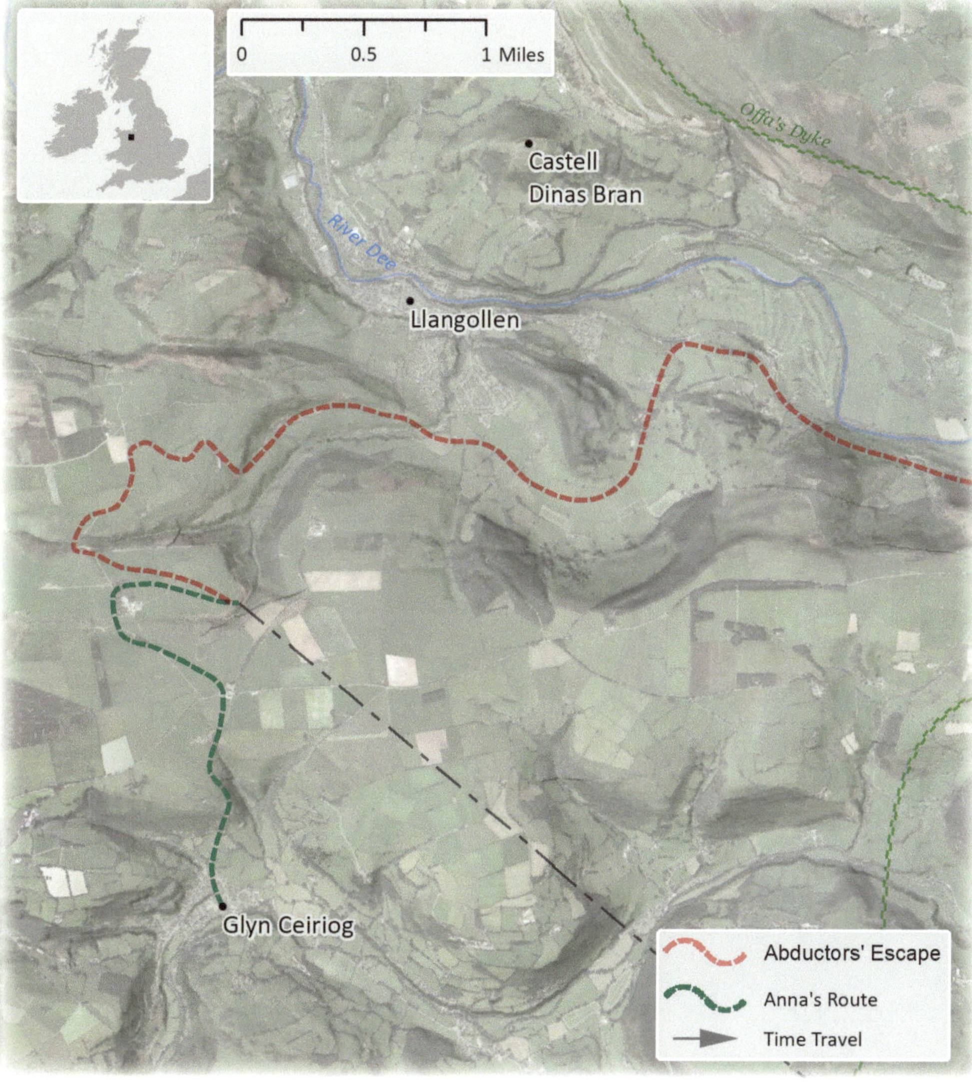

Ambush near Dinas Bran

Pursuit of Anna's Abductors

While Ieuan leads a group of men east to track Anna's attackers all the way to Beeston, Math and Bevyn examine the dead man at the bottom of the ravine. They find that he carries the colors of Robert FitzWalter, the lord of Beeston with family connections to John Balliol.

Recognizing the possible threat against Lili and Arthur, Bevyn chooses to stay at Dinas Bran to oversee its defenses. Therefore, Math rides east, reaching Beeston by late afternoon. He designates others to infiltrate the castle, where they learn that Roger Mortimer and John Balliol are behind the plot. Math and Ieuan, meanwhile, ride to Lyons Castle, thinking that John de Warenne, its lord, is an ally, but he imprisons them.

Back at Beeston, Humphrey de Bohun, who was sent by David to befriend Roger, leaves to warn Math of the treachery. When Edmund Mortimer meets him on the road, they realize that Warenne is also a traitor and construct a plan to rescue Math and Ieuan. Their plan eventually succeeds.

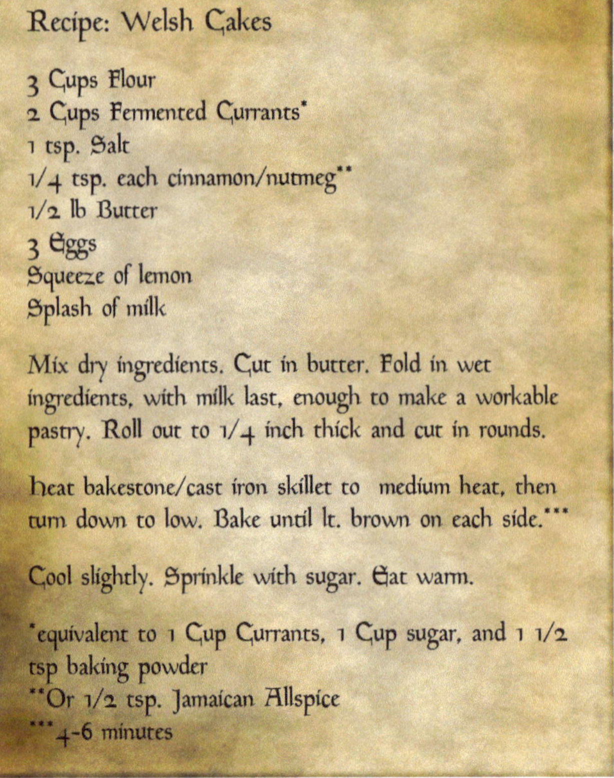

Welsh Cakes Recipe

Recipe: Welsh Cakes

3 Cups Flour
2 Cups Fermented Currants*
1 tsp. Salt
1/4 tsp. each cinnamon/nutmeg**
1/2 lb Butter
3 Eggs
Squeeze of lemon
Splash of milk

Mix dry ingredients. Cut in butter. Fold in wet ingredients, with milk last, enough to make a workable pastry. Roll out to 1/4 inch thick and cut in rounds.

Heat bakestone/cast iron skillet to medium heat, then turn down to low. Bake until lt. brown on each side.***

Cool slightly. Sprinkle with sugar. Eat warm.

*equivalent to 1 Cup Currants, 1 Cup sugar, and 1 1/2 tsp baking powder
**Or 1/2 tsp. Jamaican Allspice
***4-6 minutes

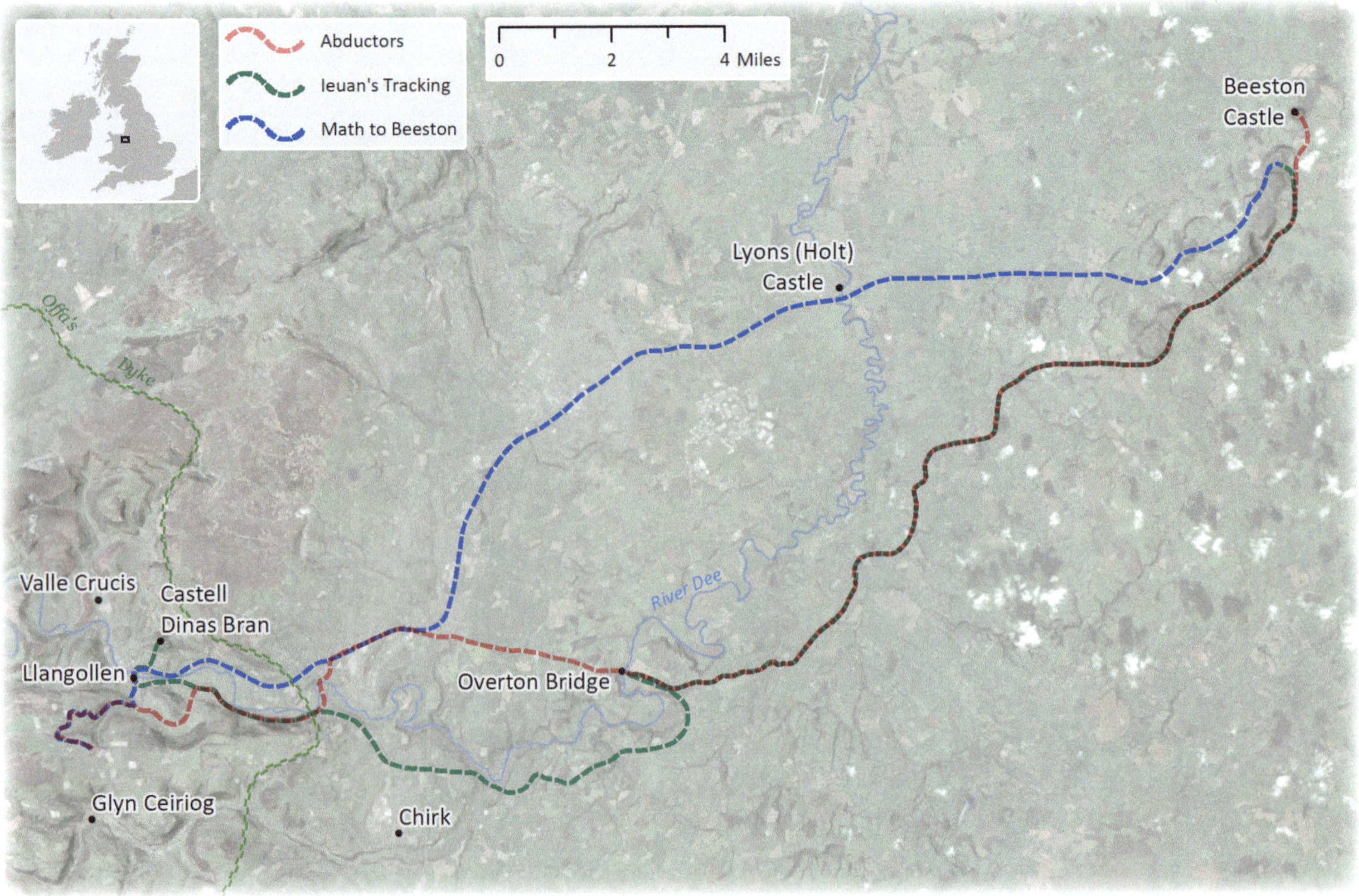

Pursuit of Anna's Abductors

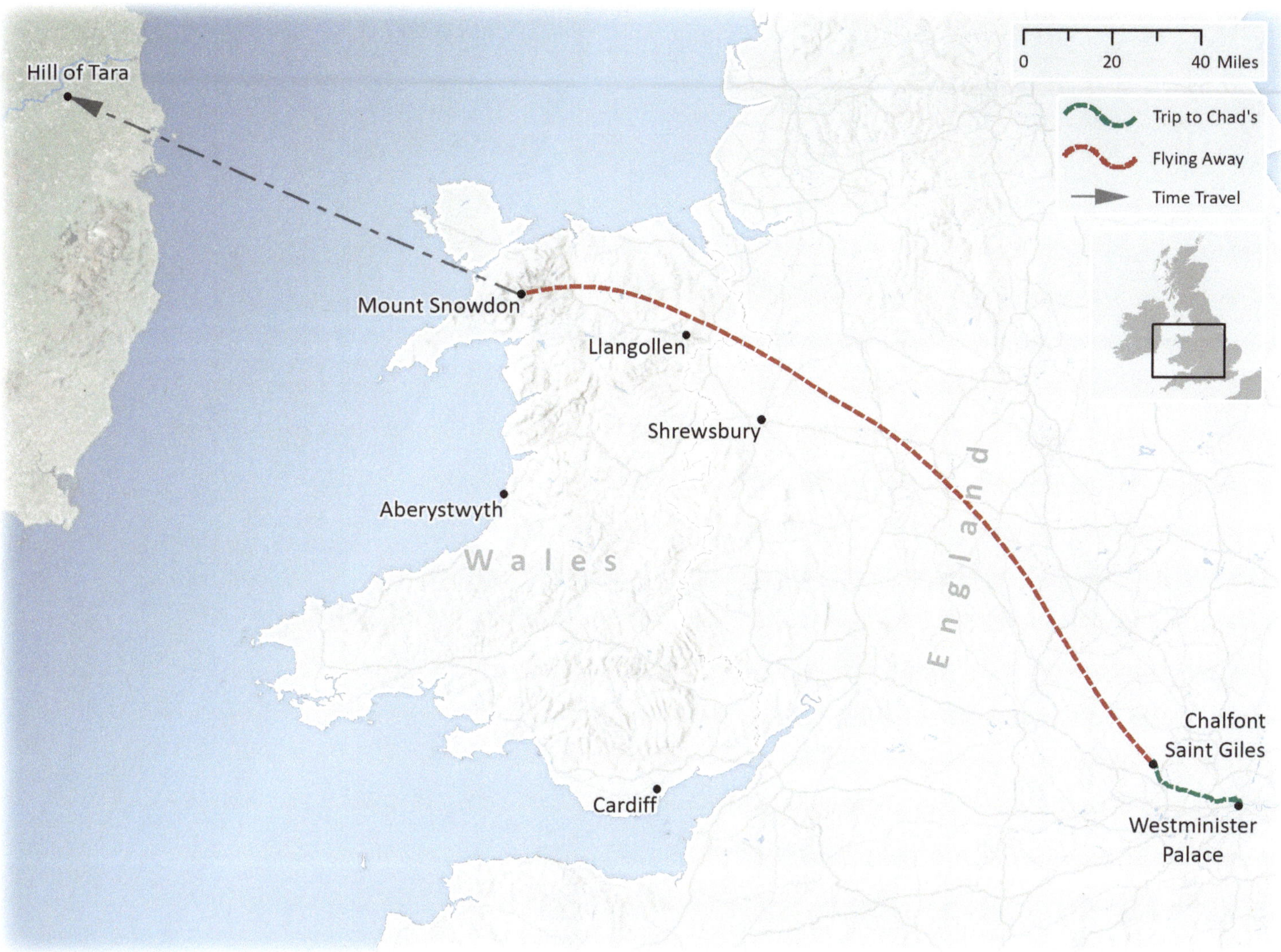

Anna in Avalon

Anna in Avalon

MI-5 agent Mark Jones and his co-worker Livia rescue Anna from the authorities in Avalon and take her to Callum's London safe house, where she reconnects with her family: Elisa, Ted, and Elen, who have moved to England in the wake of Christopher's disappearance. Ted is working for Chad Treadman, CEO of Treadman Global, who wants to 'help' the time travelers when they arrive in Avalon. Anna agrees to be taken to his compound northwest of London, where Chad convinces her to bring his offer to David.

MI-5, meanwhile, continues to pursue Anna, so Chad puts her on a plane with her family to fly to Ireland. Fighter planes are scrambled to pursue them, and they choose to fly into Mt. Snowdon rather than be captured. They time travel, arriving at Tara just as David is crowned High King.

The Hill of Tara

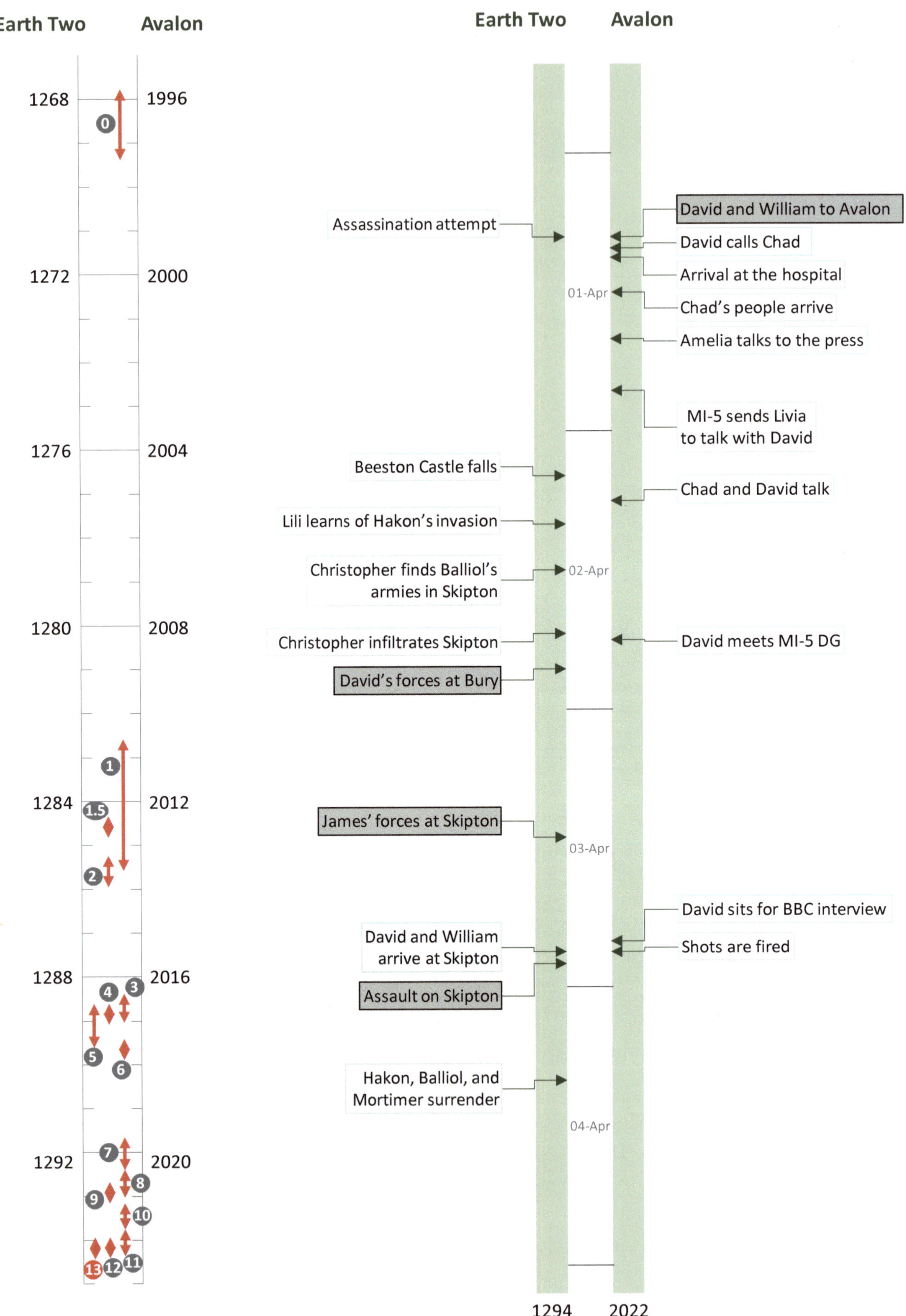

Timeline: Champions of Time

Book 13: Champions of Time

The story opens two weeks after the ending of *Shades of Time*. As William de Bohun speaks to David on the wall-walk of Chester Castle, a crossbowman on the opposite wall-walk fires on them, attempting to assassinate David. Instead, the two of them travel to Avalon. After the disappearance of David and William, the people remaining in Chester find a bloody crossbow bolt and chase down the would-be assassin. They realize David has gone to Avalon, and they must continue the campaign to quell the rebellion without him.

David's Adventures in Avalon

David and William arrive at an archery contest in Beaumaris, and William's wound makes onlookers mistakenly believe that William was shot by one of the participants. Michael, a medic, stops William's bleeding and drives David to Ysbyty Gwynedd. Chad Treadman arranges for a house, staff, and an interview with a TV personality, which is necessary because, in the two weeks since Anna left, Chad has been broadcasting David's story across the planet, in part to prevent MI-5 from pursuing him. The strategy works, and, instead of chasing David, the director sends Livia to him as a liaison.

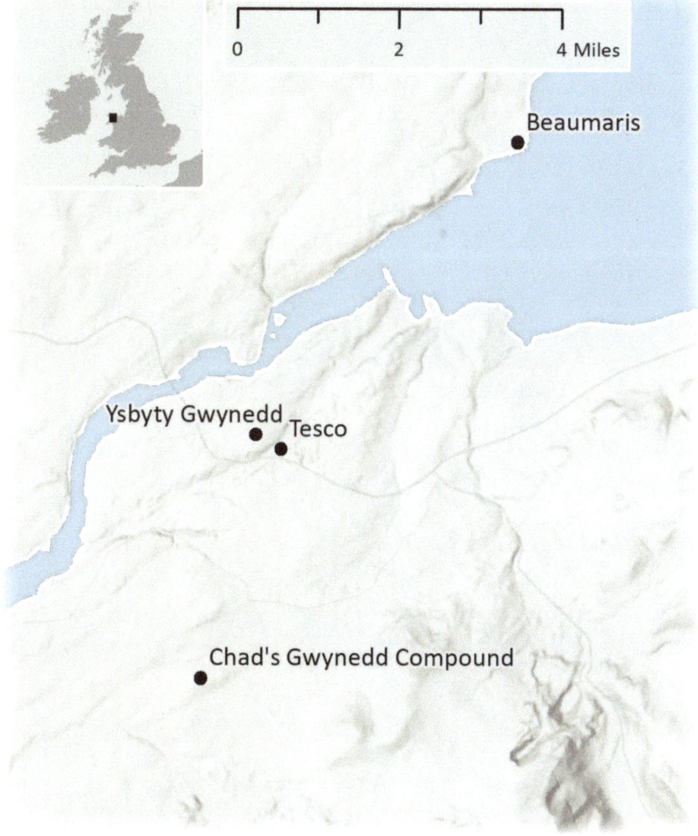

David's Adventures in Avalon

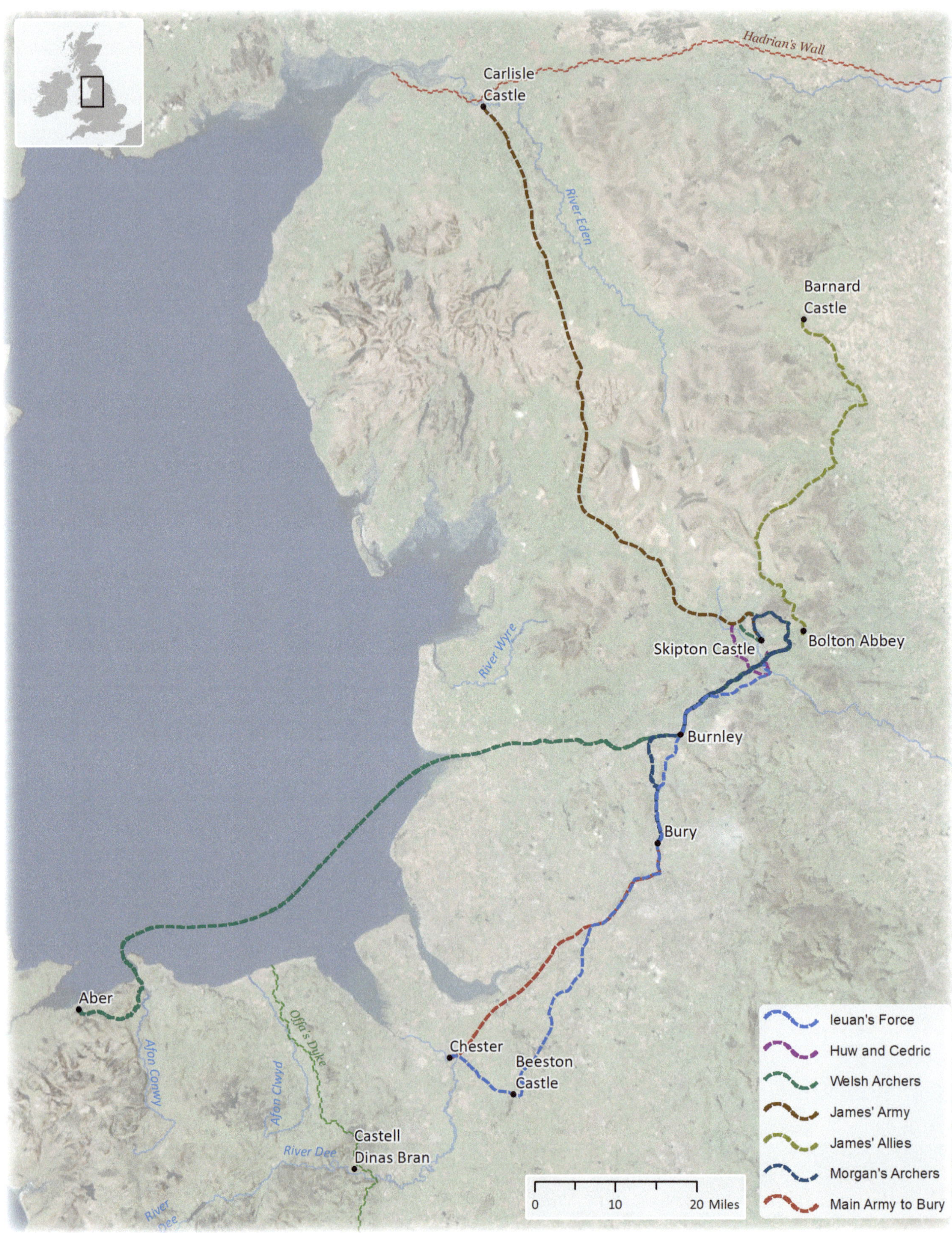

Marching on Skipton Castle

Black Mountain
from Skipton

Marching on Skipton Castle

Callum dispatches Christopher and a small team of men under his command north to warn James Stewart, who has returned to Scotland with Robbie Bruce, of what has happened. Callum and Ieuan head to Beeston, which, with the help of the twenty-firsters who arrived with Anna on Chad's plane, they take. In the process, they rescue the hostages and discover that Roger Mortimer has left the castle to ride north to meet John Balliol.

Close to five thousand men have camped in the valley around Skipton Castle. Christopher dispatches four of his men to inform Callum and James Stewart of the situation. While they wait for their army to come, he and Matha infiltrate the castle.

Battle of Skipton Castle

The friends gather on Black Hill, southeast of Skipton, with their forces. Callum decodes a message that David, who has returned to Earth Two with William, broadcasts in Morse Code from the battlement. While David and his companions take Skipton from the inside, Callum and his companions attack the army in the field. With forces surrounding him on all sides, Balliol finally surrenders. David and Callum propose to James and Robbie that Scotland form a parliamentary government with David presiding over the entire British Isles as High King.

Champions of Time is the final episode in the three book sweep that is *Outpost/Shades/Champions,* and many readers expressed concern that it is the final book in the series. It is not, but it wouldn't be wrong to say that it completes a story arc that began with *Footsteps in Time.*

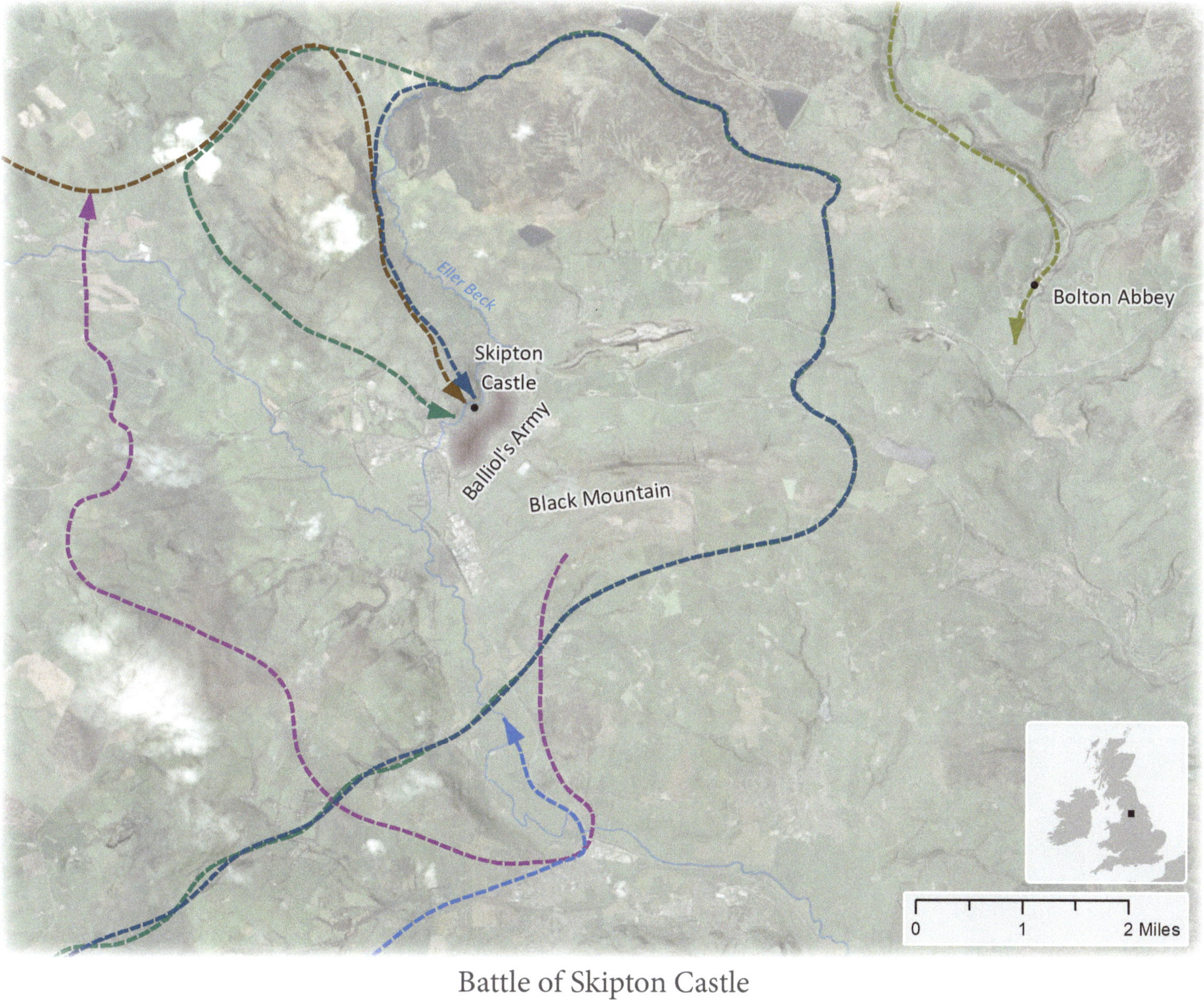

Battle of Skipton Castle

The whole series seems, to me, an
argument against building barriers
between people; where they came from
or the colour of their skin.

— Frances Yancey, reader

Chapter Seven: Conclusion

While the *After Cilmeri* series relates the adventures of one, very special, fictional family, it is also about families in general, with all their joys, frustrations, and complications. Other threads running through the series include what it means to be a leader—not to mention a king; honor, courage, and justice; and doing the right thing even when it's hard or comes at a cost to oneself. These themes are timeless and were valued and laughed at in equal measure in the medieval era as in the modern world.

At the same time, I would have to say that the blending of medieval and modern has been as difficult for me as for my characters. On one hand, ideals such as the equality of men and women, freedom of religion, and the acceptance of diversity are values that I share with my twenty-first-century characters, but they were in no way prevalent during the medieval period.

On the other hand, imposing modern standards on medieval people—and judging them by those standards—is wholly unfair and a recipe for an inauthentic story. That is certainly something I wish to avoid!

But if you come away with anything from the *After Cilmeri* series, and this particular book, I hope it is with an appreciation of how we can all find connections with each other, no matter how different our cultures and history and even if we are separated by huge distances in space and time. And I hope that, with Gerald of Wales' unnamed Welshman, you can find space in your heart for the special place that is *this small corner of the earth.*

Works Cited and Further Reading

Brown, R. Allen. *The Normans and the Norman Conquest*. London: Constable & Co, 1969.

Borrow, George. *Wild Wales*. London: John Murray, 1907.

Brut y Tywysogyon; or the *Chronicle of the Princes: Red Book of Hergest Version*, Thomas Jones, trans., ed. Cardiff: University of Wales Press, 1973.

Charles-Edwards, T.M. *The Welsh King and His Court*. Cardiff: University of Wales Press, 2000.

Davies, John. *A History of Wales*. New York: Penguin, 2007.

Davies, R.R. *Conquest, Coexistence, and Change: Wales 1063-1415*. Oxford: Oxford University Press, 1987.

—————. "Edward I and Wales," in *Edward I and Wales,* ed. Trevor Herbert and Gareth Elwyn Jones. Cardiff: University of Wales Press, 1988.

—————. *Domination and Conquest: The Experience of Ireland, Scotland and Wales 1100-1300*. Cambridge: Cambridge University Press, 1990.

—————. *The First English Empire: Power and Identities in the British Isles 1093-1343*. Oxford: Oxford University Press, 2000.

Davis, Paul R. *Castles of the Welsh Princes*. Swansea: Christopher Davies Limited, 1988.

Gerald of Wales. *The Journey Through Wales/The Description of Wales*. Lewis Thorpe, trans. New York: Penguin Books, 1978.

Gildas. *De Excidio et Conquestu Britanniae*. Retrieved from: http://www.ict.griffith.edu.au/wiseman/DECB/DECBps.html

Given, James. "The Economic Consequences of the English Conquest of Gwynedd." *Speculum 64*, no. 1 (January 1989): 11-45.

Griffiths, Ralph A. *Conquerors and Conquered in Medieval Wales*. New York: St. Martin's Press, 1994.

Hasted, Edward. *The History and Topographical Survey of the County of Kent*. Second edition. Maidstone, UK: EP Publishing, 1972 [1797].

Haug, Brynne. *Captive Cymru: Llywelyn and Gwynedd in the Wars of King Edward*. Whitman College Department of History, 2012.

—————. *This Small Corner of the Earth: Cultural and Political Identities in the Medieval Welsh March*. Whitman College Department of History, 2012.

Herbert, Trevor and Gareth Elwyn Jones, eds. *Edward I and Wales*. Cardiff: University of Wales Press, 1988.

Hobbes, Thomas. "Of Man, Being the First Part of Leviathan." Vol. XXXIV, Part 5. *The Harvard Classics*. New York: P.F. Collier & Son, 1909–14

Jacobs, Joseph. *The Jews of Angevin England: Documents and Records*. London (1893): 212-15.

—————. "England." *Jewish Encyclopedia*. 5. Isadore Singer *et al.*, eds. New York: Funk & Wagnalls Company, 1903: 161-174.

Meisel, Janet. *Barons of the Welsh Frontier: The Corbet, Pantulf, and Fitz Warin Families, 1066-1272*. Lincoln: University of Nebraska Press, 1980.

Morgan, Kenneth O. "Welsh Nationalism: The Historical Background." *Journal of Contemporary History*. 6.1, Nationalism and Separatism (1971): 153-159, 161-172.

Morris, John Edward. *The Welsh Wars of Edward I*. New York: Haskell House Publishers, 1901.

Oakeshott, Ewart. *Sword in Hand: A History of the Medieval Sword*. Minneapolis, MN: Arms and Armor, Inc. 2001.

Pettifer, Adrian. *Welsh Castles*. Woodbridge, UK: The Boydell Press, 2000.

Pounds, N.J.G. *The Medieval Castle in England and Wales: A Social and Political History*. Cambridge: Cambridge University Press, 1990.

Powicke, F.M. "Gerald of Wales." *Bulletin of the John Rylands Library*, xii (1928): 389-410.

Prestwich, Michael. *The Three Edwards: War and State in England, 1272-1377*. London; New York: Routledge, 2003.

Pryce, Huw. *Native Law and the Church in Medieval Wales*. New York: Oxford University Press, 1993.

—————. "British or Welsh? National Identity in Twelfth Century Wales." *English Historical Review* 116 (2001): 775-801.

—————. "Lawbooks and Literacy in Medieval Wales." *Speculum* 75.1 (Jan. 2000): 29-67. Registrum Epistolarum Johannis Peckham, Volume 3. C.T. Martin, ed. Rolls Series, 3 Vols. London, 1882-1885.

Rhys, John and David Brynmor-Jones. *The Welsh People: Chapters on Their Origin, History and Laws, Language, Literature and Characteristics.* New York: Greenwood Press, 1969.

Richter, Michael. *The Political and Institutional Background to National Consciousness in Medieval Wales.* Belfast: Appletree Press, 1978.

—————. *Giraldus Cambrensis: The Growth of the Welsh Nation.* Aberystwyth: National Library of Wales, 1976.

—————. "National Identity in Medieval Wales." *Medieval Europeans: Studies in Ethnic Identity and National Perspectives in Medieval Europe.* New York: St. Martin's Press, 1998.

Roberts, Brynley F. *Gerald of Wales.* Cardiff: University of Wales Press, 1982.

Russell, Paul. ed., trans. *Vita Griffini Filii Conani: The Medieval Life of Gruffudd ap Cynan.* Cardiff: University of Wales Press, 2005.

Smith, Beverley J. *Llywelyn ap Gruffudd: The Prince of Wales.* Cardiff: University of Wales Press, 1998.

Stacey, Robert C. "Parliamentary Negotiation and the Expulsion of the Jews from England." *Thirteenth Century England: Proceedings of the Durham Conference, 1995.* 6. Michael Prestwich *et. al,* eds. Woodbridge, UK: Boydell Press, 1997: pp. 77–102

Turvey, Roger. *The Welsh Princes 1063-1283.* London: Pearson Education Limited, 2002.

Walker, David. *Medieval Wales.* New York: Cambridge University Press, 1990.